ROB DELPLANQUE

She's Not The Only One

First published by RAD Publishing 2025

Copyright © 2025 by Rob Delplanque

All rights reserved. No part of this publication may be reproduced, stored or transmitted in any form or by any means, electronic, mechanical, photocopying, recording, scanning, or otherwise without written permission from the publisher. It is illegal to copy this book, post it to a website, or distribute it by any other means without permission.

First edition

ISBN: 978-1-0684032-0-0

Cover art by Manav Khadkiwala

This book was professionally typeset on Reedsy. Find out more at reedsy.com

For those who dare to dream

'And if I only could, I'd make a deal with God, and I'd get Him to swap our places'

Kate Bush, Running Up That Hill

Chapter 0

He started with the fingers.

Despite the rust that tarnished the old blades of the secateurs, their cold steel gave off a faint glimmer as he grasped them in his right hand.

He steadied himself, taking a deep breath.

He'd thought about this moment countless times; wondered if it would ever happen and, if it somehow did, how he would go about it. He'd pictured every frame; fantasised about it in every sordid detail. Down to the minutiae.

Now, finally, he was here.

Though tinged with a hint of apprehension, a sense of liberation washed over him. He felt as though he had licence to live out his fantasy and was relishing the prospect. It wasn't just him *choosing* to play out his darkest desire; he felt he *had* to.

There was an inevitability about things.

Moving closer, he calmly positioned the secateurs around the first finger of the man's left hand.

His victim in waiting.

The name of the man, he knew: Wilson Fensome.

You could argue he was usually a handsome man, although

the current terror he expressed, twisted and distorted his fine facial features. His hair, a wash of jet black, currently plastered to his forehead with sweat. His eyes, once sharp and confident, were now wide with panic and reflected the glare from the desk lamp that shone directly into his face, amplifying his fear.

By contrast, Wilson's captor was mostly shrouded in darkness. Obscured, except for a glint of steel and the outline of his twisted grin.

Crunch.

Snap.

A muffled scream tore through the duct tape which covered Wilson's mouth. His eyes scrunched tight and his face contorted in agony.

As he frantically shook his head in pain, a bead of sweat flew from his slicked hair onto his now disfigured hand.

"Ooh that sounded like it hurt," the man heckled, his eyes squinting. "Did it hurt?"

"Mmhhmmm, MHHHRRRMMM!!" came the desperate muted sounds from Wilson's plastered mouth, as he struggled in futility against his restraints.

His wrists and ankles were bound to a chair with tight cable ties while his left hand was locked in a vice, pinned mercilessly to the workbench beside him where the sole light shone from.

The shadowed man mimicked Wilson's screams. Mocking him, and clearly enjoying this moment, he hopped from side to side in childlike glee. His grin widened—became somehow, more maniacal—and was only upstaged by his attire: a black apron with white text sporting the phrase 'Just wait until you try my sausage'.

Wilson's head dropped in abandonment.

The apron-clad man's smile waned momentarily in detest.

CHAPTER 0

He pulled Wilson's head up by a handful of slick, black hair and brought him back to full attention with a sharp slap across the face.

Eager to hear his victim's voice; with a swift, follow-up motion, the man tore the duct tape from Wilson's mouth with a *rasp*.

"Why are you doing this?" Wilson cried, casting a sorrowful glance at his mutilated hand. Tears rolled and dripped from his quivering bottom lip. His eyes red and puppy-dogged.

"Oh, don't give up on me yet, Wilson. We're just getting started."

"Who are y-you?"

He paused; took a deep breath and sighed it out. "Who I am isn't important. It's irrelevant." His depraved smile returned. "But you can call me, Al."

"But, what h-have I done?"

"Something." Al nodded. His movement, slow. Measured. "You've definitely done something." He leaned in close and stared Wilson squarely in the eyes, their noses only inches apart; the desk lamp illuminating his manic face to Wilson for the first time. "And you know it!" he uttered, in a harsh whisper.

"I have a family. A beautiful family. Please. Please just let me go," Wilson blubbed. His lip still quivering with a rapid, but irregular tempo.

Al's eyes lit up with delight and he backed away from Wilson, pacing across the damp stone floor, over to a desk at the rear of the room. He returned a few seconds later, brandishing a document in one hand.

"Ah, yes, of course. The happy family," Al chimed, as he flipped the document over to expose it to him, revealing a photograph of Wilson alongside a woman and two young children. All smiles and bright eyes.

Wilson audibly gasped. The chair creaked as he recoiled. His eyes were cast with fear. "Where did you get that?"

"I'm afraid I can't say, but I hope you didn't make any plans to see them again."

Wilson's hands shook against his restraints, cutting into his flesh. "What are you saying? You-you've got me mistaken. I don't even *know* you. Please, I'm *begging* you. Whatever you want... *anything*... I'll give it to you." His voice trembled. His eyes, pleaded.

"That's exactly what you are doing, Mr Fensome. You *are* giving me *exactly* what I want. And for that, I thank you." He placed his hands together, mimicking a sign of prayer. "Now onto the next phase."

Turning his back to Wilson, Al approached a bench covered with a white sheet. He lifted the cover, revealing an array of saws, hammers, blades and all manner of other workshop tools: weathered, worn and some even rusty with age.

"Wh-what is this?" said Wilson, his voice cracking, as a mix of saliva and tears fell from his chin.

Engaging in a ritual like that of a surgeon inspecting his many instruments, Al perused his collection with meticulous care, his fingers lingering over each tool as if savouring the possibilities.

After what felt like an age of deliberation, Al finally turned to face Wilson. He raised his hand so that what he was brandishing was highlighted in a flash of the room's dim light.

A hack saw.

"No, no, no. What are you *doing*? No!" Wilson screamed. The blood drained from his face. A ghostly white visage against the dark of the expanse of which he was unable to see the extremities.

"Now, now, Mr Fensome. Please don't get carried away. And, by all means, scream all you want, but no one will hear you... Not here." Al leaned closer and, as he came into Wilson's view, he exposed his crooked teeth. "Did you know that the brain can still operate for up to seven minutes even after the heart has stopped?"

Al paused to let that thought sink in and awaited the look of understanding to gloss over Wilson's eyes.

"We've only just begun. Let's see how far we can take this before you... expire... shall we?"

Chapter 1

Slack-jawed and eyes glazed, Jack was rocked from his trance-like state.

"What do you think, Jack?" said Ralph; his voice a foghorn in Jack's ears.

"Y-yeah, sounds great, Ralph," Jack replied, blinking in an attempt to regain focus.

Jack had zoned out. Nothing new there. For months he'd been experiencing life like this: a dark fog shrouding his usually impeccable concentration.

"You didn't listen to a damn word, did you?" Ralph sighed, crossing his arms. His tone, a mix of frustration and concern.

Jack flushed. A pang of tightness rippled in his chest— a feeling that was all too familiar to him these days. Guilt. Shame. Fear. The emotions blurred together; a constant struggle that had haunted him for the past year.

"I'm sorry... would you mind repeating the question? I'm still finding it hard to keep my..."

"Your *focus*?" Ralph interjected, his voice still harsh. He paused to compose himself, softening his tone. "I get it. As much as I can anyway. I feel for you, I really do, but you've got to pull yourself together. Man, you're... you're destroying yourself, and as a friend, it's awful to see." He rustled his hair. Raised his eyebrows. "Why don't you take some time out? Do something for yourself. I'm... I'm saying this as your mate."

"I'm fine," Jack said curtly. "Forget it. Now just repeat the question, would you?" He could still taste the lingering burn of bourbon and wondered if Ralph could smell it on his breath. He leaned back in his chair.

Who am I kidding? I'm not fine. I'm very far from fucking fine.

"*Fine*? Fine," Ralph conceded, shaking his head. "Okay. I was just asking how the article is coming along. We need it for this week's edition. Is it nearly there?"

Jack Stevens worked as a journalist at *The Weekly Reporter*, a niche national newspaper known for its investigative journalism. He had worked with Ralph Wilson for over ten years, on and off, at several different publications and had known him for many years prior to that; meeting and sharing a flourishing bromance since their early days at university that was bonded over a shared love of football, booze and gambling.

Ralph was a smart guy, both in appearance and his mental aptitude. Horn-rimmed glasses and a haircut that would befit any banker working in the City were complemented by 'Sloane Ranger' attire. He hadn't always dressed this impeccably, but since his recent promotion to editor of the paper he had raised his game to suit. Jack wondered if this outward transformation had been a conscious attempt to ward off any imposter syndrome.

In stark contrast, Jack looked dishevelled. His sandy brown hair hadn't been cut in months and resembled a badly tended garden, flopping awkwardly over his eyes and tufting up at the back. Wrinkles around his eyes were more pronounced than normal and were now accompanied by dark rings. Pits of despair. His facial hair, normally kept in check, was unruly: too long to be considered stubble and not quite a beard, it was visibly flecked with grey, adding years to his already tired, pale and haggard face. Seemingly, he was doing everything he could to represent the self-destructive part that he was currently playing down to a tee.

Once considered equals, Jack and Ralph now seemed worlds apart. Over the last year Ralph had sharpened up, while Jack—due to his personal trauma—had spiralled. Previously employed in the same capacity as journalists, their working relationship had been fairly informal, but the promotion had changed all that. Now having to report to Ralph as a superior was a tough pill for Jack to swallow and their once relaxed working relationship was becoming strained.

Day by day, Ralph moved a step ahead while Jack fell several steps behind.

He's your best friend, Jack.

You're pushing him away. You've pushed everyone away.

"It's nearly there," said Jack, forcing a smile and stuffing some chewing gum into his mouth. "Just finishing up some tiny details. You'll have it for Wednesday."

Jack was writing an article about how Shoreditch is no longer seen as the cool place to hang out. He'd been piecing together a list of the top ten upcoming hipster hangouts in London. With every sentence he wrote he cringed. This was a far cry from some of his more probing pieces as an investigative journalist; having previously worked on articles that resulted in the ousting of high ranking executives and members of parliament by exposing their illicit behaviours.

How far he had fallen.

This wasn't the work of someone that had previously been

held in such high regard and Jack was embarrassed by how low he had sunk professionally. It was clear to him that Ralph had lost faith in his 'star man' and now only trusted him with the most menial of assignments.

There was some benefit to writing a piece exemplifying booze culture, however. Jack was able to legitimately spend his time in trendy (and not so trendy) bars, all in the pursuit of 'research'. Though he derided the hipster culture, he couldn't think of a better way to keep his job while actively disguising his burgeoning drinking habit. He felt in equal part, grateful *for* and ashamed *of,* that fact.

"If you're sure," Ralph muttered, casting a rueful glance over Jack's desk. It was a chaotic mess that mirrored Jack's declining mental state: three discarded takeaway coffee cups, a family-sized pack of antacids, scattered papers, a notepad bearing childlike scribbles and doodles, an assortment of ballpoint pens that seemed to have organised themselves through the whims of natural physics alone after being dropped from a distance, and a half-eaten packet of crisps. Amidst the clutter and standing out over all of this, like a lighthouse beam in a dark night at sea: a picture of his wife, Lisa.

"I'll get it done," Jack said, firmly. Noticing the look of disdain on Ralph's face, Jack shifted his posture, sat up straight and aligned the ballpoint pens into a neat row, in a vain attempt that he hoped would give the impression he had his act together. "I have the material. I just need to review the first draft. I'll do it at home this evening and I'll get something for you to take a look at in the next twenty four hours, okay?"

"Okay." Ralph nodded, though the disappointment in his expression remained. "Don't let me down on this, Jack. We're short on content for this edition as it is and the last thing I need to hear from my superiors is that we're adding weight to the 'print is dead' debate."

"I'll get it done," Jack repeated, surprised at his own assertion.

Ralph ran his hand across his cheeks and through his well-kempt beard. He opened his mouth halfway, as if he had something more to say, but said nothing. Looking Jack in the eyes, he gave a subtle nod, turned and ambled away from Jack's desk and back to his corner office.

* * *

Following his conversation with Ralph, anger and anxiety scratched away at Jack. His stomach churned and his armpits had broken out into a ferocious sweat. He buried the emotions. Locked them away along with other recent shames in his own savage prison of resentment and self-loathing.

Unable to concentrate effectively with the rampant levels of brain fog that were taking over him, Jack decided he'd be better off heading home sooner rather than later to finish off his draft.

Home.

A relative safe haven where the pressure of work could be lifted, though never entirely eased. A bottle of bourbon would help with the rest—Jack's go-to medicine of recent times.

He packed up his laptop along with his notepad and a couple of ballpoint pens, stuffed a packet of tobacco into the front pocket of his stonewashed jeans and grabbed the half eaten packet of crisps. Making his way to the lift, he reached into

CHAPTER 1

the packet, grasping at the crisps like a claw crane in a video arcade.

He pressed the button to call the lift and tapped his foot in impatience as he waited for it to reach the third floor.

He hesitated.

Thought twice.

Not wanting to see any colleagues, Jack changed course and headed for the stairs. He raced down three flights, relieved not to run into anyone and burst out into the city street.

Even for March, it was a cold and dreary day and it hit Jack like a jolt of electricity. The wind cut through his leather jacket, stinging his face and numbing his fingers as he struggled to light a cigarette. He pulled his chin down into his chest, bracing himself against the chill and hurried towards the nearby tube station, shouldering his way through the relentless onslaught of human traffic.

He pulled hard on his cigarette; the icy breeze inducing a wincing pain as it scratched at his smoke-scorched lungs.

Nearing the station, Jack was approached by a man in a crumpled suit. It hung off his bony frame like a soggy rag. Every wrinkle and stain told a story of damp streets and sleepless nights, a life unravelling at the seams.

He pleaded for spare change and the sight caused Jack's stomach to flip. The man's hollow eyes mirrored his own and the encounter seemed like a haunting reflection of a potential future. A premonition, perhaps, of things to come.

He kept his head down, avoided the man's gaze, and hurried into the station.

As Jack headed down the escalator towards the platforms, he took the time to scan the faces of those travelling up in the opposite direction. Every nameless face looked the same. Headphone-donning, phone-watching, fatigued, expressionless.

Perhaps there was *one* expression that littered the anonymous faces. One expression that was held in common; and one that Jack could relate to: Sadness.

Is everyone sad? Or am I just projecting?

There was a unique kind of solitude that came with travelling on the underground. An anonymity that Jack was grateful for on this day in particular, when he was actively trying to avoid those he knew. Happy to blend into the meandering herd of unknowns. Invisible.

And there was an eerie quietness to life down here. An unnatural silence.

No one spoke.

On the escalators, the stillness was broken only by the faint hum of machinery and the occasional shuffle of feet. Most passengers stood idly on the right, clutching the handrail; their gazes fixed on nothing in particular as they drifted off into their own thoughts.

Those in a rush would walk (or even run) down the left side, their urgency bordering on competitive. And woe betide anyone who misguidedly chose to stand on the left. This breach of the golden, unspoken rule was enough to push even the most stoic commuter to the brink.

As was standard with the British, and true to the stiff upper lip cliché, the anger would be stifled and bottled up. And on rare and extreme cases, when restraint had reached boiling point, you might even catch a muttered 'prick' slipping out under someone's breath.

Oh, the sweet relief of British anger.

CHAPTER 1

Waiting on the platform for the train to arrive, Jack—a veteran commuter—knew exactly where to be so that the doors would open precisely where he stood.

His carriage.

There was a sense of homeliness and familiarity to riding in the same carriage each day. A sense of territory. He'd taken this trip countless times and had it down to a fine art without having to give it any conscious thought.

A moment later the train arrived with pinpoint accuracy and, as the carriage door opened, Jack's chest lightened upon realising that it wasn't full. Choosing to leave the office early meant that he'd been spared the enforced armpit-sniffing, claustrophobia-inducing, snugness of the rush-hour commute. *Small mercies*, he thought, as he took a seat next to the carriage door.

I need a drink.

As the train departed the carriage rattled around him and he rested his sweat-soaked head against the, less than comfortable, perspex partition, letting his ragged breath slow to a natural rhythm.

* * *

Jack arrived home as the sun was dipping behind his riverside apartment block. He flashed his access fob and entered the lobby, nodding in acknowledgment to Karl, the young, sharp, slick-haired concierge who greeted him with a smile. Jack avoided the exchange of any words, desperately wanting to reach the solitude of his flat and shut his door to the outside world.

He rode the lift up to his flat, which was situated on the eighth floor of the nine floor block. Entering, he let out a sigh. One of relief.

And then another.

Of disappointment.

The two-bedroom modern apartment had once been lavishly presented and inviting, but it now mirrored the decline of Jack's mental state. Chaos. Empty beer and bourbon bottles adorned the side tables, an ashtray overflowed with cigarette butts and numerous takeaway boxes with half-eaten remnants littered the dining table.

Jack traipsed through to the kitchen, poured himself that well needed vat of bourbon on ice and headed out onto the balcony. The view overlooking the river was spectacular. The famous arch of Wembley Stadium visible in the distance to the north and, on a clear day, the summit of the Shard to the east. But Jack barely noticed anymore.

Sitting down on a plastic patio furniture chair, Jack took a sip of his bourbon and set it down on the matching table alongside. He rolled a cigarette with practised ease, lit it and took in a huge drag.

His thoughts drifted to Lisa.

What had she felt in those final moments?

A tear formed in Jack's eyes, pooled at the corner and dropped directly into the glass he was cupping in both hands. The tear created ripples across the surface of the drink, distorting the reflection of his own face staring back at him. A wave of pain and guilt crashed over him, knotting his stomach and burning his chest. A visceral feeling that threatened to devour him. He wiped the tears from his eyes and sniffed. A vain attempt to contain his emotions.

What was it your therapist said to you?
Allow your feelings to be felt.

Jack reached for his phone and scrolled through his photos until he reached a collection of cherished memories featuring Lisa.

Stopping on one particular video, he hovered over it for a few seconds before pressing play.

The video showed Lisa dancing in this very apartment while cooking and drinking wine. She caught a glimpse of Jack secretly filming her, turned a shade of red, gave the camera a wink, laughed, blew a kiss and mouthed "I love you."

The clip, although short, brought back a wave of treasured memories and Jack's face curled into a tear-soaked smile.

He played the clip again, hoping it would bring him some sense of peace.

It didn't.

Couldn't.

The circumstances around her death haunted him constantly.

He couldn't let go.

I'm so lost without you.

His smile contorted with anguish and he placed the phone down on the table and stared at the clouds across the river. He took another sip of his drink and closed his eyes.

"I miss you so much... I'm so sorry, Lisa," he whispered, his voice trembling. His words were barely audible against the clinking of the ice in his glass as his hands shook in symphony with his sobs.

He remained sitting there on the balcony, still and weeping as the cloud's hues turned from white to red and the London skyline awoke with a sparkle.

"I'll find who did this... I promise. I won't rest."

Chapter 2

"It's close, I'll give you that... but I think it still needs more work," said Ralph. "I'm not excited by it. There's no *heart* in it."

Jack grimaced as the words fell from Ralph's mouth. He knew only too well it wasn't good enough. Last night, his pain had consumed him. Unable to face the work, he'd fallen into bed in a drunken stupor and his grief had followed. He'd tossed and turned, only to be jolted awake by hallucinatory flashes of his wife in her last moments every time he drifted into slumber: her face, a fixed scream of terror; the whites of her eyes bloodshot from struggle.

And this morning? Waking up from an inebriated haze, he'd scrambled to cobble together a tighter narrative and polish his words into something mildly coherent. The result? An embarrassment.

"I'm going to give it to one of the junior writers to tidy up, before print," Ralph continued, his eyes darting away. He ran his hand through his hair and looked back at Jack. "You look like shit, mate. I really think you should take some time out. You have plenty of holiday time you haven't taken. Take a week. Take *two weeks* if you need. Get your shit together."

Jack couldn't hold Ralph's gaze. He looked down to his own fidgeting hands. "You might be right. I... I haven't been taking good care of myself recently. Time off might be good for me, so long as I keep... busy. I worry that without work, I might... I might lose my *mind*." He exhaled, relieved but resigned. Time off might ease the burden, but it wouldn't lift the weight in his chest.

The thought of handing over his work to a junior writer would normally feel like a dagger piercing through his pride, but it barely registered.

They'll do a better job than I can right now.

"I think you're already losing your mind a little and that's my concern. Yeah, definitely make sure you keep yourself busy. Go see some family. How's your sister doing? Or your dad?"

Ralph's mention of family caught Jack off guard. He flinched in realisation that he'd not spoken to his twin sister, Rachel, in over a month, despite living in the same city. And his dad, with whom he'd grown particularly close to since his mother's death three years ago, now felt like a stranger; he couldn't even remember the last time they'd spoken.

"Yeah, I'll certainly give Rach a call. Not sure if it would be good for me to go back home to see my dad or not though. I'll think it over."

"Take all the time you need, it doesn't have to be just a week or two. We can cover for you here. I just want to make sure my best man is fighting fit and able to produce his best work, without me having to breathe down his neck. I don't enjoy being your boss, you know?"

"I know," said Jack, raising a slight smile and looking up to meet Ralph's eyes again. He could see the compassion in his friend's face, prompting a surge of warmth that ran through his stomach. "I appreciate you having my back."

"No problem. I'm not just your boss. I'm still your friend. Take the rest of the day and do whatever you need to clear your head. Call me if you need anything and only come back to work when you're fit and ready, okay?"

"Okay," said Jack, with a subtle nod. "And thanks, Ralph. Really. Thank you."

* * *

Leaving the office, Jack made a pit stop at a bar not a hundred metres down the road. A dive he wouldn't usually consider, but convenient enough to take the edge off before dealing with the arduous tube ride home.

Upon entering, Jack was hit with the familiar smell of stale beer and man sweat. He took a quick scan.

At this time of day, the bars were quiet, and this was no different—only three other punters.

One sat on a stool, propping up the bar, a half-drunk pint of ale in front of him, muttering incoherently to himself. Combat trousers, a ragged checked shirt, and a greying beard paired with a mullet—he looked as dishevelled as the place itself.

The second was an elderly lady sitting alone at a table with a G&T, a tabloid newspaper, and a small, scrawny dog asleep beside her.

The third was a stringy, pale man losing a battle with a fruit machine and audibly bemoaning his bad luck.

Is this kind of establishment my level now? Am I as sad and desperate as these three losers?

As Jack approached the bar the bartender looked up from his phone, set it down and walked over to stand opposite Jack.

"What can I get ya?"

"A pint of IPA and a straight bourbon."

No pleasantries needed here.

"One for me, too," Mullet may have mumbled. Jack ignored him, and waited impatiently for his drinks, tapping his fingers fast and rhythmically on the etched woodwork.

As the bartender returned, Jack immediately picked up the glass of bourbon, slammed it down in one, the burn barely registering, placed the glass clumsily back on the bar and paid. He thought he saw the bartender scowl, but dismissed it, grabbed the beer and walked over to find a table, as far away from the others as possible.

Taking out his phone, he trawled through his contact list and stopped on the number for Rachel.

After four ring cycles she picked up.

"Hey, bro. Long time no speak. How you been?" chimed the voice on the other end of the line.

Jack raised a loose smile at the sound of his sister's voice. "Hey, Rach. Yeah it's been a little while. Sorry, I've been a little... out of sorts recently," he said. "I have been meaning to call."

"That's cool. I was meaning to check in, too. Work's been hectic, but that's a lame excuse for being so rubbish."

"Yeah, fucking work. Actually, that's... that's the thing. I've decided to take some time out. Just for a little while. Would be good to see you. Don't suppose you're free any time this week?"

"Is everything.... Is everything *okay*?" said Rachel. The concern in her voice was striking. "You don't sound like yourself."

Is it that obvious?

"Things have been better, to be honest. I've still been finding it hard with work to... to... to concentrate." He paused. "To tell you the truth, Ralph recommended I take some off."

"Oh, I see. Makes sense. He may be your boss now, Jack, but he does know you better than anyone, so he's probably right."

"Or he just doesn't want to deal with my flakiness." Jack was joking, but there was a subtext of seriousness to what he said. He had no doubt that Ralph would be relieved to be free of him for now.

"Don't think like that, Jack. I'm sure he's just looking out for you. I'd like to, too, so yeah let's hang out. Come over to my place... tomorrow? I'll cook."

"Okay, sounds great. I'll bring a bottle."

"Bro... you're not still... leaning on the drink too much, are you?"

Oh shit.

Jack's stomach knotted. "No.. No, not at all," he lied.

"Good to hear. And you know me, I'm always up for a glass or four of wine. Oh, Jack, I'm really looking forward to seeing you, I'll knock up something special."

"Thanks, Rach. Sorry again for not being in touch sooner."

"Not a problem. And hey, what are big sisters for, eh?"

"Every time." Jack sighed. "You're only ten minutes older, you know?"

Since they were kids, Rachel had teased Jack about being the older one. Over thirty years later and she still continued to bring this up.

"Yes. That is true, but I never get tired of saying it," Rachel beamed. "See you tomorrow, bro. Seven okay?"

"Ideal. See you then."

As Jack hung up the phone his shoulders dropped, and for the first time in days, his chest didn't feel like it was wrapped in barb wire. Rachel had a way of grounding him without even trying.

He took an unrestricted deep breath and sipped his pint, rather than gulping it down.

* * *

Jack's face dropped as he opened the door to his flat. Hit by the stench of food decay, stale tobacco smoke and beer, he was struck by a sudden call to action. He opened the door to the balcony, allowing fresh air to waft through his decomposing abode; sounds of the city below dancing through along with the breeze.

He bagged up the leftover takeaway cartons, empty beer and bourbon bottles and the contents of the ashtray. Moving on to the kitchen, he cleared away dirty plates and cutlery into the dishwasher and switched it on. He gave the worktops a wipe down, took the bin bags down to the refuse area and returned back to his flat. Pleased with the sight he was now greeted with, he let out a sigh of relief and proceeded to make himself a quick snack of poached eggs on toast along with a cup of strong, black coffee.

With his appetite sufficiently satiated and feeling slightly wired from the coffee he reached for his laptop and browsed the news. *"Knife crime sees 10% rise in London", "President Trump imposes tariffs on China imports", "Ten car pileup on the*

CHAPTER 2

M1, kills 3". He clicked onto the bookmarks bar and tapped on a link for a site called 'Nethunt'.

Nethunt was a site for unsolved crimes and unexplained incidents. Postings were most commonly related to people missing or murdered where the cases had gone cold and victims' families or friends had taken it upon themselves to dig deeper with the help of the hive mind of the internet, hoping to generate some new leads or lines of inquiry.

Trawling through the reams of posts, there were threads of all manner of unsolved mysteries: *'What happened to Jeff Hawkins? - Dad of two disappears after leaving to return video tapes in 1986 and never returned', 'Unexplained celebrity deaths', 'Big cat on the loose in Lincolnshire. Was it a puma?'* A lot of time spent by armchair detectives, retirees and the unemployed, wasting their time on this nonsense was Jack's overriding belief.

Generally, he didn't care for these forums, but he did have one key interest in them. In his desperation he'd added his own thread onto the site a couple of months after what had happened to Lisa, hoping that someone could shed some light on things and give the police more to follow up on.

Susan Reeves, the Senior Investigating Officer of Lisa's case had ceased the investigation over 6 months ago. She'd said to Jack that they had '*exhausted all lines of inquiry*'. No forensic evidence. No eye witnesses. No suspects.

Jack had been left devastated by the police's loss of interest in his wife's case and tried anything he could think of to help resurrect the investigation—hoping beyond hope that someone might be able to offer some new angle or some new evidence. Something of use that the police had not considered or were not aware of. Something that he could use his skills as an investigative journalist to dig into.

So far all of his attempts to reignite the fire had fallen short.

In an act of futility, Jack checked his notifications on the site to see if anyone had responded to his post, knowing full well that he would have received an email informing him of anything new.

He sighed as he was presented with a '*Sorry, no new notifications*' screen.

Jack had been pushed aside by the police since the investigation closed, but the journalist in him couldn't let it rest. He would persistently call Susan to see if there were any new leads and suggest ideas about how they could further their inquiries and how he could help.

His intentions were desperate yet genuine, but Susan, a stern, no-nonsense woman, had heard it all before. While initially compassionate with Jack's countless attempts urging her to reopen the case, Susan's patience had faded over time, like a photograph left out in direct sunlight for too long.

His constant appeals had clearly become a nuisance and now Susan wouldn't answer his calls, let alone respond to the anguished voicemails that he'd left too frequently.

As Jack despairingly pulled at the metaphorical door, seeking answers, the police only tightened their grip, shutting him out further.

* * *

The next evening, Jack had trimmed his facial hair before leaving his flat. Not clean-shaven, by any means, as he didn't want to have to contend with the constant upkeep of daily shaving, but at least trimmed to a point where he could pass as presentable. Anything he could do to reduce the likelihood that his sister would worry about (or comment on) how he was doing was a bonus.

Rachel lived in a quaint Victorian end-of-terrace, in a quiet London suburb, with her fiancé David. *Never* 'Dave'—risk shortening his name at your peril.

David was an affable guy and Jack had struck up a close friendship with him over the years. They both worked in central London, making it logistically easy for them to meet up for drinks after work, and they ensured they habitually made the most of this opportunity to indulge themselves.

David worked in the finance sector and in keeping with this stereotype he liked to frequent the more upmarket cocktail bars in the City. During those heady days he had introduced Jack to Old Fashioned cocktails, which ended up being their go to tipple. In hindsight Jack had wondered if maybe this was where his affinity *for* and reliance *upon* bourbon had stemmed from.

Very much a lady's man, David enjoyed the company of women, but seemingly never overstepped the mark. At least he hadn't when Jack had been around him. He was curious though. He'd always wondered if David was just reigning in his character a little when the two of them were together because of the fact he was engaged to his sister. He hadn't witnessed anything untoward in their time together, but his gut had picked up on a level of sleaziness in David's character which Jack had chosen to ignore.

Arriving at his sister's, Jack knocked on the front door with his free hand; the other holding a single bottle of Shiraz. The door chain was released with a rattle and Rachel opened the door to greet Jack with a warm smile, highlighting the slight crow's feet wrinkles around the corners of her eyes.

"If it isn't my little brother. Come in. Shoes off, you know the drill."

"Still so house proud, eh?" said Jack, walking into the entrance hall and stooping down to take off his shoes. "This is for you," he added, handing her the wine.

"Thanks! Shiraz. This will go perfectly," beamed Rachel. She walked on down the hall, leaving Jack to place his shoes by the doormat. "We're having duck," she announced over her shoulder.

Walking through the hall, Jack was hit with the inviting aroma of home cooked, fine dining. Salivating, he walked on into the kitchen where Rachel proceeded to uncork the wine, pour two glasses and hand one to Jack.

"Cheers," Rachel said, clinking her glass against his.

"Cheers, sis. Thanks for having me over. I must say, this all smells delicious."

"Let's hope it's as good as it smells. You hungry?"

"Starved." Jack paused for a moment. "Where's David?"

"Working late. *Again*," Rachel huffed.

Is he actually working?

Rachel shrugged. "Jesus, you look shattered, Jack," she said, quickly changed the subject.

Maybe the beard trim only helped to highlight *the dark rings around my eyes.*

Fuck.

"Yeah, a rough few days," he said, rubbing his eyes. "Deadlines, you know? Still, I got the piece I was working on pretty much completed, before I took this time off." He blew air from his cheeks. "I guess I need it."

"Looks like you do. Dinner's gonna be a while yet, let's take these through to the living room and have a sit down," said Rachel, gesturing at her glass of wine.

Rachel's living room was in stark contrast to Jack's: two matching corner sofas, freshly plumped, with numerous scatter cushions; an Afghan rug positioned precisely and perpendicularly between them; a number of original oil paintings adorned the walls—David's attempt to market himself as an art buff, though Jack knew he didn't know the faintest thing about art; ornate stand-up lamps in two opposite corners of the room provided subtle, ambient lighting; and a large wood burner, positioned at the far wall, roared invitingly. Above it, on the mantelpiece, was a single photograph of Rachel and David. Jack's first thought was *showhome.* His second, *why no TV?*

He sank into one of the sofas, sighing at the firm yet yielding cushioning and placed his glass of wine down on a side table.

"I wish you'd tidied up a little, sis," Jack teased.

Laughing and looking slightly embarrassed, Rachel said, "Well it's been a while since we had the guest of honour here, so I thought I'd make it nice for you."

"It's incredible, Rach. Makes my place look like a pig sty." Jack reached for his glass of wine and took a sip. "Have you heard much from Dad recently?"

"A little. He's keeping busy. He seems good. I make sure I call him once a week. How about you, have you spoken to him?"

"Not for a long time, to be honest. Things have been strained since Lisa... you know." Jack's throat tightened, a familiar ache settling in that came with the struggle of uttering his wife's name. He coughed, trying to push it down. "It's like he's not sure what to say to me anymore, like he's afraid of saying the wrong thing, or maybe of not saying anything at all."

Rachel looked at Jack with compassion. "You know how Dad is. He's not good with his emotions, that's all. You know that. He shuts down when he doesn't know what to say. He probably thinks he'll just make things worse." She cringed. "Maybe you should go up and see him. Might be easier in person and you have the time at the moment to get away for a bit. I'm sure he'd love to have the company. Might be good for both of you."

Jack nodded in agreement and paused to think through the idea. "Yeah, maybe I'll give him a call," he said, finally, although instantly dismissing the thought. He wasn't in the frame of mind to commit to anything in particular right now.

"Good. You should." Rachel took a sip of wine and then continued. "Did you want to talk at all about Lisa?"

Hearing someone else say her name caused Jack's stomach to flip.

"What's there to say? She's gone," he said, dryly, his voice, thick. "The police have stopped the investigation and they've made it clear there's nothing more they will do for me. For *us.*" The words felt heavy, final. He shook his head, staring into his glass. "Whoever did this is walking free."

He blinked several times. His eyes ached with unshed tears, but he held them back. His hand trembled, forcing him to hold the glass tighter.

"Sorry. I didn't mean to bring it up. I just wondered if there were any developments or if you wanted to talk about her at all."

Jack took a long sip. "I'd rather not, sis. I'm doing okay.

Really." He knew he was lying, but it was easier than going down the route that led to pity. "Moving on is hard though, you know?"

"I can't imagine," said Rachel, a sullen tone to her voice.

An undertone of awkwardness hung heavy as Lisa's name lingered in the air. Reverberating. Neither said anything for maybe a minute. They both sipped wine in silence, until Jack couldn't stand it any longer. He changed the subject. "So, what's with David working late all the time? Are the markets in that much turmoil?"

"Oh, I don't know." Rachel sighed. "He just seems to be so *distracted* lately."

A buzzer pinged in the distance. A look of relief washed over Rachel's face. She rose quickly and hurried back to the kitchen.

"Saved by the bell," Jack muttered to himself.

* * *

Rachel served up dinner for herself and Jack: roast duck, dauphinoise potatoes, assorted steamed vegetables, and a thick red wine sauce. As she put a plate down in front of Jack, he noticed a spare place laid on the table for David. Looking up, he saw Rachel glance at it too, a sombre expression painting her face.

The elephant in the room loomed larger than life.

"This is delicious, Rach. Incredible," said Jack, savouring the first bite and groaning with satisfaction. He took a sip of wine to wash it down. The full bodied, smokiness of the Shiraz blended perfectly with the aftertaste of the duck. His sense of taste was slightly subdued these days, due to his incessant smoking, but even that couldn't detract from the fact that this was an amazing meal and it stood out as the best he'd had in recent memory. "And the wine's a winner, too."

"Glad you like it. Just a little something I knocked up," Rachel said, with a wink. "And yeah the wine does go perfectly."

"Mmhmm," Jack agreed as he stuffed another forkful into his face.

* * *

The light of the golden hour outside had begun to fade into twilight and Jack and Rachel had settled into a comfortable silence when the faint sound of a key in the front door's lock interrupted the stillness, causing Rachel to glance up.

The door creaked open and David entered the hallway.

"Hi love. Sorry I'm late."

"Hey you. That's okay, there's still some dinner for you. Oh, and Jack's here, too... we're having duck."

"Hiya mate," Jack hollered from the kitchen table, looking over his shoulder towards David.

"Hey, Jack. Sorry I didn't realise you were coming over," said David. "I'll be right with you guys, just gonna grab a quick shower. Need to clean the office vibe from my soul before socialising."

"It'll get cold. Have a shower after eating, would you?" Rachel pleaded.

"I'll only be a few minutes. You two crack on and I'll be down

CHAPTER 2

in a mo," David called back. He was already halfway up the stairs.

"He won't be long," said Rachel.

Don't make excuses for him, Rach.

* * *

Jack was helping Rachel clear the plates away as David reappeared. They'd been able to push aside the awkwardness of the moment and had moved on to reminiscing about their childhood, when the two of them had been inseparable and getting up to all kinds of mischief, driving their parents to their wit's ends at times. Rachel recalled a story to Jack about how the two of them, aged around six, had taken old tins of paint from the shed and painted the windows of their bedrooms, while their parents were out sunbathing in the garden. Jack laughed, like he hadn't in ages.

Tears streamed, but for once, not of sadness.

"Much better," David announced, as he entered the kitchen, looking fresh-faced, but with a subtle edginess. Something in his posture or expression—a flicker of something—made Jack uneasy, though he couldn't pinpoint why.

"I left you a plate. It's probably a bit cold now," sighed Rachel.

"Thanks babe. I really did need to freshen up. Sorry. I'm all yours now. How about I eat this and make us all a cocktail? Martinis?"

"Just the ticket," said Jack, drying his hands and going over to greet David, who responded by giving him a burly man hug.

Rachel remained silent as David opened another bottle of red wine, filling their glasses almost to the brim before draining what little remained into his own. He sat down and tucked in to his meal, but Jack noticed something strange — David ate slowly, each bite seeming forced and each chew, sluggish. Finally, he pushed his plate aside, half-eaten.

"That was delicious, sweetheart. Really delicious. I... I don't feel like I have much of an appetite at the moment, though. Sorry. Maybe I'm coming down with something. Anyone want the leftovers?" He shifted in his seat and reached for his drink. He took a sip, placed his glass back down and stood up. Pointing at Jack and raising his eyebrows, he said, "Martinis?"

"Sure. Can I help?"

"No mate, you sit right there, I'll knock up the best dirty Martini you've ever had," he said, as he walked over to the kitchen cabinets and retrieved three martini glasses. Placing them down on the worktop, he motioned to Rachel. "Can I get you one, love?"

Of course they have martini glasses.

"I'll stick with the wine."

"Okay, if you're sure. Do we have any olives?" David said, as he shrugged and placed the third Martini glass back in the cupboard.

"In the fridge," said Rachel, a shortness in her response.

David checked the fridge, returned with the olives and continued preparing the cocktails with practised precision.

There was an icy atmosphere between Rachel and David that caused Jack's chest to tighten. His hands began to fidget and he reached for his phone—a distraction technique he often employed to put himself at ease.

He swiped aimlessly through sports headlines, scrolled

CHAPTER 2

through social media for notifications. Nothing.

He turned his attention to his emails and his heart rate spiked as the app opened.

He had one new email.

No subject.

Unknown sender.

The ominous nature of this uninvited email triggered a visceral reaction. A cold sweat prickled his skin, a single bead tracing down his spine.

Opening it, a wave of nausea hit Jack like a punch to the stomach.

The blood drained from his face.

His hands trembled violently and he dropped the phone onto the table with a clatter.

The clatter shattered the cold silence. Rachel glanced at Jack, concern flickering as she caught the panic in his eyes.

Vivid flashes of Lisa's tortured body came screaming into Jack's mind and his peripheral vision faded into oblivion as he focused solely on the email.

Five stark, bone-chilling words filled the screen:
SHE'S NOT THE ONLY ONE.

Chapter 3

"What's wrong?" said Rachel, looking over at Jack.

Jack couldn't speak. He sat there, motionless, looking down at the screen of his phone in disbelief. Totally unaware of his surroundings.

David walked over to the table and set the two Martinis down. He looked concerned, but said nothing.

"Jack!" shouted Rachel, after a few seconds of silence. "Talk to me. What's going on?" Still no response. Rachel put her hand out to touch Jack's and softening her tone now, she said, "What is it? Is everything okay?"

The touch of his sister's hand brought Jack back to reality. He nodded in acknowledgement of Rachel's presence, paused for a moment and said, "My phone. An email." He gulped. "I think it's about Lisa."

Rachel audibly gasped. "What?" She reached for Jack's phone to take a look. Reading aloud, she repeated the words from the email. "*She's not the only one?*" Her brow furrowed and she looked back towards Jack. "What does it mean?" she whispered.

"I don't know," muttered Jack, shaking. "I don't know the sender... it's a gibberish email address, but it has to mean

CHAPTER 3

there's more people out there..." He trailed off. "Like Lisa." He reached for the Martini glass and swallowed the drink in one huge gulp, without bothering to remove the olive skewer. He gasped.

"Jesus, Jack! Calm down," said Rachel, grabbing the now empty Martini glass from him and passing it to David's accepting hand. "How do you know that this has anything to do with Lisa? Even if it does, this could be any old hack just messing with you. All it says are those five words."

"It has to, surely." Jack's words floated in the air. Hollow. "Surely...it fucking has to."

Doesn't it? That familiar friend of desperation was clawing at Jack's consciousness.

David placed the empty glass down on the kitchen worktop and returned to the table. "Let me take a look," he said, as he reached to take the phone from Rachel. Pausing to read the email, he continued, "I think Rachel's right, mate. There's not even any other information here. Just those five words. Could be any old nonsense. It could be just any old spam email, but for you it resonates because of what happened to Lisa. We see what we want to see, you know?"

Jack grabbed the phone back from David. "A spam email would typically have a link though, wouldn't it? You know, to entice you to click on it."

"Maybe. Maybe not," replied David, shrugging.

"It's got to mean something," Jack said, shaking his head. "I just know it." He stood up, grabbed his jacket from the back of his chair and started to walk out of the kitchen and into the hallway.

Rachel started after him. "Where are you going, Jack?"

Jack, trying to put on his shoes with an incredible sense of urgency, struggled to do up his laces, giving Rachel the chance to catch up with him. She grabbed him gently by the arm, stooped down to his level and looked him in the eye. His eyes were bloodshot and watering.

"Just stay for a while and let's talk, okay?" said Rachel, her eyes mirroring Jack's.

"I have to go." He paused to wipe his eyes, finished tying his shoelaces, and stood up, straightening his jacket. "I really appreciate the dinner, sis. It was great to see you... and David, too. But I really feel I need to... be alone with... this."

"Jack," Rachel said, her voice trembling, "I know you're hurting, but you don't have to go through this alone. If this is about Lisa... if it's real... you *shouldn't* be on your own. Please, just stay tonight," she pleaded, her voice cracking.

David, now hovering by the kitchen door, looking out into the hallway and leaning casually against the frame of the door, said, "Of course, you can stay here, mate. Maybe no more Martinis though, eh?" He cringed—presumably realising the bad taste of the joke, as Rachel gave him an icy stare. He coughed and added, in a more sombre tone, "anything you need."

"I'm fine. Honestly." said Jack, addressing both of them, and trying to convince himself as much as anyone. He pulled Rachel into a hug, holding on longer than usual. "I'll call tomorrow, I promise."

"You'd better... I mean it."

"I will." Breaking the embrace, Jack said softly, "I love you, sis."

"Love you too, bro. Please stay safe."

Jack nodded, then turned to David. "Take care of her."

Without waiting for a reply, he stepped out into the night.

CHAPTER 3

* * *

Jack's head was hive-busy. A nest of rattling thoughts.

For a fleeting moment, a thread of quiet rationality cut through the chaos:

Maybe the email was from my posting on Nethunt.

Someone might have reached out.

He sat down at the dining table, immediately reached for his laptop and logged on to check the site.

No notifications.

He cradled his chin in his hands as he wondered where else this message could have come from. Coming to no immediate conclusions, he ambled to the kitchen and poured himself a large glass of bourbon, took a sip and returned to the dining table.

He reached for his phone to check the email again.

"She's not the only one," he muttered aloud, his voice trembling.

He lit a cigarette, took a shaky drag and rolled his drink around in his glass.

Still staring at the email, he exited it and his breath caught in his throat when another popped into his inbox.

No subject. Same sender.

He felt his heart thump in his chest. A heavy timpani drum beat.

He tapped to open the new email.

No words this time. Just a link.

Jack's stomach twisted. He knew better than to tap on email links from anonymous senders, but the temptation screamed at him.

His thumb trembled, hovering over the link like a hummingbird in flight.

I'm not going to tap on that link.

But... what if they're trying to tell me more about Lisa?

Jack moved his thumb up to the 'reply' icon.

A reply would be safer.

The blank email screen stared back at him as he started to type. He wrote a short, cautious response, giving nothing away about himself and being sure not to mention Lisa:

'I'm not going to click on a link from an anonymous email. Who are you? What are you trying to tell me?'

He finished his cigarette and stubbed it out in the ashtray, singeing the tip of his finger in the process. He noticed how the ashtray was already starting to fill up again.

He downed his drink and, with a shaky breath, he sent the email.

Doubt crept in immediately.

Should I have sent that?

Fuck it. What's done is done.

He refilled his glass and tramped around the room, his restless energy consuming him.

His mind worked overtime, the demon of desperation sinking its claws deeply into Jack's soul.

He darted back to his phone to check for a response, knowing full well no reply would come so quickly—if at all.

His pulse spiked as he saw that there *was* a new message—not from the original sender, but a '*delivery unsuccessful*' notice.

He shuddered.

How can this be possible?

I only received an email from this address a few moments ago.

CHAPTER 3

Had they deleted their account to cover their tracks, already?

The question gnawed at him, but deep down, Jack already knew what he would do. The decision had already been made in the deep, dark recesses of his mind.

He took a moment. Paced around his living room and scratched his neck, even though there was no itch to scratch.

Lit another cigarette.

Another glass of bourbon.

More pacing.

Finally, he sat back down, his hand trembling as he gripped the phone. He stared at the email, his thumb quivering over it.

He paused for a second—holding on to the illusion of free will—took a breath, then tapped on the link.

Jack blew air from his cheeks as a news article popped up. A wave of relief. And then one of confusion. It didn't appear to be a phishing email after all, but he couldn't imagine why an anonymous person would send him this.

The article was short and succinct:

POLICE APPEAL FOR WITNESSES IN VICTORIA PARK MURDER INVESTIGATION

Police, investigating the death of a young male in North London, are appealing for witnesses.

Police were called to Victoria park on Friday morning after the body of a young male was discovered by a local dog walker. The man was found dead as a result of stab wounds in Victoria Park, North London and has been identified as Nathan Brown, 36, of Hackney, North London.

Enquiries are ongoing and the police are appealing for witnesses who may have been in the area between 10 p.m. on Thursday evening and 8am Friday morning.

Senior Investigating Officer, Susan Reeves said: "Our thoughts are with the family of the deceased at this time and we would like to appeal to anyone who may have any information in this case, to assist us with our inquiries and help us bring the perpetrator to justice.

"As yet, no suspects have been identified.

"If you have any information that you think could help our investigation, please call the Metropolitan police, or contact Crimestoppers anonymously."

Jack feverishly read the article several times, scanning its brief contents for a clue he might have missed. A detail that would be relevant to him. Something that he needed to know.

The name Nathan Brown didn't mean anything to him and he didn't know anyone from Hackney. His eyes widened as he noticed the name of the Senior Investigating Officer on this case:

Susan Reeves. The same detective who had worked Lisa's case.

Jack's mind dredged up unwanted memories of what had happened to Lisa a year ago and he realised his forehead had begun to drip with sweat.

A single bead dropped onto the screen of his phone and, like a tiny magnifying glass, it enlarged the font size of some text above the article title.

The date.

This is from three months ago.

CHAPTER 3

Why is it being sent to me now? And why, anonymously?
He wiped his brow with a shirtsleeve.

Standing up, slightly jelly-legged, Jack gulped down his glass of bourbon and went to the kitchen to pour another. His head pounded. He took a large sip, a futile attempt to calm the voices which were screaming in his mind.

Why was I sent this?

What could this mean?

Does it have anything to do with what happened to Lisa?

A flash of Lisa's face, distorted with terror, entered Jack's mind. He took another sip, placed the glass down, went to the bathroom and splashed some cold water on his face. He shuddered from the sensation.

Looking at himself in the mirror, it was a face that he barely recognised now. The dark rings around his eyes, the wrinkles that had only been slight a few years ago, were now etched solidly into his brow. His hair, a strewn mess. His eyes, wild. He took a few deep breaths to calm his nerves and slow his rampant thinking, all the while staring at himself intently in the mirror. "Pull yourself together, Jack," he said aloud to his reflection.

Finally, a thought of some utility popped into his ravaged mind:

Keep digging, Jack. Maybe there's more I need to find here.

Drying off his face, Jack returned to the living room and reached for his laptop. Trying hastily to log in to the Nethunt site, he mistyped his password, paused, cracked his knuckles and tried again.

Upon accessing the site, he navigated to the search function and typed in the name of the victim from the article: '*Nathan Brown*'. He clicked on the search button and results came back almost instantly. There was one main thread that appeared in the search results, titled: *'Nathan Brown – Unsolved Victoria Park Murder'*.

Jack clicked on the link.

The thread explained the case in much more detail than the article, and there were reams of information for Jack to sift through with numerous subposts linked from the main thread. He first read through the outline of the case that had been posted on the forum:

Nathan Brown was found dead on Friday November 23rd 2018 in Victoria Park, as a result of stab wounds sustained in an attack, by an unknown assailant.

As yet no suspects have been identified and no witnesses have come forward.

Please can you help find Nathan's killer and bring me some form of justice.

Nathan was wearing gym clothes when he was attacked and it was likely he was out for his evening run in Victoria Park at the time.

He typically went out for an evening run around 9 p.m. twice a week on Tuesdays and Thursdays and would always run through the park which was only a few minutes walk from where he lived in Hackney.

As far as I know, Nathan didn't have any enemies and I think this was an unprovoked attack, although the evidence does seem to show that he was targeted for some reason, but you won't find this out through the press.

I've added a number of subposts to this thread which provide some further insight into the details of the case that aren't being

CHAPTER 3

shared by the police, in the hope that someone can help me piece this together and figure out who killed Nathan and for what reason.

Nathan was a good man; kind hearted and loyal. He was liked by all who knew him and he was a great brother to me.
Please help in any way you can to bring his killer to justice.

Jack realised that the post had been written by the sister of the deceased and glanced upwards to see the username of the person who posted the thread—Jennifer Brown.

A tear formed in his eye as he reflected on the pain he had been going through and knew she must be feeling the same way. Hopeless, lost, angry, desperate were the first words that came to mind.

After reading the outline of the case, Jack scanned down to see one of the subposts, also submitted by Jennifer, titled: *'Key Evidence – The Debt is Paid'.*

He drew a sharp breath, clicked on the link, and read the contents of this second post:

One of the compelling pieces of evidence in this case (which has not been reported by the police) was that when my brother's body was found, by a local dog walker, he had noticed first that Nathan's gym top had been ripped open, and words had been scrawled on his back with a permanent marker pen. It seemed as though a message was being sent to someone through this killing of my brother.
The words were clear to see without the dog walker having to move the body and simply stated:

'THE DEBT HAS BEEN PAID'

If anyone has any information about what this might mean, please reach out on this thread or send me a private message. As far as I know, Nathan didn't have any debts and hadn't got in with loan sharks of any sort. He did have problems with money in his past, but he seemed to have put these behind him and was actually recently doing really well for himself, so I don't know what this could mean.

Please scan the other subposts for more information on other evidence and reach out if you think you can help me in any way at all.

"The debt has been paid?" Jack whispered to himself.

What has this got to do with Lisa?

He rolled another cigarette and took a long drag, as if sucking the very life out of the thing, before proceeding to the next subpost in the list.

This one was titled: *'Key Evidence – The photograph'*.

Jack's heart skipped a beat.

The title of this post resonated much more with him and his hands shook as he clicked on the link.

This second post showed a photograph of a photograph. Presumably of Nathan. The photograph was smeared red. At first Jack thought that there had been a problem in the processing of the photo; maybe a lens flare.

His body tensed as he realised that the photograph was actually smeared with blood.

He drew in a shaky breath, took a sip of bourbon, stubbed out his cigarette in the overflowing ashtray and carried on to read the text below the image:

CHAPTER 3

A significant piece of evidence that the police have not shared is that Nathan's body was found with a photograph pinned to his clothing, as shown above.

The police would not release this evidence to me, but the person who discovered the body took a photo on his phone and shared it with me directly through this site.

It pains me to do so, but I wanted to share this here, so that it might make sense to someone who is reading this.

The photograph is one that is of Nathan and looks as though it was taken covertly while Nathan was sitting in a coffee shop.

I have no idea who took the photo, when, or where this was taken. If you think that you can help explain this, then please comment directly on this post, or reach out to me, via direct message.

As Jack read this post his mouth widened. His peripheral vision disappeared and only his laptop was in focus. As he stared at the screen the background of the room seemed to move away from him rapidly as if in a dolly zoom shot in a movie.

He felt as though he was falling.

Hurtling towards the ground at a thousand miles an hour.

This was why he was sent the link, he thought. This is the similarity. Lisa's photo.

'She's not the only one'? Could Nathan Brown be the *other one?*

Could the person who killed Nathan be the same person who killed Lisa?

With his fingers trembling, Jack began to type a message to Jennifer.

Chapter 4

Lisa had been declared dead on a Saturday. The darkest of Saturdays in Jack's life. After reading about Nathan, his memories came flooding back in an excruciating stream of flashes. He couldn't hide from them now. Not even the booze could contain them this time.

He remembered it all.

Vividly.

Saturday 24th March 2018

Birdsong. Cerulean blue skies. Early Spring blossom. A new dawn. The early days of Spring were always Jack's favourite. On the morning of that fateful day, he and Lisa had eaten eggs benedict with a cafetière of freshly brewed Guatemalan coffee on the balcony of their newly purchased apartment, overlooking the river while the sun rose in a burst of orangey-red haze.

They had shared the usual meaningless chit-chat.

The sort of meaningless chat that actually meant everything. Meant they were entirely in sync and totally at peace and

CHAPTER 4

infatuated with each other.

He had known that the apartment was way above their means and had questioned how Lisa had somehow pulled together the majority of the deposit for the place. She had said never to ask how she got 'the scratch together', as she put it, and Jack had agreed. She had joked about being the breadwinner in their relationship, but he knew that her salary as a marketing executive wouldn't have stretched to this.

"Considerable bonus?" he had asked, to which she had responded with *"Something like that,"* winked, and moved on to another topic. That was the end of it. Jack had never asked again, although it had played on his mind. Niggled at him ever since.

Ignorance is bliss.

Jack and Lisa held an incredible amount of trust in each other; the level of trust that he'd previously only known to be shared between childhood friends. They'd been together for twelve years at this point—married for four. And yet, Jack could still remember the first time he ever laid eyes on Lisa, as if it had happened yesterday...

* * *

Ralph had introduced Jack and Lisa those twelve years ago, at a dinner party he and his wife, Barbara, had hosted. Barbara didn't know Lisa directly, but had been introduced via a mutual friend, Shelly, who took frequent gym classes with Lisa.

Shelly, already married, already bored, got off on the idea of playing matchmaker and had suggested that Lisa would be a perfect fit for Jack, the eternal bachelor.

At the dinner, the two of them had—not so subtly—been seated next to one another and Jack had been instantly fascinated by Lisa, and not just by her captivating looks: the long straight blonde hair, high cheekbones, full lips and piercing eyes which taunted Jack with a sexual mystery. She spoke eloquently. Passionately. And this only added to her allure. He couldn't stop looking at her; scanning every detail in wonder. Imagining kissing those lips. Imagining her wanting him.

Lisa's vivacious way mesmerised him in a way no other woman ever had and he hung on her every word like a dog waiting expectantly for a treat. It was clear she was also interested in him, too; laughing at his appalling jokes and touching him fervently on the arm or hand during the evening. The frequency of the touching correlating perfectly with the amount of wine consumed in an $x=y$ symmetry.

Jack had forgotten about the other guests at the party that night. He was totally enchanted with Lisa and seemingly, she, with him.

As the evening drew on they had settled together into a sofa in the living room, each cradling a glass of wine in one hand; their idle hands frequently in contact with the body of the other. By the end of the evening they were in each other's arms and had gone home together. Just three months later they had moved in with one another.

Shelly shamelessly took all the plaudits.

Eternal bachelor Jack was no more.

* * *

CHAPTER 4

That Saturday evening, Jack sat at a large oak table at his local pub. He sipped a pint. Before fully swallowing, he took a bite of a double cheeseburger with extra chillies, washed it down with a second sip and responded to Ralph. "Yeah I guess, I could stay for another couple." Wiping his mouth and clearing the errant strand of melted cheese from his bottom lip, he continued, "I'll check with the boss."

"You can't leave me here with Steve all alone, mate. There's only so many of his tawdry jokes I can handle in one day," Ralph said, looking over at Steve with a smirk.

Sitting up straight in feigned upset, Steve retorted, "Whatever, guys. Tawdry? That's a big word for you, Ralph. I'll have you know the guys at work consider me quite the comical genius." He smiled, exposing his broad, Essex teeth. "Maybe you're just not my audience."

Steve, a friend of Ralph's, who he'd introduced to Jack several years ago, was one of those ageless lads. Always fun on a night out. Constant banter. Forever single. The archetypal Peter Pan. The sort of guy you would invite out for a night on the booze, but never anything that was less superficial. Small doses were required when dealing with Steve and Jack had known that Ralph's comment was at least partly said in seriousness.

Steve was area manager of a sales team for a large multinational corporation and he exuded the misguided confidence of many a salesman. He had an air of optimism that was unwavering. It was hard to keep him down and that attitude made him great fun to be around, but only ever in short bursts.

His enthusiasm was tiring.

"That's what you get for being the boss," snorted Ralph.

Jack took his phone from his pocket and sent a quick message to Lisa:

'Hey babe. I'm just out with Ralph and Steve at the mo. Having a good old catch up. Any chance you'd be okay to get the train back tonight? Let me know if it's a problem though and I'll come and pick you up. I'm easy either way, don't want to leave you hanging for these guys. Xxx'

Jack always typed three kisses to Lisa.

Steve downed his pint. He followed this up with a grunt, and a tensing of his arm muscles in a ritualistic, mini celebration. "Another round, gents?" Steve propositioned.

Ralph gave a subtle nod, without looking at Steve. His interest, firmly fixed on the football.

Steve's eyes moved over to Jack.

"One sec, mate," Jack said. "Just waiting for a message back from Lisa. I've not finished this one yet. Get yourself and Ralph one and I'll grab myself one in a mo, if I get the all clear, yeah?"

"Fair do's," said Steve, as he stood up and removed his wallet from his ironic skinny jeans. "Back in a sec."

"You know he's gonna get you one anyway," said Ralph, momentarily turning around from the TV to face Jack, raising his eyebrows in an expression that Jack decoded as *'typical Steve'*.

Jack's phone buzzed in his pocket. A response from Lisa:

'Okay babe. Yeah that's fine. I know you need your guy time and I'm fine to have a bit of me time too. I think I'll head to the gym after work instead. You can make it up to me later though, okay? Oh, and don't let Steve lead you astray! Love you Xx'

Lisa only ever sent two kisses.

Jack looked over at Steve, waiting impatiently at the bar which was three-deep with punters, caught his eye and gave

CHAPTER 4

him a thumbs-up gesture. 'Good man' Steve mouthed back and proceeded to squash his way into the baying herd.

* * *

A flurry of feathers. A swarming flock of birds darting towards his face. The birds, pecked holes in his cheeks and tapped their beaks on his head, trying to drill into his frantic brain. A rhythmic, hollow, procession of taps.

Jack came to. The banging sound of his dream instantly replaced with the realisation that there was a knocking at his door. He pried himself off the sofa, wiping crusty drool from his face with a lazy hand.

"Mr Stevens... Are you there? Mr Stevens?" came a voice from beyond.

Slowly getting to his feet in a delirious haze and walking like a badly conducted marionette towards the door of his apartment, Jack hollered, "Just a second!" He winced from both the boom of his own voice and the rhythmic battering of the incessant knocking.

Jack took a look at his watch, squinting to read the dial of the face.

1:30 a.m.?

Why would someone be knocking at my door at this time? And where's Lisa?

"Lise? Baby?" Jack slurred, as he continued to traipse toward the apartment door, tripping over one of his shoes left awkwardly in the middle of the hallway.

No response.

Reaching the door, Jack stretched his eyes wide and rubbed his hands on his cheeks in an attempt to right himself. He opened the door.

In front of him were two men. Tall. Beards. Uniforms.

Police officers?

Oh shit, what have I done?

"Mr Stevens?" said one of the men, while brandishing a form of identification. Both were looking squarely at Jack. Furrowed brows.

"Yes," Jack said, responding in a way that sounded like a question.

"I'm DI Andrews of the Metropolitan Police. This is DS Hathaway. May we come in?" he said, gesturing with an open hand.

"What's this about? It's one thirty in the morning."

"It really would be better if we came in," insisted DI Andrews, his eyes, desperate.

Hathaway was now looking at his own feet.

Jack said nothing for a few moments and stared blankly at the officers.

"Please," urged Andrews.

Without saying a word, Jack led the officers through the hallway and into the living room. He quickly tidied away his errant shoes and socks, while Andrews and Hathaway took a seat on the sofa.

"Perhaps you should sit down, too," said Andrews, perching on the edge of the sofa. The tone of the officer's voice was melancholy. Jack obliged, taking a seat at one of the dining table chairs a few feet away from the sofa.

Andrews cleared his throat. "I'm afraid we have some bad news, Mr Stevens. Yesterday evening, your wife, Mrs Stevens...

CHAPTER 4

" He shifted his posture, shared a glance with Hathaway and then focused back on Jack. "She... was the victim of an attack—"

"What do you mean, attack?! Where's Lisa?" Jack exclaimed, interrupting the officer. Thoroughly awake and highly animated. His eyes, ocean-wide.

Andrews removed his hat, held it in his lap and leaned forward so far he was almost falling off the sofa; all the time meeting Jack's gaze. "I'm sorry, sir. Lisa... your wife... It seems she was attacked last night. She was found by a passer-by in—"

"Where is she?" Jack pleaded, interrupting again.

"I'm so sorry to have to tell you this," Andrews continued. Jack noticed a tear forming in the officer's eye and his bottom lip quivering. "Your wife... Lisa... she's..." He paused, took a deep breath and gripped his hat tight. "She's dead."

Jack's eyes squinted. His head span. His mouth opened.
No words.

Chapter 5

Rain ran in rivulets down the window beside Jack as he sipped his coffee. Sitting alone in the booth of the cafe, he looked out at the pavement outside and watched as the water pooled on the surface of the uneven paving; the splashes of heavy rain creating distortions in the patterns of the slabs.

He sat and waited for Jennifer to arrive. Having reached out to her on Nethunt he'd asked if they could talk about Lisa's case and the similarities with that of her brother's, hoping that together they may uncover more details that would help them mutually find answers. Jennifer had responded almost immediately—sympathetically and sensitively—seemingly relieved that there was someone else out there with a shared sense of grief. She'd suggested meeting up in person to talk and Jack had suggested a cafe that he knew well, was often quiet during the morning on a weekday and served, according to his tastes, incredible coffee.

Morgan's Cafe was inspired by 50's style American diners, but in a subtle and classy way. Booths, with seating upholstered in leather and a solid wood table in the centre, could seat 4 people comfortably and were placed equidistantly along two of the walls. A few tables were scattered on the main floor; one of which was being tended to by a young waitress, clearing away a couple of leftover coffee cups and a plate with the remnants of a pastry. Soft jazz music filled the air in an ambient, non-intrusive way.

Much like a pub, the coffee bar was lined with a number of stools. Apart from Jack, the only other customer was propped up on one of the stools, idly munching on a baguette and making sporadic chit-chat in between bites with the woman serving from behind the bar.

As the waitress finished clearing the table she came over to Jack. He noticed her name tag: '*Lisa*'. He winced.

"Can I get you anything else?" she said, brightly.

Making sure not to address her on a first name basis, he replied "Another flat white wouldn't go amiss. Thanks."

"Sure thing. I'll bring it over shortly."

Jack watched as the waitress walked away. His stare transfixed and lazy.

His gaze was averted by noticing something in his peripheral vision—the door of the café being opened, accompanied by the jingling of a bell.

A young woman, late twenties perhaps, entered, shook off an umbrella and placed it in a receptacle by the door. She wore a neck scarf, jeans and a tight fitting jumper that showed off an athletic physique. She took a second to straighten up her windswept hair and then walked slowly through the café, her eyes darting from side to side as she surveyed the place.

She caught Jack's eye and started towards him.

"Jack… Is it Jack?" she said, glancing down at him. She blinked and bit her lip.

Jack was lost for words for a second. She was ravishing. Long brown hair, beautiful clean complexion, dimples at the corners of her mouth and bright green eyes. His gaze lingered just a little too long.

"Jennifer?"

"Yes, or just Jen," she said, nodding her head slightly. She reached out a hand and Jack stood up to shake it.

"Please take a seat," Jack said, motioning to the opposite side of the booth. "Can I get you a coffee?"

"Thanks. Yeah, that would be great. Cappuccino? I need something to warm me up now. It's horrid out there."

Jack ushered over the waitress, who promptly came back to the table. He ordered a cappuccino and she shuffled back to the coffee bar to prepare the drinks.

"Yeah it's pretty brutal out there," agreed Jack, cringing at the fact that he was so blown away by the sight of her that he could only resort to small talk about the weather.

"Oh my God, I just want to say thank you so much for reaching out to me," said Jennifer, with animated hands, as she took a seat in the booth and placed her bag beside her. "You don't know how good it feels to finally have someone to be able to talk to about this."

Jack picked up on some nervousness about Jennifer as she fidgeted with the contents of her bag. *Was it nervousness?* He wasn't sure. He didn't know her from Adam. Or should that be Eve? This might be her normal demeanour, he considered, but this situation was anything but *normal*—two bereaved strangers meeting at a random location for coffee to share their stories.

I wouldn't blame her for being nervous.

Jennifer pulled out a phone and a notepad, set them down on the table between them and rested her hands in her lap.

Jack felt a rush of anxiety; his armpits started to sweat.

CHAPTER 5

Perhaps it was the sight of Jennifer more so than the situation itself. She wasn't at all what he expected.

Before he had time to stop himself he noticed that he was unconsciously mirroring her nervousness by fidgeting with his own phone and pointlessly checking his pockets.

Jennifer looked up at Jack with those big green eyes of hers and it brought him into the present moment. In a conscious effort to cease his fidgeting, he put his phone on the table, face down, and clasped his hands.

"Yeah, I know what you mean. People can be sympathetic, but they don't really get how I feel. Thanks for suggesting to meet up. It's really nice to speak face to face." Jack paused for a second, not sure if he should ask the question that was on his mind, but went ahead anyway. "I was actually wondering if you reached out to *me*?"

"What do you mean?"

Realising he was clearly wrong about this, his anxiety ratcheted a step higher. The tempo of his pulse raised.

"Umm, you see, I uh, got this message from someone that led me to Nathan's case. I wondered if... if *you* might have sent it?" Jack picked up his phone, brought up the original email that he had received from the anonymous sender and showed it to Jennifer.

"*She's not the only one?* How creepy?! No, I never sent this to you. Oh God, that's made the hairs on the back of my neck stand up."

"And then there was this," Jack continued, showing the follow-up email. "This link took me to a news article about your brother's de..." He trailed off . "About your brother."

"Oh wow. I can understand why you thought it might be me, but I'd not actually heard about your wife's case. Also, there's no way I'd just leave it hanging cryptically like that. How rude." Jennifer smiled at Jack and he smiled back. He was picking up on a warm, casual nature from her and he felt his anxiety calming; his pulse steadying.

The waitress approached the table and set the two coffees down. "Cappuccino," she trilled, as she slid the frothy mug over to Jennifer, "And a flat white," she pointed to the mug she'd set down in front of Jack. "Can I get you any sugar?"

"Please," said Jack.

"Not for me, thanks."

The waitress returned with a pot of brown sugar, set it down and walked back to the coffee bar.

"Mmmmm. That's just what I needed," sighed Jennifer, cradling her coffee mug in both hands and looking intently at Jack. "Did you not reply to the email? I know I would've."

"Yeah, I did. It failed to send. It's as though... I don't know... whoever sent the email, disabled the account after sending the messages."

"Creepier and creepier." Jennifer put down her coffee and shuddered. Jack wasn't sure if it was involuntary or not. "You said in your message that there were some similarities in what happened to Lisa. Like what?"

The anxiety kicked back in. Jack knew that he wanted to talk about the details, but whenever he let himself think about it, his body tightened and his throat went dry. He took a sip of his coffee.

Why didn't I go for decaf?

"I find it a little... difficult to talk about, so you might need to bear with me."

Jennifer reached out a hand to touch Jack's. "I understand. Take your time."

CHAPTER 5

The touch of Jennifer's hand steadied Jack. Gave him the strength to tell his story.

"She... Lisa, was going through Battersea Park. She'd often walk through the park from her gym when heading home. That's where she was found. She'd been... stabbed." Jack's chest tightened and he felt a tear forming in his eyes. He took a few seconds to pause. He felt Jennifer's hand squeeze his. Clearing his throat, he continued. "Her throat had been slit and she... w–was just left there... to d–" Jack's voice cracked; he couldn't say the word. A tear dropped onto the wooden table and he reached for a napkin to wipe the tear from the surface. A vain attempt to try and stifle the emotion. "Whoever did this. Whoever killed her. They... pinned a photograph to her body." Jack sniffed. Wiped his nose. "Sorry, this is really hard." He withheld the detail that he was originally supposed to pick Lisa up from work on that day. There was no need to share that guilt.

"Jesus, this definitely sounds the same. Was the picture of Lisa?"

"Yeah, a picture of her and not one I... recognised," said Jack, as he took a sip of his coffee. He gulped hard, forcing it down his tight throat.

"Were there any words on her body like with N–Nathan?" said Jennifer, stumbling on her words.

"No, nothing like that." Noticing that she, too, was struggling a little now, Jack gave her hand a reciprocal squeeze. "At least not from what the police have told me."

"Did she have any enemies?"

"No. Lisa? No. No way. She was the most kind-hearted person I've ever known."

"Anything strange about how she'd been acting? Sorry if

this is a little intrusive."

Jack looked up in the air, recalling in his mind the days and weeks leading up to Lisa's death. "Nothing that stands out. I've been over this in my head so many times." Looking back down, he met Jennifer's eyes. "I can't think of any reason she would be targeted. And it certainly looks like both she and Nathan were targeted... doesn't it?"

Jennifer sighed. "Yeah, it really seems that way," she said in a whisper, as she took her hand away from Jack's and began nervously twisting her fingers through her hair.

"And you can't think of any reason for Nathan to be targeted? In your post on Nethunt you said he had problems with money in his past." Jack raised his tone at the end of the sentence, leaving the comment sounding like a question.

Moving her hands back to cradle her coffee and take a sip, Jennifer replied, "Yeah he did have some gambling problems in his past. He could get himself in some financial trouble because of it."

"Any serious trouble?"

"No, not that I know of. He actually seemed to be doing really well for himself."

"How so?"

"Well, he'd got a better job and must have been making decent money. He'd just bought himself a brand new car. A BMW. Always a show off, was Nathan." She looked down at the table for a brief moment before reverting her gaze back to Jack. "Do you think that's what this is? Do you think it's about money?" Her eyebrows were raised at the centre, creating a furrow in her brow. A puppy dog expression. Her bright green eyes looked pleadingly at Jack. Emerald eyes that were full of questions.

CHAPTER 5

"It might make sense with those words that were scrawled on him. What was it? The debt has been paid?"

Jennifer's eyes were etched with grief. "Yeah that's what it said... And you say Lisa's body didn't have these words. Just the photo?"

"Yeah that's right. No words. Just the photo," Jack confirmed, shaking his head and giving a shallow shrug.

Jennifer looked as though she was about to say something, but instead took another sip of her coffee. Setting the cup down on the table, she opened her hands and said, "I know this might sound weird, but do you think I could see where it happened? With... with Lisa?"

"You want to see where Lisa was—"

"I just know that I needed to see where Nathan was... f-found. It might be helpful to compare the sites? I don't know..."

Jack paused for a moment. He didn't know what good it would do, but resolved that it couldn't do any harm. "I guess so. Would you want me to take you?"

"I would really appreciate that. I don't know why, but I feel if I could see the place I might understand more. That's if you wouldn't find it too hard and if you're not too busy... Are you not working today?"

"Yeah that's not a problem. I've got my car parked around back and no, I'm not working today. I'm actually having a bit of time off right now, so it would be good to have the company to be honest."

"Okay, great. What do you do, when you're not having time off?"

"I'm a journalist. For the Weekly Reporter. Do you know it?"

"That's so cool! Yeah, I know it. I read it most weeks,"

Jennifer beamed. "I was actually reading a piece yesterday titled *'Time to ditch Shoreditch?'* about how the hipster culture is springing up in other parts of London and that there's now more trendy areas to hang out."

Jack felt his face going red with embarrassment and couldn't help but burst out laughing.

"What's so funny?"

"Well you see, that's actually my piece."

"No way!" Jennifer exclaimed, reaching out and grabbing Jack's hand again.

"Yeah, honestly. It's the piece I just finished before taking some time out."

"Oh wow. To think, I was just reading it yesterday and now I'm sat across from the writer! What a small world. I loved it by the way, it was a great piece. It's given me lots of ideas of where to go with the girls on our next night out."

Jack's self esteem received a well needed jolt with Jennifer's apparent enthusiasm for his work. He also felt a sense of relief that the piece had made it to print in time, and was actually quite impressed with the article title. Presumably the junior writer who'd picked it up from him had come up with it, as it was better than his draft title: *'Drinking from the ditch'*. He'd have to thank them, whenever he finally came back to the office, for sifting through his garbled nonsense and putting it into some sort of coherent structure.

"Haha. I'm really glad you liked it. It was actually quite cathartic to write. Gave me a chance to get paid for getting drunk and to berate hipster culture all in one fell swoop."

"*Cathartic. Berate,*" echoed Jennifer, with raised eyebrows. "I can tell you're a writer, just by dropping in those fifty cent words."

CHAPTER 5

Jack flashed a smile towards Jennifer and she mirrored him. Averting his gaze, he glanced out of the window and took a final sip of his coffee. "Okay, looks like the rain's easing off. Let's get out of here, shall we?"

* * *

The drive to Battersea park was surreal. Here was Jack taking a strange new woman to visit the site where his wife had been brutally killed. It should have felt like a morbid experience—a road-trip of the macabre—but for some reason it didn't seem that way. He and Jennifer made casual chit-chat on the journey; talked about where they grew up and what life in London had been like for them since moving here. Jack was surprised that, having known Jennifer for only an hour, she seemed to have this calming effect on him and he was now feeling—for him at least—quite at peace.

A state he hadn't known for some time.

Parking the car on the west side of the park, the two of them walked through Central Avenue, past the bandstand, a couple of lonely tennis courts and up to the northeast corner. Heading away from the main tree-lined pathway, which was awash with joggers and dog walkers, they wandered off on a narrow path, over a slight ridge to an area which was more densely populated with trees, longer grass and out of sight of the main thoroughfares.

This was it. The spot where Jack had been told Lisa was found.

Near one of the trees, a withering and decaying bunch of

flowers lay. Jack's flowers. He would visit this site every few weeks and place a fresh bouquet on the ground near one of the trees here.

He didn't know the exact spot of his wife's death, but he always picked the same tree to leave fresh blooms.

Approaching the site, Jack stopped; almost forcibly, as if his body wouldn't let him proceed. Silently, he pointed a sole finger towards the flowers.

"Is this it?" Jennifer said, looking at Jack with raised eyebrows.

He nodded.

"And are these *your* flowers?"

Struggling to find words, Jack coughed in an attempt to spring his vocal cords into action. "Yep," he muttered.

Jennifer surveyed the scene while Jack hung back. He rested his hand on a nearby tree, as if needing support.

After a minute or so of idly raking leaves with her feet and moving fallen tree branches with her hands, Jennifer turned back towards Jack. "I don't know what I'm looking for, Jack. I guess I just figured something would spring out at me."

"Yeah this might be a big waste of time. Is there *anything* that's similar to Nathan's site?"

Jennifer glanced around for a few seconds, looking pensive. "Yes. Lots."

"Really? Like what?"

"It's a park," Jennifer said, as she gave a wry smile and stretched her hands out either side of her, bringing Jack's attention to the obvious.

Jack's forced smile faltered as he felt a soft tickle brush the back of his hand. Glancing down, he saw a butterfly— a pale, fragile creature—perched there. Its wings, traced with delicate patterns, quivered as though sharing a silent secret. He watched, transfixed, as it fluttered away, disappearing into the trees in a whisper of motion.

His eyes lingered where it had rested—and froze. What it had hidden beneath its delicate wings now came into focus.

At first, he thought it was just the rough pattern of the bark, but no.

It was something sharper. Deliberate. Intentional.

Uneven grooves carved into the wood that seared into his mind like fire.

His breath caught in his throat as he leaned closer, his fingers trembling against the wood.

His heart began to hammer, loud and wild.

Colour drained from his face.

"I don't know why I thought we'd find anything. If there were any clues here I'm sure they'd be long gone by now, eh? Thanks for indulging me though, I'm sure this wasn't easy for you. Shall we go?" Jennifer said, glancing at Jack, whose gaze was fixed on the tree in horror. "What is it, Jack?"

Jack said nothing.

Couldn't say anything.

Jennifer hurried over, her voice rising. "Jack? Are you okay?" He didn't respond, his eyes fixed on the tree as if rooted in place. Transfixed. Perplexed.

Jennifer's eyes followed Jack's gaze to where his hand met the rough texture of the tree trunk. Squinting, she strained to see what had captured Jack's attention. Finally, she made out faint etchings in the wood; barely visible, just above Jack's trembling hand.

Etchings of words.

Five words.

'THE DEBT HAS BEEN PAID'.

A few moments of stunned silence passed as they stood and stared at the etchings on the bark. Finally Jennifer managed a few stuttered words. "It's the same. Th-the same as Nathan. It's definitely the... th-the same words."

Her face was white.

Jack staggered away from the tree, his hand remaining outstretched towards the etching. Seeing the inscribed words and the sudden realisation of what this meant had hit him like a hammer blow. His knees buckled and he planted himself down on the wet, leaf-covered ground.

Looking down at Jack, Jennifer said, "Do you know what this means, Jack?" His eyes were glassy. Unresponsive. She answered her own question. "It must *definitely* be the same person who kill—" she trailed off. "Who did this to Nathan."

Jack's body shook from the emotional shock and the feel of the cold earth. He lifted his gaze up to meet Jennifer; his eyes, wild and determined. "They must... they must have missed it," he said. His voice, barely a whisper.

"Who? The police?"

"Yeah. They never said anything about this. They must have missed it." Looking away from Jennifer now and back over to the tree, he continued, his head shaking, "I guess I missed it, too."

Looking back over at Jennifer, he noticed a compassionate colour in her gaze. He felt she wanted to say something, but she remained quiet.

Needing to fill the silence, he said, "Maybe Susan will reopen the investigation when she hears about this." His words were hollow. It was a prayer not an expectation.

CHAPTER 5

"Susan?" Jennifer stooped down to Jack's level, looking him in the eye.

"The SIO on Lisa's case. She was also the SIO on Nathan's case, wasn't she? You must have spoken to her during the investigation into Nathan's death."

A flash of recognition. "Oh, Miss Reeves. I never got on first name terms with her. You must have spoken to her a lot to be on first name terms."

Jack sighed. "Too many times perhaps. She wanted nothing to do with me in the end. And she hated it when I called her by her first name... forever insisting that I refer to her as '*Detective Reeves*'. I did at first, but my patience soon wore thin."

With the initial shock abated, Jack put out a hand, indicating he wanted help getting up from the wet ground. Jennifer obliged, helping him up to his feet.

"I guess my journalistic tendencies didn't do me any favours. Too keen to question what they were doing and how they were doing it," Jack said, as he dusted off wet leaves from his mud soaked jeans. "I think I've burnt my bridges there. I guess you could say I'm now quite cynical about police procedure. Perhaps... perhaps if you called her to tell her about this? About what we've found here? I don't think she'd be too pleased to hear from me."

"Of course I will, Jack." Jennifer paused for a second, took a breath and then continued. "They had given up on Nathan's case, too, you know, but maybe with this link between the two they'll be forced to reconsider."

"Perhaps. I hope so," said Jack, a cynicism to his voice.

"I'll call them as soon as I get home, okay?"

"Thanks. And thanks for meeting with me, Jennifer—"

"Jen," she interrupted, broadcasting a warm smile.

"Jen. Okay, Jen. Thanks for coming to meet with me, Jen. I don't know how I would have handled finding this on my own," he said, as he pointed at the etching in the bark without looking directly.

"I'm glad I could be here when you found it. It works the same for me, too, you know?" Jen reached towards Jack, putting her hands on his shoulders and looking him in the eye sincerely. "I've not had anyone to share this with who could relate either. Even my parents have given up and closed themselves off to it. They've become totally withdrawn."

Jack felt a familiar pang of unease at Jennifer touching him. Guilt. His chest tightened. It should have felt comforting, but instinctively he knew he shouldn't have another woman's hands on him. And certainly not at the site of his wife's death.

He gently shrugged his shoulders and puffed out his chest, giving Jen a subtle message that he wasn't comfortable. Without the need for words, she got the message, removed her hands and put them awkwardly into the front pockets of her jeans, rocking back and forth on her heels, as she gazed at the ground.

"Give you a lift home?" Jack finally offered, after several moments silence.

"Sure. Thanks, Jack."

* * *

From Battersea Park, it was a short fifteen minute drive to Jen's flat in Balham. The shocking nature of the revelation they'd uncovered had resulted in Jack and Jen remaining quiet for the majority of that journey. Stony faced. Shaken.

On their route they passed Clapham Common and as they did Jack felt a wave of unease. He glanced over at Jen and was unsurprised to see that she also seemed on edge. They had both suffered tragedy associated with London's parks and seeing another one today was triggering.

Needing to slice through the silence and break the unbearable tension, Jack motioned to a road leading away from the Common.

"I used to live around here, you know?"

"Sorry?" Jen replied, clearly lost in her own thoughts.

"Yeah, straight out of uni. I rented my first place around here, with my mate, Ralph."

"Really? Me, too!" Jen fidgeted with her seat belt, adjusting her position, so she could turn to face Jack and see out of the window where he had pointed.

Jack's chest lightened with a feeling of relief that the icy silence had been broken. "Seems like so many people start out their post-grad London life here, eh?" he said.

"Sure does. So many poncy estate agents in their cheap Topman suits, thinking they own the place," said Jen, with a slight smile. "How long did you stay around here?"

"Too long. I lived with Ralph for a few years and then when I met Lisa we lived here together for several years. Until we could afford our own place. Then I finally got out. It was never really my scene."

"I felt the same, but as you can see, I didn't move far."

"Yeah, just a couple of miles, eh? How do you like Balham?"

"It's okay, I guess," mused Jen. "More authentic than Clapham, I reckon. Whereabouts do you live now?"

"West. Chiswick area."

"Oh, how the other half live?!" Jen chuckled.

The normality of the conversation brought a gentle feeling of contentment.

Jack smiled.

* * *

"This is me, here," said Jen, pointing to a small Victorian terraced house. Jack pulled up alongside the kerb, put the car in park and switched off the engine.

"Looks nice. You live alone?"

"Yeah I do for now. I had a room-mate until a few months ago. She moved out and got a place with her boyfriend. To be honest, I love it. It's actually been really nice having my own space. It's not the whole house, it's a flat conversion and I have the first floor."

"Not many of these houses aren't flat conversions these days."

"So true," Jen replied, as she grabbed her bag from the footwell. "Thanks again, Jack, for today. It's really helped being able to talk this through with you. And I'm glad I could be there with you when we found... well... you know."

"I know. You're welcome. And thanks for being there for me, too."

Jen undid her seatbelt and leant over to give Jack an embrace, which he welcomed and reciprocated. Breaking the embrace, she looked Jack in the eye and said, "We'll get justice for Lisa and Nathan. We'll find who did this. Together."

Jack said nothing, instead choosing to offer just a faint smile

CHAPTER 5

and a nod.

"Thanks for dropping me off. I appreciate it. I'll give Miss Reeves... Susan... a call in a mo and I'll let you know how it goes, okay? Speak soon, yeah?"

"Thanks, Jen. Yeah, speak soon. Take care of yourself."

"You, too," said Jen, as she stepped out of the car.

Jack started the engine and drove off, leaving Jennifer with a casual wave of the hand, the voices in his head calmed. For now.

* * *

Leaning forward in her leather high-back executive chair and staring intently at the words displayed on her monitor, Susan clicked the end of a ballpoint pen rhythmically and incessantly. Her focus, suddenly disturbed by the trill ringing of her desk phone.

"Jesus Christ," she muttered, dropping the ballpoint pen and reaching for the handset. "Reeves," she snapped.

"Ma'am. It's DI Andrews, ma'am," the voice on the other end of the line said, quavering.

"What is it, Andrews? I'm quite busy preparing for this briefing. This better be good." There was only one thing Susan hated more than being interrupted and that was a lack of assertiveness. Here she was contending with both at once.

"Sorry, ma'am. I have a call for you. From a Jennifer Brown?"

"Jennifer Brown? Why do I know that name?"

"She's, uh, the uh, sister of Nathan Brown." The statement

sounded like a question.

A flash of recognition. "Oh yes, the Nathan Brown case. What does she want? Can't you deal with it, Andrews?"

"She says she has some new information and has requested to speak with you about it directly."

Susan's eyes narrowed. "New information? Okay, I guess you better put her through."

The phone line clicked as the call was transferred.

"This is Susan Reeves. Who am I speaking to?" probed Susan, knowing full well who she was speaking to—a typical tactic employed by Susan, giving her the control and allowing her to start on the front foot.

"Miss Reeves? This is Jen Brown."

"Hello, Miss Brown. What can I do for you?" Susan's voice courteous, but abrupt.

"I'm sorry to interrupt you, I'm sure you're busy, but there's something I need to... I've got some information I need to share with you."

"I assume this is about Nathan?"

"Actually no... Well, yes and no, but more about Lisa Stevens?"

"Lisa Stevens?"

"Yes, the woman who was killed last year in Battersea Park. I think you worked her case, too."

Susan's interest was piqued and her frustration resurfaced as she remembered the difficulty she'd had dealing with Lisa's husband.

What was his name?

Oh, yes. Jack.

Jack Stevens.

Susan sat up straight in her chair, picked up the pen and

proceeded to click the end of it in the same, habitual, rhythmic fashion, with her free hand.

"Miss Reeves, are you still there?"

Susan hadn't spoken for several seconds; her mind occupied in the past. Finally, she responded, "What does this have to do with you and Nathan?"

"Well, everything and nothing. I mean, not *nothing*. This is big. This could blow things wide open. I... I'm sorry. If I could just... explain."

Susan was picking up on an anxious, animated tone to Jen's voice and decided the best course of action was to slow the conversation down.

"Okay, Miss Brown. Please relax and take your time. Take a breath." Susan took one herself. "Now. One step at a time. Please tell me what this is all about."

"Thanks, Miss Reeves." A pause on the end of the line, as Jen took a deep breath, before continuing, "You see... I met with Jack, the husband of Lisa Stevens—"

"Why were you meeting with Mr Stevens?"

An audible inhale from Jen. "He-he'd reached out to me online and it turns out we had reason to believe there were... *similarities* between Nathan's and Lisa's cases."

Susan's brow furrowed. "What similarities, exactly?"

"Do you remember the photo that was left on Nathan's body?"

"Yes, I remember."

"You see, Lisa had the same kind of thing left on her."

"Yes, I remember that similarity. I worked both cases, so I'm well aware of that detail." Susan sped up the tempo of the clicking of her pen; her frustration, growing.

"Of course, Miss Reeves. I know you'll be aware of that," Jen replied, her voice trembling. "But there was something else."

"Something else?"

"Yes. You know that Nathan was found with words written on his body."

"Yes, of course, but Lisa's body didn't."

"Her body, no, but—"

"Go on," ordered Susan.

"But we found something. We visited the site where Lisa had been killed and we... we found... we found those words."

Susan stopped mid-click and sat bolt upright; her eyes, wired. "You found those same words at the site where Mrs Stevens was killed?"

"Yes, Miss. On a tree. We found the exact same words etched into a tree there. The debt has been paid."

"I don't think so, Miss Brown. We checked that area thoroughly, for days, with several very experienced officers... and you're telling me we missed something this obvious?"

"It's faint. It wasn't obvious, but it's definitely there."

"How the hell did we miss that?" Susan muttered, her voice sharp with disbelief. "You're sure?"

"One hundred percent."

The recollection hit Susan like a punch to the gut and the image of Nathan's body with those words written on it seared into her mind in a vivid flashback.

Nathan Brown's murder, along with that of Lisa Stevens' had remained unsolved and had itched away at Susan's conscience for months. She abhorred a closed case. Especially a murder. The thought that someone capable of doing that to another human being, and to still be wandering the street as a free man, left her simmering with a deep unease. Not to mention the effect that lack of an arrest had on her exemplary record.

CHAPTER 5

She'd pushed to keep both of these cases open, but the higher-ups had prohibited her from continuing with the investigation, citing cut-backs and limited resource. It was a fight she constantly faced and she'd learnt to pick her battles wisely.

Susan took a deep breath and exhaled sharply. "That is significant. Very significant. I'll get some officers to go out to corroborate this. Thank you for calling, Miss Brown."

"Thank *you*, Miss Reeves."

Susan placed the receiver down and took a moment to gather her thoughts.

How had we missed this?

Maybe I should've put up more resistance to closing the case, but if what Miss Brown says is true I might be able to reopen it.

Looking out across her immaculately clean desk, she stared intently at the two photo frames positioned in the far corner. Photos of her two young daughters. Taking a deep breath, she picked up the phone and swiftly dialled an internal extension.

"Ma'am?" came the voice on the other end of the line.

"DI Andrews, get us a car. We're going to Battersea Park."

"Battersea Park? What about the briefing?"

"Forget the briefing."

Chapter 6

"I can't do this," he muttered to himself as he stared into the mirror, his piercing dark eyes glaring back at him.

The voices in his head screamed: *But you have to do this.*

He took a shot.

Another shot.

Winced.

He looked down at a photo. A photo of a man. A stranger to him, yet he knew two things. Where he would be. And when.

The clock was ticking. Only eighteen hours remained.

Failure wasn't an option.

Tonight was the night.

With trembling hands, he donned a ribbed black jumper, cargo trousers and a dark beanie hat. Slowly and methodically he laced up some heavy walking boots and tucked a hunting knife into a holster that he had fastened securely to his right calf. He pulled his trouser leg back down to conceal the holster and stood up straight, arching his shoulders back in a feigned show of strength and confidence. Lastly, he tugged on a pair of leather gloves, scrunched his fists and pulled them taut until the fit felt natural and his fingers were dextrous.

With a heavy head he reached for the photo again and took

CHAPTER 6

another glance. It depicted a man he knew to be named as Brett Anderson. Youthful, good looking. He had a prominent brow, which gave a slight Neanderthal look to his appearance.

So many questions entered his mind as he stared at this unknown face:

Why him?

What had he done to deserve this fate?

Did he have any family?

He gently folded the photograph, slid it into the back pocket of his cargo trousers, drank another shot, took a deep breath, gritted his teeth and left.

* * *

On the dark city backstreet, he stood and waited in the shadows. Still and unseen. There was a faint glow from the lights of busy streets that ran parallel, and a hum of noise that floated on the air, but here it was comparably as quiet as a vacuum.

The air was thick with a stench of rot from overflowing rubbish bins and a solitary, discarded traffic cone—the usual orange tint, tainted with a layer of grime—lay on its side, half submerged in a murky puddle. The broken cobblestones were covered unevenly by a light drizzle from earlier in the evening and glistened in the faint light.

A rat scurried by, its claws clicking on the cobbles, as it darted past the man's feet and into the bleakness beyond.

Lifeless, like a palace guard, he had no earthly sense of how long he'd stood here. The seconds passed like hours.

In the darkness his senses were heightened. His eyes, now

accustomed to the low light, could see vividly and sharply. His nostrils were aflame with the acrid rankness of the bins that flanked the alleyway. The tightness of the knife holster attached to his leg throbbed away; a constant reminder of the inevitable. He could hear the blood pumping in his ears, slow and rhythmical. Surprisingly slow, considering the task ahead of him.

The silence broke. He heard a door squeak open a few yards back from him in the dark side street. He remained steadfast. Still and ready.

The door ground to a close and he heard wet footsteps proceeding in his direction.

Pressed against the cold brick wall, he cautiously turned his head to glimpse who was coming.

The target.

Is it?

He had to be sure. He squinted his eyes, forcing clarity. The heavy brow was a giveaway.

It *was* him.

He watched with patience as the target walked past him, confident that Brett was totally unaware of his presence lurking in the shadows.

Unseen.

His heart skipped a beat as he noticed that Brett was a much larger man than he had expected. He must have been six foot four and heavy set with broad shoulders. A looming presence.

He didn't give his mind a chance to think about the risk he faced, instead focusing on action as he silently removed the hunting knife from his leg holster and moved stealthily out of the shadows towards Brett.

CHAPTER 6

With the end of the alley in sight, he knew he had no more than thirty metres with which to ensure he caught up to Brett and completed the deed, without risking contact with another person. His pace was paramount.

His pulse quickened as he followed. Matching the cadence of Brett's steps to reduce the likelihood of being heard, he took longer strides, allowing him to gradually catch up to his target, while maintaining the element of surprise.

In lockstep—and nearing his target now—he lunged, grabbing Brett's collar and yanking him back while bringing his knife-wielding hand towards Brett's throat.

Brett was quick to act, his hand shooting up like a reflex and grabbing hold of his would-be assailant's wrist with astonishing force and pushing it back, causing the man to falter.

He hadn't been prepared for the strength of his target.

In the struggle for the knife, Brett wheeled around to face him—a look of shock and disbelief in his eyes—while still firmly restraining the hand which brandished the blade.

The swift turn from Brett caused the man to lose his grip on Brett's collar. Acting instinctively, he formed a tight fist with his left hand and threw a punch into Brett's stomach, forcing him to arch over as the wind was taken out of him.

"Wh-what is this?" Brett bellowed, through gasping breath, still clutching the man's knife-wielding hand in a vice-like grip.

Raising his knee swiftly, the man caught Brett in the jaw with a crack that echoed against the walls of the narrow alleyway. The strike sent Brett tumbling, forcing him to lose his grip on the man's wrist.

The man leapt towards Brett and raised the knife to bring it down, but Brett moved quickly, grabbing his assailant's feet and pulling hard, causing him to fall backward—the knife clattering to the side.

In a flash, Brett leapt on top of him. A bear of a man. He felt a thunderclap in his head, as he received a solid punch to the face. And then another. His nose buckled and his eyes instantly filled with tears.

As Brett continued to rain punches down, the man brought up his right arm to protect his face, while his other searched wildly for the fallen knife.

After a few dizzying seconds, his gloved fingertips felt the touch of steel and he clawed the knife towards him as he was subjected to a relentless shower of strikes.

Wrapping his fingers around the blade, he felt a sharpness, as it etched into the palm of his hand through his leather gloves.

Momentarily managing to free his right arm amidst the barrage of blows, he launched a well-timed right hook into Brett's bleeding jaw, staggering him just enough to firmly grasp the knife's handle.

Brett shook his head, fighting the daze from the hit, but the man seized the split second of opportunity. With force and precision, he thrust the knife hard and true into Brett's sternum.

Brett let out a gurgling scream, arched upwards and then fell onto his back, the knife protruding from his chest.

As Brett fell, his attacker quickly scrambled to his feet and stood over Brett's quivering body. Blood from his surely broken nose dripped relentlessly. He reached down and pulled the knife out of Brett's chest with a wet, crunching sound and plunged it deep into his victim's stomach.

CHAPTER 6

"Wh-why?" gargled Brett, blood pooling in his mouth and running down the sides of his face.

"I'm s-sorry. I had no... choice," he said, his voice quavering, as he readied the knife again—this time stabbing it down into Brett's jugular.

Brett's face twisted in horror. His lips parted. His teeth, bloodied.

As the man tugged the blade free, blood gushed from the wound, spraying over him in rhythmic squirts. He raised his hands to cover his face in a vain attempt to avoid the spurting jets.

He'd never seen so much blood.

Brett's body convulsed as he took his last, dying breaths.

The torrent of blood ejecting from his gaping neck wound slowed as his pulse withered.

Nausea stirred deep within the man and he gulped hard to force it down. With his hands shaking wildly, he reached into his back pocket, retrieved the photo and placed it on the blood-soaked chest of his victim.

"I'm sorry. I had no choice," he repeated in a whisper, as he wiped blood from his face with his gloved hands.

His breath caught in his throat in a moment of panic, as a thought struck him.

Fuck. I need to write the words.

Gagging, he moved over to the pool of blood beside Brett's lifeless body and began scooping it into his hands. Fighting the reflex of bile that inched up his throat, he acted fast and with purpose, smearing the blood on the wall beside him in deliberate strokes.

He reached into a pocket, retrieved his phone and took a

snapshot of the scene, grimacing as the flash went off. He checked the image. Red. The screen was smeared with blood, the scarlet cast amplifying the horror of the scene that he'd created.

He turned and hurried away, choking on blood, tears and vomit, as the bloody mural behind him screamed the words:

'THE DEBT HAS BEEN PAID'.

Chapter 7

Susan lay on her back with her arms across her chest, reminiscent of a vampire in an old Hammer Horror movie. Corpselike. A rhythmic buzzing awoke her abruptly and she sat up, robotically, removed her gel eye mask and peered over to the bedside table where her phone vibrated heavily against the wooden surface. Squinting to adjust her eyes to the bright light from the phone's display, she checked the vital information that would determine whether she answered the call.

Time: 05:45.

Fuck.

Caller: Superintendent Hale.

FUCK.

"Sir," Susan said, answering the call. Her voice gruff. Without presence.

"Reeves? Apologies for the early call."

"That's okay, sir. What can I do for you?"

"There's been another one."

Without asking she knew what he meant. "Where? When?"

"An alleyway in Chinatown. Last night. I'll text you the address. Can you get over there?"

"Of course. I'll be right there."

The line went dead.

* * *

The familiar site of yellow police tape greeted Susan as she arrived at the scene, along with a number of eagle-eyed tourists already propped up against the cordon, keen to get a glimpse of the horrors that lay beyond.

Forcing her way through the throng, Susan caught the gaze of DI Andrews who edged towards her and raised the tape for her to duck underneath and into the exclusivity of the crime scene.

"Can't we get these people out of here?" said Susan, with frustration.

"Amazing how many people show up to a crime scene at five in the morning, eh, ma'am?"

"And smack dab in the centre of London. Just what we need." She rolled her eyes. "Haven't these people got better things to do with their time? How sick do you need to be to want to catch a glimpse of a murder rather than stay in bed."

"I got you a coffee," said Andrews, gesturing to a cup in his left hand. "Cappuccino. Oat milk. One sugar. I figured you'd need it."

"Thanks, Andrews," said Susan, accepting the takeaway coffee cup with a nod. She took a sip, licked her lips and narrowed her eyes. "What are we dealing with here?"

"Walk with me."

Susan walked on with Andrews, past several parked police cars; their lights echoing from the walls of the narrow confines

CHAPTER 7

of the alley, creating a tunnel of flashing blue, amidst the dark of the early morning. She gave a knowing nod to a number of other officers as she was led further into the crime scene, following the forensic evidence markers; numbered and laid out in a haunting procession, like a nightmarish treasure hunt.

"Forensics have been here for a couple of hours already," remarked Andrews, gesturing over at two officers wearing white coveralls.

"Thanks, DI Andrews. I'll go chat with them. See what they've uncovered so far. Could you do something about that baying crowd back there?" Susan pointed with her eyes as she gave an icy stare to the herd of onlookers at the perimeter of the cordoned off area. "Get them to move back? We don't want the press getting too close to this."

"Sure, ma'am... Let me know if you need anything."

"Of course."

Susan nodded and turned back towards the scene, leaving Andrews to go and deal with the voyeuristic public. Nearing the epicentre of the scene, the flicker of lights alerted her to the wall of the alley where the bloody message was displayed; the crimson red appearing black under the strobing blue lights.

"There's no missing this one," Susan muttered under her breath, as she let out a sigh.

Edging closer, Susan noticed a body lying on the ground, alongside marker number 1. A brutal scene was opening up to her. She stifled a gulp and shuddered as an icy chill ran up her spine. Even after doing this job for twenty five years she was still shocked at the depravity of people and the horrors that they could commit. She choked down the acid reflux inching up her throat.

Keeping her distance to ensure she couldn't contaminate

the scene, Susan ushered one of the forensic detectives over to her. Acknowledging her request, the detective got to his feet and wandered over to her, pulling down his face mask, but keeping his hood in place.

"Ma'am," said the forensic detective, addressing Susan.

"Morning, Detective…"

"Raines," he added.

"Detective Raines," Susan echoed, with a nod. "What do we have?"

"Young white male. Multiple stab wounds."

"Murder weapon?"

"None found yet."

"Any prints?"

"No, ma'am. And based on initial analysis it doesn't look like we're going to get any."

"Damn."

Raines said nothing, staring at Susan with questioning eyes.

"I've obviously seen the bloody note he left for us," said Susan, her eyes darting to the wall. "Looks like the same MO. And what's worse… he's getting more brazen. More ballsy with every killing. Was there a photo this time?"

"We've taken lots," said Raines, his eyes blank with confusion.

"No, I mean was there a photo left on the body?"

"Oh. Yes. Sorry, ma'am. We've bagged that already. A photo of the victim, I believe, although it's hard to tell with the state of his face."

"Okay, well I'm sure I'll get to look over it later. What else do we know?" inquired Susan, giving a cursory glance across the crime scene.

"The victim is a Brett Anderson, according to the ID in his

wallet. Initial findings are that he's been stabbed at least twice, in the chest and jugular. The latter seemed to be the fatal blow and caused massive blood loss, as you can see from the pool near the victim's head." Raines relayed this information without the blink of an eye and all the while looking squarely at Susan. It was said with a dryness and a sense of normalcy of someone who had become completely desensitised to the horrors of what people are capable of. Susan knew that she would never be able to react so unremarkably to such an horrific situation. Or at least she hoped that she wouldn't. She'd always said to herself that if she started acting in a manner this detached and emotionally closed off then she'd consider it a sign that the job had broken her soul and that she should call it a day. Not only for the sake of herself, but also for her kids. How could she raise them effectively if she had become this numb? That thought terrified her, but not as much as leaving the job. It was all she knew how to do.

All that she ever wanted to do.

Continuing his gruesome tour of the scene, Raines said, "It appears as though the assailant used the victim's blood from the pool to write the note on the wall. We can see smears on the ground where it looks like he used his hands, presumably gloved, to apply the blood."

"Jesus," muttered Susan. She took a glance further up the alleyway, noticing more evidence markers leading away from the scene. "I'll be right back."

Susan started to walk away from the body and up towards the far end of the alley, glancing across at the parade of forensic markers as she did so. There was a pattern of what looked like blood droplets leading up to the end of the alley and she squinted to focus more clearly on them for a second. A thought, like a fire being ignited, suddenly popped into her head and she paced with purpose back to Detective Raines.

"Detective?"

Raines had turned to go back to his business of bagging evidence, but promptly directed his attention back to Susan. "Yes, ma'am."

"These drops of blood on the way up the alley, what do you make of them?" Susan questioned, pointing with her eyes and a slight nod of the head, up towards the end of the alley.

"Not sure yet, ma'am. I assume they're from the victim and show where the assault began. We're waiting for a blood splatter analyst to get here and give their thoughts."

Susan brought her gaze back to Detective Raines, her eyes wide.

"What do you think it is?" he asked.

"I think they look like they're from someone leaving the scene, not entering."

"Ma'am?"

"You can see from the pattern that they seem to be spaced further apart the further you go up the alley, as if the source was from someone hurrying away. Could still be the victim's blood, but it could be that our killer was injured in this encounter. The victim is a big guy from what I can see, yeah?"

"Yeah. He's a large build that's for sure."

Susan gave a closed mouth grin and raised her eyebrows; tilted her head to the side. "Maybe our killer bit off more than he could chew this time."

Raines's eyes widened. His eyebrows disappeared from view under the hood of his coveralls. "It's possible, of course. We'll certainly be testing all of the blood samples to see if we have any DNA evidence that belongs to someone other than the

CHAPTER 7

victim."

"He might have made a mistake this time, Raines." Susan's eyes grew ever wider. "We might have just caught ourselves a break."

Chapter 8

A spring day which felt full of promise. The clouds had parted, making way for the warmth of the midday sun, drying the rain pools of previous days. Evaporating. Rising up, like a phoenix, to be born again and shed from the same sky on a different day.

In another place.

The change in weather and his recent meeting with Jen had given Jack cause for hope. A sense that he wasn't alone. Despite this, his head was still buzzing with questions: *Who had killed Lisa? Who had killed Nathan? Why either of them? What did the words 'the debt has been paid' mean?*

As a distraction—and to clear his head—he'd taken himself out for a walk along the Thames path. He walked casually, hands in his pockets, admiring the serenity; the sounds of soothing music playing in his ears, courtesy of his wireless earphones. He often walked while listening to ambient music. No matter the site or situation it always had a way of creating a relative sense of peace within him. A grounding. Drowning out the chaos. Or, on a day like today, amplifying the serenity. It was working. The voices in his head were calming.

Along the river, by his side, rowers streamed past. Oars

CHAPTER 8

stroked rhythmically. Muscle and sinew flexed. Gentle intersecting waves coalesced. And, all the while, the high frequencies of occasional bird song overlapped and complimented the sounds that streamed from Jack's phone.

The moment of peace was short lived—suddenly broken by the chiming of Jack's phone ringing in his ears. He reached into his pocket to check the caller.

Ralph.

I bet he's calling just to check up on me.

"Alright, Ralph."

"Hey, Jack." There was an awkward pause before Ralph continued. "How... how are things, mate?"

"I'm doing okay thanks, mate. Just out for a walk. You know. Taking in some sun." Jack tried to sound nonchalant, but his face reddened as he realised how fake he must have sounded.

"Good for you, man. Can't beat some vitamin D after the winter we've had."

Jack waited for Ralph to continue, filling the silence with a passive grunt.

"So have you been keeping yourself... busy?" Ralph continued.

"Yeah, kinda. Well, I've been trying to. The time off has been helping, I think. It's good just to have time for some... self care."

Do I sound believable? Not sure I believe it myself. God knows what Ralph thinks.

"Cool. Yeah I'm glad it's helping, Jack."

"How's work?" said Jack, moving the focus of the conversation away from himself.

"Busy, as usual. You know how it is."

"Yeah, I bet. Do you need me to come back—"

"Oh, no, mate. That wasn't why I was calling. I'm not going to rush you back to work. I was serious when I said I wanted you to take some time out."

There's something off here. He's not calling just for a catch up. There's something on his mind.

"So you were just calling for a chat?" Jack probed, his chest tightening.

"Actually, no." Ralph took an audible deep breath and sighed it out. "Well, I do want to see that you're doing okay, but there... there was something else. Have you... have you seen the news today?"

What is he getting at?

"The *news*? No. I try to avoid it at the moment, it's a bit of a busman's holiday really. Why?"

"There's reports of a murder in Chinatown last night..."

Jack could sense the hesitation in Ralph's voice and knew there was more to this. He kept probing. "Okay, so what of it?"

"I've heard from some of my contacts that the police are trying to keep the specifics quiet right now. Worried that people may be fearful."

"Fearful?"

"Well, it seems that this victim might be part of a serial."

"Why do I get the feeling there's more you want to tell me here, Ralph?"

"Yeah... Sorry... I realise I'm drip feeding you a little here. Bear with me." Another deep breath. "So, from what I hear there's been three murders all sharing the same characteristics." A sigh. "And... Lisa was one of them."

What the fuck?!

Jack's stomach flipped and his head spun. He stopped in

his tracks, mid-stride. Several seconds passed without him uttering a word.

"Jack? You still there?"

Jack's chest was tight. He took a few deep breaths to regain some focus on the moment. "I'm still here," he said, dryly. "So th-there's *three* now?"

"You knew about another one?"

Jack sensed how outlandish this would sound, but without hesitation he answered the question. "Yeah, this is going to sound strange. I, uh, I actually met with the sister of the second victim the other day." He paused as he heard an audible gasp from Ralph. "Nathan Brown was his name."

"Jesus, Jack. You met with his *sister*? What the hell?"

Jack cringed, but with belief in his resolve he didn't let Ralph's words shake him. "Yeah, alright, I know it might sound weird, but we figured we could compare notes and maybe help each other, or find a new angle. But now you're telling me there's *another* one?"

"Shit, Jack. Don't go all investigative reporter on this. I think you need to leave this one to the police."

Jack's skin prickled.

"Yeah, that worked out really well with Lisa's case, didn't it?" he barked. "Why did you even call to tell me about this?" The suggestion that Jack stay out of it was like a red rag to a bull. The news about a third killing only feeding his motivation.

"Sorry, pal. I didn't want to stir things up and make it worse. I just figured you should know about this and I wanted to see if you wanted to talk about it at all."

"Okay, I do appreciate the info. Honestly, I do. It's really important that I know, but don't tell me what to do with this information, mate. I won't just sit on my hands while Lisa's killer is out there."

"Okay," Ralph snapped. He paused and adjusted his tone, speaking more softly now. "Okay, Jack. Okay. Do what you want with the information. Let me know if I can do anything for you. Just stay safe."

"What was their name?"

"Who?"

"The third victim. What was their name?"

"Anderson... Brett Anderson. Does the name mean anything to you?"

Brett Anderson?

"No... I don't know anyone by that name. Thanks, pal. I've got to go, but I'll call you soon."

Before Ralph had the chance to say anything else Jack hung up the call. There was no more that his friend could do for him right now and he could think of only one person he wanted to talk to.

He stood still for a few moments, planted on the river bank, looking pensively at the horizon as the sun played its bouncing reflections across the water. He looked back down at his phone, took a breath, and called Jen.

Chapter 9

Beep. Swoosh. Clunk. The familiar sounds of the tube doors closing rang out as Jack boarded the carriage. He scanned the car and noticed one available seat between an elderly lady—pen in hand, concentrating hard on the Metro crossword or sudoku—and a man who was, to put it mildly, somewhat portly; his gut stretching out beneath his agonisingly taut shirt and his heavy arm eclipsing the armrest.

With a sigh of resignation, Jack sidled over to the empty seat and squeezed himself into place. With the rotund man refusing to budge his trunk of an arm, Jack was forced to lean uncomfortably over into the elderly lady's personal space. She gave him a suspicious look, scoffed and folded the corner of her newspaper away from him, like someone in an exam shielding their paper to avoid being copied from.

"Three across, nine letters is 'interfere', by the way," said Jack, with an awkward, smug grin.

After his conversation with Ralph that morning and learning the news of another killing, seemingly showing the same modus operandi, Jack had only one thought on his mind and that was to reconnect with Jen.

Since their meeting a few days ago he'd found his mind

drifting to thoughts of her frequently. Although they'd only spent a few hours together, she had ignited something within his soul.

Something he hadn't felt in years.

Was it the shared trauma? The shared sense of purpose? Or some kind of sexual chemistry?

He wasn't sure, but he felt driven by an undeniable need to see her. A sense of kismet; as though they had been destined to cross paths.

* * *

Arriving at Jen's home, Jack smoothed his jeans, straightened his jacket and checked his reflection in the screen of his phone, before knocking on the door. Within a matter of seconds the door opened.

"Hi, Jack," Jen said, as she greeted him with a warm smile.

He noticed a tint of rosiness in her cheeks.

"Hey."

Jack's pulse spiked. He was mesmerised by Jen's appearance as much as the last time he'd seen her. She was wearing jeans with rips at the knees, a loose-knit woollen cardigan that dropped playfully off her left shoulder and a T-shirt, presumably for a band that he'd never heard of. She oozed style and sexual energy seemingly without being aware of it, or even having to try.

She's way too cool for this old dog.

Jen's eyes glanced down. "Oh, you bought wine!" she exclaimed, with a bright smile.

CHAPTER 9

"Well, I figured it'd be rude not to bring an offering."

"I'm pretty well stocked, but that's really kind. And, hey, you can never have too much booze."

Don't I know it.

"I'm sure we could both use a glass or two," she said, as she graciously accepted the bottle and ushered Jack inside.

"Or *three*. Shoes off?"

"Totally up to you. Come on in and make yourself at home. I'll crack this bottle open." Jen turned away and walked up the hallway to the kitchen.

Jack slipped off his shoes and entered Jen's flat. A thought dawned on him and he realised that this must have been the first time he'd been invited into a woman's home since the early days of when he and Lisa had got together.

Taking the first steps into another's private life was something which he believed should be cherished. A sign of trust. That someone is willing to open up their personal habitat and display their idiosyncrasies, foibles and preferences to potential prejudice or criticism is not something that should be overlooked or taken for granted.

Jen had opened up her world to him and he felt not only grateful for this but also surprised at how relaxed she seemed about the situation.

Would I be quite as relaxed if this was the other way round?

Following Jen's steps, Jack walked up the hallway, his attention drawn to a few wall-mounted canvas prints of idyllic, sun-soaked landscapes. He paused beside a collage of photographs that were pinned to the wall. The images showed Jen and a number of other women that depicted a life full of vibrancy, love and connection—the women's laughter practically radiating from the glossy snapshots.

A life well lived, he thought, as he smiled, feeling both inspired and envious in equal measure. Men could have similar experiences and memories from their lives, but rarely would they collate this evidence and hang it on a wall, or at least Jack was yet to meet someone who did.

Entering the kitchen to see Jen wrestling with a corkscrew, Jack remarked, "Looks like you could do with some help there".

"Urrnngghhh. Don't worry. I got this," Jen grunted.

"At least let me fetch the glasses. Where do you keep them?"

Still wrestling, Jen motioned with her head to a cupboard up to her left. "Just up there. Thanks, Jack".

Jack reached up and grabbed a couple of wine glasses and placed them down on the worktop, beside Jen. He heard a 'pop' and looked up to see she had finally succeeded in rescuing the cork from the bottle. Slightly flushed, and with a broad smile of satisfaction, she poured two large glasses and handed one to Jack. He took a sip, then another in quick succession and leaned against the worktop in an attempted casual manner.

An awkward silence hung in the air between them for a moment and Jack felt the elephant in the room looming large. His chest felt tight and he was hesitant to broach the subject, but he couldn't think of anything else to break the silence. He dove straight in.

"So..." His mouth was dry. He took another sip of his wine. "D-does this name Brett Anderson mean anything to you?" His chest tightened further.

Jen was clearly caught off guard. With wide eyes, she said "Oh, wow, we're straight into this are we?" She paused for a moment and took a drink before continuing. "No, I've never heard of the guy. Have *you*? And how did you hear about it? I haven't seen anything on the news."

CHAPTER 9

Jack shook his head. "Same. I've never heard of him either. I heard about it from Ralph."

"Oh, your friend you mentioned? How come he's in the know?"

"Well, friend, yeah. Nowadays he's my boss, too. Being in the reporter game and with the contacts you pick up along the way, you get to know about the news before anyone else, so he reached out to me with it."

Jen took another sip of wine.

"This is all so crazy isn't it?!" Her brow furrowed and her eyes narrowed. "It's only been a few hours since you told me, but I'm struggling to come to terms with it, to be honest. They were killed in exactly the same way, with the same message displayed? It really sounds like a serial killer, doesn't it?!" She shuddered. "How did Lisa and Nathan get caught up in this? It seems they're..." Jen tailed off, looking at Jack, but not at him; through him.

"Linked in some way?"

Jen took a sharp intake of breath. "Exactly. But... how? They don't appear to have any connection to each other."

Jack pushed away from the worktop and moved towards Jen. Reaching out with one arm, he placed a hand on her shoulder and looked at her in the eye. "We're gonna find the connection, Jen. We'll figure this out. I know it won't bring them back, but we're gonna find the bastard behind this."

Jen stared back at Jack and gave a comforted smile. "I hope you're right. I'm with you on this. All the way. But... where do we go from here?"

Jack shrugged. "I'm not sure yet. Something will come to me. But I'm sure as hell not going to rely on the police."

"Yeah, I'm with you on that, too," Jen scoffed.

Running his hands through his hair and looking up to the ceiling, hoping for some inspiration, something occurred to Jack. "One thought," he said, "Do you have any way of getting into Nathan's email, or social media? Anything like that? It might be one thing to try. If we could understand what may have been going on for him in his personal life at the time, then we might find some clue to all of this."

Jen's eyes grew wide and she gave a nod. "I'd actually thought of that before, but for some reason I had some resistance to even trying to get into his emails. Like it was... an invasion of privacy, or something."

"Yeah I get that." Jack lowered his head, his stomach knotting with guilt at the suggestion. "Sorry if the idea's made you uncomfortable."

"Don't apologise, Jack. It's a good idea." She paused, squinted and looked to the side, as if deep in thought. "I guess he'd want me to try anything that might be able to help bring him justice. Have... have you tried to get into *Lisa's* personal stuff?"

"I haven't, no. But I *will* try. Lisa was always very big on being cyber secure though, so I don't imagine it'll be an easy one to crack, but I'll give it a shot."

Before Jack had finished speaking, Jen scooted over to the dining table at the back end of the kitchen, where a laptop rested. She powered it up. Her fingers hovered over the keyboard and she looked up to the ceiling for a moment. She drew a deep breath, focused down at the computer and began typing.

"What are you doing, Jen?"

"There's no time like the present, eh?" she said, raising her gaze from the laptop with a look of enthusiasm and determination. "I'm trying to hack Nathan's email."

"Wow. You don't mess around. Any idea what his password could be?"

Jen continued to tap away; the look of determination turning ever more so into a look of dejected frustration with each failed keystroke.

"No idea." She sighed. "I'm trying the obvious things. Pet names. Pet names with a one at the end. Previous girlfriend's names. Favourite movies. Et cetera, et cetera. No joy so far."

Jen continued tapping away for several minutes, while Jack watched on in silent prayer. Eventually she conceded to the futility of the situation and calmly closed the laptop, in surrender.

"I'm not getting anywhere, Jack." She took a deep breath and sighed it out. "I will try again, but that's enough for now. I need to think clearly about what the password could be. I'm just typing the most random shit now," she said, as she gave an ironic laugh.

"At least you gave it a shot. And yeah, don't give up. Give it another try tomorrow, eh?"

Jen stood up, moved away from the dining table and grabbed the half finished wine bottle. "Right. Enough of this morbid talk about serial killers. Let's go through to the living room and relax and get stuck into this wine. What do you say, Jack?"

You read my mind.

"Sounds like a plan. Lead the way."

* * *

Entering the living room, Jack was now given further insight into the woman behind that broad smile and nonchalance. An overwhelming bohemian vibe washed over him that he hadn't expected.

In one corner, a sprawling vintage violet L-shaped sofa was scattered with mismatched floral and animal-patterned cushions. A reclaimed wooden coffee table, shaped like a yin-yang, sat beside it, and a cascading spider plant spilled over a chunky wooden bookcase, partially obscuring the books on its top shelf.

To the side of the bookcase was a battle-hardened brown leather armchair with a bright yellow knitted throw casually strewn across one of the armrests. In between the armchair and sofa was a vivid, patterned rug which spanned the width of the room, its intricate patterns weaving a kaleidoscope of hues across the floor.

Jen sat down on the sofa, tucked her legs under herself and motioned for Jack to join her, as she placed her glass of wine on the yin-yang table. Jack obliged, smiling as he sat. He took a sip of his drink and sat pensively for a moment, taking in the ambience.

With narrowed eyes, he further scanned the room with growing intrigue. A Buddha statue sat proudly atop the mantelpiece, sharing its perch with a lava lamp—already warm and pumping its purple lava up and down within the encased red liquid. Mismatched lamps scattered throughout the room cast overlapping pools of soft light, creating a warm, dreamlike atmosphere.

A sanctuary. Eclectic. Bohemian. And unapologetically so.

"You've really nailed this new age vibe, Jen," Jack teases, gesturing towards the scattered ornaments and furnishings with his glass in a wide arc.

Jen chuckled. "You just wait 'til I get the tarot cards and incense out."

Jack reciprocated Jen's laughter. "I jest, but I really like it. I feel like there's a lot to know about you that I wouldn't have realised." He took a sip of wine and smiled. "Thanks for having me over."

"The pleasure's all mine. I'm not sure there's much to know about me, but I'm happy to be an open book. What do you want to know?" Jen shrugged and fidgeted on the sofa. "Oh, and this isn't just part of your investigative journalist routine, is it?"

Jack held his hands up. "Not at all. I'm honestly curious. Listen... we've got the *darkest* situation in common, and rather than having just our shared trauma to talk about, I'm interested in getting to know the *real* you." He placed his glass down, leaned forward and clasped his hands together, forming a faux sign of prayer. "Indulge me, would you?"

"Okay, Jack." She took a sip of her wine and licked her lips. "Let's do this tit for tat though, okay? You ask me a question and then I get to ask you one. No fibbing and no refusing to answer."

This will be very interesting.

"Deal."

"Okay. Shoot. Hit me with your best shot, journo."

"Okay, here goes... Where did you grow up?"

Jen rolled her eyes. "Wow... Where did you grow up? *Really*? Is that your opener, Jack?" she teased. "You'd better be prepared for more of a personal grilling from me. Besides, I'm sure I told you this before. When we were in the car together?"

"Easy now. I'm just getting started," Jack retorted. "You did tell me a little, but it was very brief. This is how us 'journos', as you put it, start off. We don't dive straight in. We make sure our interviewee is comfortable before we start with the probing questions." He picked up his glass and leaned back, settling into the softness of the cushions. "Oh, and that's the last of my interview techniques I'm gonna give away and I only gave that up because I don't want you to unnecessarily think I'm boring."

"Oh, well I can't wait for you to be *necessarily* boring then."
I walked into that one.

"Just answer the question, joker."

"Well, if you must know, I grew up in a typically dull, small town in Hertfordshire."

"What's the name of the town?"

Jen wagged a finger at Jack. "Oh, no, no, no, Jack, that's two questions. My turn." She pointed at herself and flashed Jack a warm, cheeky, bright-eyed smile. "How old were you when you lost your virginity?"

Jack recoiled, nearly spilling his wine. "Jesus! Right for the jugular."

"I did say you'd be in for a grilling."

"Fifteen," he said, his face reddening.

Jen raised her eyebrows and gave a smug grin. "How was it?"

"That's two questions."

"Dammit! Touché, Jack."

Jack winked and took a sip of wine. "We'll make a journalist of you yet, Jen. This is one of *your* interview techniques, isn't it?" His eyes narrowed. "Take someone back to an awkward moment in their life, so that they feel vulnerable and you have the upper hand in the conversation. Am I right?"

CHAPTER 9

Jen shrugged. "Maybe. You're not the only one with some tricks up their sleeve. And '*awkward moment?*' It seems that you've answered the second question anyway, so I win." Jen paused to take another sip of wine. "Anyway... your question."

I need to raise my game.

"Any tattoos?"

Clearly unfazed, Jen got to her feet, undid the top button of her jeans and pulled them down slightly on her left hip, revealing an intricate tattoo of a wolf howling at the moon.

"That's n-nice." He coughed to clear his throat. "Where did you get that done?"

Jen pulled her jeans back into place and fastened the top button before replying. "You do realise that's another question."

"And you do realise that I didn't ask to see your tattoo, right? That would have been another question right there, but you seemed to miss that trick."

"Very shrewd." Jen pursed her lips and nodded slowly. "Okay, let's quit it with trying to trip each other up and just... let the conversation flow, okay?"

That would be more my style. Play it cool, Jack.

Jack reached for the bottle, topped up his glass and reclined back into the sofa.

"Please," Jack said, as casually as he could muster. The sight of Jen's bare hip had quickened his pulse. He took a long sip of wine to steady himself.

Jen returned to her position on the sofa alongside Jack. She appeared satisfied with Jack's agreement to let the conversation flow. "I got the tattoo when I was backpacking in Thailand around five years ago. It's totally cliché."

"Doesn't seem that cliché to me. I don't think I've seen another tattoo of a wolf howling at the moon, but what do I know?"

Jen, blushed and paused to top up her wine. "With the rest of the context it really is." She laughed nervously at herself. "If you must know, I got the tattoo after having quite a spiritual experience while dosed up on mushrooms at a full moon party in Koh Phangan."

"I think I probably had a very different time to you when I travelled around Thailand," said Jack, laughing. "No drug fuelled spiritual enlightenments for me, sadly. I smoked some weed a couple of times, but that was about it. I was out there during my thirties, but maybe I would have done things a bit differently if I was in my twenties... I did try the whole full moon thing, but it wasn't really my bag. Too much techno music and too many people off their tits."

"Who knows, old man, maybe we were there at the same time and I was one of those people 'off their tits'," Jen remarked, with that same cheeky smile; the dimples in her cheeks adding a layer of inviting warmth to her beaming face. She polished off her glass of wine and stood up. "This bottle's done, Jack. Wanna stay for another? I'm keen to hear more about your past adventures. We can share travel stories."

"Yeah, absolutely. I was hoping you'd suggest that."

"Cool. I'll be right back." Jen picked up the empty bottle and made her way out to the kitchen.

Jen was gone for several minutes and Jack remained seated on the sofa enjoying a sense of welcome comfort. He reflected on this feeling and realised how much he was really enjoying this moment. He wasn't sure if it was the booze, the conversation, or his obvious attraction to Jen. He concluded it was probably a perfect cocktail of all three and for once he shouldn't overthink it.

CHAPTER 9

"Do you like gin?" a voice echoed from the kitchen.

"Who doesn't?!" he replied almost instinctively.

"Great. I'm rustling up a couple of my signature cocktails."

"Cool. Can't wait to try it."

A few minutes passed while Jen tinkered away in the kitchen; the rhythmic clatter of ice, cracking of eggs and the popping of a cork echoed.

She re-entered the living room carrying a tray with another bottle of red wine and two immaculate looking yellow cocktails with a white foamed top.

"Voila!" she said, as she put the tray down on the table and gestured proudly with open hands towards the fruits of her labour, like a magician at the close of one of their tricks.

Jack picked up one of the cocktail glasses and admired it.

"I call it the Jen Fizz," she gushed.

"It's really quite something. So beautiful I almost don't want to drink it. How do you get this foam to stand so tall like that?"

"A magician never divulges their secrets; you should know that, Jack. Anyway, just drink it. You'll enjoy it."

Jack obliged and took the most delicate of sips, not wanting to disrupt the presentation of the drink too much. The taste was a feast for the senses; sweet, tangy and tart.

"Oh my God. That's incredible!"

"I thought you'd like it. It's a bit of a speciality of mine."

"I love it. Wow. Another thing I've found out about you tonight. You're an expert mixologist."

Jen blushed. "I don't know about all that. It's the only cocktail I make, unless you count gin and tonic."

"You're a dark horse, Miss Brown. For sure, a dark horse. Full of surprises."

What other wonders are you hiding?

* * *

Dusk arrived and was eroded away with the setting of the evening sun; giving way to night. A disordered arrangement of empty glasses and bottles, textured with a spectrum of colour by the dim light of shaded lamps, lined the coffee table and cast shadows over the vibrant rug.

Time moved with perpetual velocity, yet here, in this bohemian sanctuary carved out for two, it felt suspended.

Jack leaned back on the sofa, swirling the remnants of his glass of wine. His cheeks, warm from the alcohol. He was inebriated, but his focus was still sharp; his senses heightened by Jen's presence delivering a heavy dose of adrenaline and dopamine.

The light-hearted nature of their conversation had turned deeper with each drink, revealing glimpses of the person behind her teasing smiles. A connection had blossomed. It was tangible; palpable. Electric.

During a pause in the conversation Jack reached forward to grab his drink. With a mirrored symmetry, Jen did the same. He wasn't sure if it was an accident or not, but they both reached for the same glass.

Their hands touched.

Fleeting, yet it sent a jolt through Jack. A spark that felt both foreign and natural at the same time.

He looked at her. Their eyes met and lingered for a beat longer than they had before.

CHAPTER 9

Jen's gaze softened. Her lips parted ever so slightly.

Jack's pulse drummed in his chest and an invisible force pulled him closer . He was helpless to fight the urge.

Jen mirrored his movement.

Edging closer.

Closer still.

Their lips met.

The kiss was soft at first—tentative—but quickly deepened, fuelled by a spark, like a rush of electricity that coursed through Jack's veins. A euphoric wave that brought all senses to life.

Jen moaned sensually and started unbuttoning Jack's shirt. Her touch slow and deliberate. As it fell open she placed her hands on his warm, exposed chest. His heart was beating thunderously but steadily and he responded instinctively, his hand cupping her cheek, thumb brushing her jawline, as his other hand fell to the small of her back and pulled her closer, lifting her T-shirt slightly, exposing smooth, warm skin.

Jen broke the kiss momentarily, her breath mingling with his as she looked into his eyes. Her expression a mix of desire and tenderness that left Jack shaken.

Without thinking, he murmured, "I want you," the words escaping unbidden but undeniably true.

Jen answered with a kiss, her hands tangling in his hair as she pressed herself against him. He moved with her, lifting her T-shirt over her head, her tousled hair framing her flushed face. The sight of her, vulnerable yet confident, sent a fresh wave of heat through him.

His lips trailed along her neck, savouring the softness of her skin.

Jen's hands moved to his belt, her fingers deft and unhurried, sending ripples of anticipation through him.

Time seemed to fragment, the moments melting into one another, as the world beyond the bohemian walls of Jen's home faded to insignificance. Forgotten, for a moment.

Breaking the kiss, he whispered, "Are you sure?" His breath warm against her lips.

He needed to hear it, even as every fibre of his being seemed to already know the answer.

Jen responded with a slow, deliberate nod, her lips brushing against his as she murmured, "Oh, I'm sure."

Her voice carried a depth that caught Jack off guard—a mix of longing and certainty that somehow made him feel both weightless and anchored all at once. He leaned in again, their lips meeting in a fervent, unspoken agreement, the spark between them now a roaring flame.

The night stretched ahead, charged with the promise of discovery—two souls finding solace and connection in the most unexpected of moments.

As they fumbled, the purple lamp in the background continued incessantly to pump its lava.

Chapter 10

Susan was apprehensive. That afternoon, she had received an anonymous tip-off about an alleged murder in an abandoned barn near a small village in the Surrey Hills. The call hadn't come through any of the usual channels; it hadn't been routed through from 999 call centres or from the Metropolitan Police headquarters.

It had been a call directly to her mobile.

This was uncharted territory. She had never received a call like this on her personal phone, and it unsettled her, raising many questions:

Who was it that called?

How did they get my number?

Why had they chosen to call me directly and not go through the police?

Susan had taken the bait.

After receiving the call, she reached out to Detective Raines, a forensic specialist on the force, and asked him to accompany her. Discretion was key. No one could know.

She'd shared with him the details about the circumstances of the tip-off and, as she had no way of verifying the veracity of the call, she wanted to keep the circle small and not involve the hive, for fear of opening herself to scrutiny or wasting resources unnecessarily.

Driving in first gear, Susan approached the barn slowly in her squad car, with Raines riding shotgun in the passenger seat.

The sun was still above the horizon but had started its downward trajectory, pushing the golden hour into full swing and casting a subtle, muted light on the idyllic setting.

The fields surrounding the barn were aglow with a yellow hue and the greenness of the trees had a vivid and hyperreal characteristic, only ever displayed at this time of day, at this level of diminished lighting.

A beautiful and otherworldly setting—Susan only wished she was here under better circumstances.

She put the car into neutral and applied the handbrake a few yards in front of the barn. Raines opened the boot and retrieved his case of forensic tools, and with heavy steps, they made their way towards the sinister building that faced them.

Susan squinted as the setting sun shone in her eyes, gazing at the looming structure of the barn. Dilapidated. Discarded. A husk.

A battered and age-ravaged brick exterior gave way to a roof with several tiles missing, resulting in an eerie howl as the gentle breeze played through the missing slats like a macabre set of pan pipes.

An ominous presence.

"What's your gut saying, ma'am?" said Raines, as the two of them stood and stared at the barn. Their feet, planted. Rooted.

Susan shook her head. "I don't like it... Not just the building, but the nature of the tip-off. Feels a bit like we're... walking into a trap."

CHAPTER 10

Raines's brow furrowed. "Shouldn't we call this in? We don't know what we're dealing with here."

"Not yet, Raines. Not yet," she said, maintaining her steely gaze on the decaying building. "If we get in there and it's nothing we won't have wasted anything and no one will need to know about our little field trip... If, on the other hand, it *is* something, and I pray it's not, then I'll immediately call it in and deal with the consequences." She met his eyes. "This was my call, okay? You won't be to blame for not following procedure." She reached out and placed a hand on Raines' shoulder. "I appreciate your discretion, detective."

He studied her for a moment and nodded. "Right you are, ma'am... Let's do this."

Susan led the way to the battered building and approached with caution—pulling a taser from her hip holster.

The front of the barn that faced them had no obvious point of entry, so they made their way round to the side where they found a brittle wooden door.

There was no mistaking the fact that this was the entrance they were looking for. Susan's heart hammered, and she gasped as she laid her eyes on a morbid personal greeting.

On the door, smeared in what she could only assume was blood were four scarlet words:

'WELCOME DETECTIVE — THIS WAY'

Raines exhaled and, with a calmness that was out of place, said, "So we're calling this in now, right?"

Susan shuddered. "You're free to do as you want, Detective, but I'm not calling this in yet. Not until I see what we're dealing with."

With a gloved, trembling hand, Susan reached out to the handle on the barn door. She was scared. All her experience screamed at her not to open the door without backup, but she felt powerless to control the urge to see what lay beyond.

She turned the handle.

"Police!" Susan shouted, as she opened the door and barged through into the barn's interior, wielding her taser.

The scene that unfolded left her reeling. She gagged and tasted the burn of stomach acid in her throat, but somehow had the fortitude to keep herself from vomiting.

Raines staggered and held onto the door frame for balance.

"So n-now we're c-calling this in?" he stuttered.

"One s-second, Raines."

The holes in the roof's slats let shuttered light into the barn's interior in a way that illuminated the scene chaotically—a lump of flesh here, a trace of blood there.

"Torch, Detective," Susan ordered.

Raines steadied himself and obliged by reaching into his forensics kit to retrieve a floodlight of a torch. He switched it on, further illuminating the scene in a sweeping arc of white light.

"My God. What the *FUCK* happened here?!" said Susan. She felt tears forming and wiped her eyes with her wrist. "How could someone do this?" Her breath hitched in her throat as she tasted the metallic tang of blood.

Raines remained silent. His hand, holding the torch, shook, causing the light to bounce erratically.

Susan stood, trembling. Never before had she encountered anything remotely as depraved as what was on display here. Although she prided herself on mentally preparing for anything she could conceive, she never would have imagined a sight like this.

At the far end of the room, a sturdy but old wooden chair

CHAPTER 10

stood, its occupant a naked human torso, severed yet eerily upright, as if awaiting judgment.

The arms, both amputated at the shoulders, hung loosely—still attached to the chair via cable ties. Both legs had also been amputated: one above the knee, the other slightly below. Like the arms, they both remained loosely attached to the chair, dangling to the side—again secured in place with cable ties.

The left hand of the victim was clamped in a vice atop a workbench to the right of the chair. Fingerless—except for the pinkie—it had been severed from the body by the same reckless amputation.

As if this wasn't enough to kill the victim, they had also been decapitated and disembowelled.

Susan's eyes flooded with tears. She retched, and coughed to keep from vomiting. "How could someone inflict so much... so much pain and suffering on another human?" her voice cracked.

Raines had dropped to his knees—still wordless.

"I c-can't believe the barbarity that I'm witnessing here. You ever s-seen anything like this, Raines?"

Raines looked down at the congealed, bloodied ground, glinting in the torchlight. "Can't say that I have," he whispered. He took a long, deep breath and raised his gaze to meet Susan's eyes. "And I've seen some awful shit in my time... Pardon my French, ma'am."

Forcing herself to regain her composure, Susan wiped her eyes again and focused on the left side of the barn's interior, where a bloodied trail led to a canvas of the grotesque.

She squinted.

What is that?

She knew. And the wave of nausea in her stomach knew as

well. She gulped it down.

"What do you think this is?" Susan whispered, her voice barely audible above the howling wind breezing through the broken roof.

With a voice dry with irony, Raines said, "Looks like intestines to me, ma'am." His grip on the torch was tight, his knuckles white.

"I can see that," Susan snapped. "But what about the way they're placed? Is it random?"

Raines blew air from his cheeks. "Yeah, looks random enough to me."

Feeling another wave of nausea, Susan headed to the door, being careful not to disturb any evidence and took a step outside. She coughed, gagged and shed tears while trembling at what she had seen inside.

"You okay, ma'am," said Raines, his voice echoing from inside the barn.

"I just need a moment," Susan spluttered.

I might need much more than a moment.

From outside Susan could hear the familiar sound of a camera shutter. Raines had begun to photograph the scene. She shook her arms and head violently, trying to erase the thoughts in her mind and once again regain her composure.

It had limited effect, but enough to give her the strength to re-enter the scene.

Standing at the doorway, Susan looked back at the hideous blanket of entrails sprawled haphazardly across the damp, stone floor.

Her head felt light. Dizzy. She took a breath, relinquished her grip on the barn door and took a step inside.

Her eyes narrowed.

CHAPTER 10

Her pulse quickened.

Something wasn't right... There was an order to the placement.

Gaps. Deliberate intervals between lumps of human tissue.

No.

That can't be right.

But it was.

"They're words!"

"Huh?"

"The entrails. I think they spell something out. Shine some light over here, would you?"

She stepped closer. A wave of nausea crept up her throat as she traced her gaze along the lumps of red flesh that stretched out in front of her. Her pulse thumped in her ears.

She didn't want to see it. But the letters were there. Staring back at her.

Oh, God. The depraved fucking bastard.

She traced the first word with her forefinger and mouthed the word.

"T... H..."

"THE..."

Her throat went dry.

"D-DE-DEBT..."

She wanted to look away, but she was helpless.

"H-H-HAS..."

"BEEN..." She knew what was coming next.

"P-P-P-"

"PAID."

A chill ran through her. She shuddered, her heart hammering against her ribs. And that's when she saw it.

The 'I'.

It was different from the rest.

This wasn't intestines.

Her stomach flipped.

A severed penis formed the stalk of the letter.

And... as her eyes darted up...

Oh, God...

In place of the dot at the top...

A head. A *human* head—eyes frozen in a mix of terror and surprise.

The mouth was locked in a twisted grimace and... there was something clutched between the teeth—

A photograph?

Susan waited for Raines to finish photographing the area before she staggered towards the man's decapitated head.

She crouched down to get a closer look and as she'd feared— there, between the sparse array of teeth was a photograph, slightly glazed with blood, but still quite clearly depicting that of a family. A man. A woman. Two young children.

Susan winced at the sight, and tears began to stream down her face. A torrent. Unrelenting.

She sniffed, wiped away the tears and, although it was a dark place to go, she forced her mind to do what she knew best—step into the mind of a killer.

Her instincts kicked in.

This wasn't frenzied. It wasn't spontaneous. Whoever did this had planned every detail and engineered the horror. The entrails weren't discarded in a rage—they were placed. Arranged. Like a collector showcasing their most prized work.

The killer wanted her to see this. To understand it.

And that terrified her.

CHAPTER 10

Raines approached Susan. His face was ashen. His eyes, vacant. "So... do we call this in now?"

"Y-yes, Raines." Susan sniffed. She looked up to meet Raines's gaze with mascara-streaked cheeks giving her a gothic appearance not wholly out of place given the setting. "We call this in."

Chapter 11

An air of serenity. A bluish grey cloud danced in the gentle summer breeze as Jack exhaled cigarette smoke into the warm, metropolitan air. He leaned casually against the wall, his right leg bent behind him, as he admired the vivid blue sky with its peaceful hue amplified by the subtle shading of his Ray-Ban sunglasses. His tousled sandy hair accentuated his softly tanned skin, which faded into a now well groomed crop of facial hair.

It had been three months since Jack's relationship with Jen had begun and his life had seemingly started to get back on track. His drinking was under control and his overwhelming obsession with solving Lisa's murder seemed to have lost its perceived urgency in his life.

Jen had filled a hole inside of him in a way that he thought nothing or no one ever could.

A door opened beside where Jack leaned.

"You know you should really knock that habit, too, mate." It was Ralph. "This Jen character has been good for you so far. I can tell. Quite the positive influence. You're back here squirrelling away like the good old times and you don't smell of booze. At least not all the time. You were a total cliché, you

CHAPTER 11

realise that, don't you?"

Jack laughed at Ralph's overt observations. He certainly couldn't argue. He *had* been a cliché.

"She seems to have got you straightened out though," Ralph continued. "I still think it's all kinds of fucked up that you've both been directly affected by the same serial killer, but hey, who am I to judge? I just put it down to the sex. She must be dynamite in the sack, Jacky boy. I can't think of another reason that you'd want to lose that troubled, semi-functioning alcoholic, journalist, caricature that you've built up for yourself, almost as a brand."

"Have you quite finished, you fat twat?"

Ralph snorted. "Well I may be a bit fluffy around the edges these days," he said, as he rubbed his stomach, "But at least I don't look like Pete Doherty during his days on the smack."

"Nah, you're just content with looking like him after he got off the smack and started piling on the pounds, you fat knacker."

Jack was glad to be working again and his improved self had brought back the best in his relationship with Ralph, too. It felt like old times. They would wind each other up just like they did during their university days and in the years after, while living together and chasing both women and careers — swanking around in their cheap Topman suits, thinking they knew it all. He could see a glint in Ralph's eyes when he was bantering with him, that he hadn't seen for over a year. It beat the collective look of disdain, disappointment and pity any day.

A vibration in Jack's pocket as his phone rang. He glanced at the caller.

"Sorry mate, I've got to take this. It's my sister."

"No worries. I've got to go grab some lunch anyhow, before this next pointless meeting. Catch you in a bit, mate." Ralph patted Jack on the back, walked around the corner and was quickly out of view as he merged into the masses of a busy London street.

Jack extinguished his cigarette on the wall and answered the call.

"Hey, sis."

"Little bro! How's tricks?"

"Actually really good," Jack replied, and for once he really meant what he said. He *was* good and for a second he was taken aback as he had a moment of realisation that he'd almost forgotten what it was like to *not* feel good. "How about you? What's up?"

"Nothing much. You know, same old. I was just calling on the off chance... I was just wondering if you fancied meeting up with me and David for dinner and some drinks tonight? To be brutally honest, I really want to meet this chick who's turned your life around!"

"*Chick?* Since when did you start referring to women as chicks?"

"I'm just trying to sound cool and carefree. Indulge me. I'm sorry... *Woman.*"

"Haha. Well I'll give my *woman* a shout and see if she's able to join. Sounds nice. Always a treat to see you guys. I'll drop you a message to confirm, once I've checked in with her."

"Great. And yeah, make sure she can come along first."

"What time are you thinking? And where? Don't make me journey all the way across London, please."

"How's seven at the Roebuck. You know where I mean?"

"Yeah I know the one. The one near your work. That's fairly

central, so that should be pretty easy. I'll get back to you in a bit, sis."

"Great. Really hope we get to see the two of you."

Jack hung up the phone and dropped Jen a message. He rolled another cigarette and smoked it while waiting for a response, remaining in his carefree pose as he leaned against the wall.

His phone pinged a minute later. Jen was in.

* * *

Jack and Jen entered the Roebuck, arm in arm, at seven p.m. on the dot. He was dressed typically casual with a loose-neck black T-shirt and blue slim-fit jeans, while Jen was sporting a tight white T-shirt and a short denim skirt.

The Roebuck was one of those traditional pubs that had been refitted and turned into a gastropub—open plan, lots of tables, and Peroni on tap as standard. Jack's opinion of a gastropub was that it was an overused term for a place that had had the soul ripped out of it, served slightly better-than-average wine and food, and made you pay—undeservedly—through the nose for the experience. His sister was a fan, though, so he was happy enough to indulge her choice.

Jack and Jen sauntered through the pub over to a table where Rachel was sitting, waiting for them.

"Hey, sis." Jack greeted his sister with a warm embrace, kissed her on the cheek and then loosened the hug to introduce Jen. "This is Jen. Jen meet Rachel. My big sister by all of a few minutes."

"Hi Rachel. God, it's so nice to meet you. Jack talks about

you all the time."

"He does not! But, wow! So nice to meet you at last. Jesus, you're gorgeous. Well done, Jack." Rachel leaned in for a hug and Jen obliged, willingly.

"No David?" said Jack.

"Not yet. He's on his way back from work... He'll be with us soon. Busy as always. You know David."

Jack sensed frustration in his sister's voice.

"Sure. I know David. So how long have you been sitting here on your own? I thought *we* were early."

"Oh, only ten minutes or so. I was too excited!" Rachel beamed. "Well come on, sit down. We get table service here, you know?!"

Jen and Jack sat down across the table from Rachel, Jack making sure that he and Jen sat almost uncomfortably close together. He couldn't keep his hands off her—his desire for her was so strong, constantly craving her touch. He rested a hand on her bare thigh. The spark ignited, and Jack was electrified.

"It's so nice to meet you, Jen. Seriously. And it's so nice to see the two of you together." Rachel had a glint in her eye, clearly pleased to see Jack happy. "So, how's things going for you two?"

Rather than answer himself, Jack glanced over at Jen, hoping to hear how she would tackle this question. And not just that—he was keen to know what she would say about him.

Come on, Jen. Indulge me. Tell me how you think it's going.

"Well..." Jen shifted in her chair and placed a hand on Jack's. "It's been a bit of a roller-coaster few months. It all started so fast, but it's been really, really great." She looked Jack in the eye, her vivid green eyes lighting up his soul.

CHAPTER 11

"That's amazing. I do love a good romance story. So, are you in... *love*?" Rachel teased.

"Sis!!"

"What?? I'm just teasing."

Jack was blushing. He side-eyed Jen and noticed she was too. He hadn't said those cherished three words to her, and neither had she to him. He had thought it, felt it—but he didn't dare say it. It seemed too soon, and there was a lingering sense that saying it would somehow feel like a betrayal of Lisa.

"Okay, sorry. But can I address the proverbial elephant?" said Rachel.

"And what would that be?" Jack rolled his eyes and sighed. "The serial killer link?"

"*You* said it. Thanks for not making *me* say it. I don't want to make you guys feel awkward."

Jen squeezed Jack's hand.

"Well I think you failed miserably there, sis."

Fortuitously a waiter approached to break the air of unrest.

"Can I get you guys some drinks?"

"Oh yes please," said Jack, as he blew air from his cheeks. "What do you fancy, Jen?"

"I guess they don't do a Jen Fizz," she laughed. "So I'll just go for a G&T, please."

"Same for me. Make them doubles please, good sir. How about you, Rach?"

"I'll stick on this wine, I think," said Rachel, motioning to her half-drunk glass.

"So another Sauvignon Blanc?" the waiter clarified.

"That's the one. Thanks!"

"Coming right up."

The waiter left to fetch the drinks and the welcome break

from the awkwardness allowed Jack the space to come to terms with discussing the obvious burning topic.

"Since you ask, Rach, that link is of course the thing that caused us to meet and maybe, just maybe, it had an influence on the intensity of our first meeting, but our relationship is not built on that, okay?" Jack was frustrated about having to answer the question and justify his relationship with Jen, but he'd expected it. He didn't blame his sister for asking about this, as he figured it was only natural that she'd want to understand more about how the two of them got together and whether it was healthy and not built on a shared trauma or joint obsession. He actually appreciated his sister's forthrightness to raise the topic as soon as possible, so that they could move past it, rather than it remaining an unspoken concern.

Jen rubbed Jack's hand in apparent support and entered the conversation. "Yeah, Jack's right, you know? Neither of us expected this to happen, but there was a chemistry that was clear for both of us and had nothing to do with our shared experiences. I'm just glad we met... regardless of the circumstances."

Jen's response was everything that Jack could ever want to hear. He felt a warmth in his stomach, reciprocated the hand squeeze and gave her a smile of sheer satisfaction.

Rachel smiled widely. "I'm so glad to hear this. You guys make an absolutely gorgeous couple and I'm really pleased for both of you. Sorry. I didn't mean to make this an awkward moment, but I figured it would be good just to get that out in the open."

"You're right, Rach. Apology accepted and thanks for broaching the subject."

The waiter returned with the drinks and set them down on

CHAPTER 11

the table just as Rachel's gaze seemed to be averted.

"There he is," said Rachel.

Following Rachel's eyeline Jack turned round in his seat and spotted David walking through the door and heading over to their table. As David approached, Jack stood up and offered an embrace. David accepted the embrace loosely and gave Jack a hard pat on the back. So hard, it almost winded him.

"Alright Jack. Good to see you, pal."

"You too, mate," Jack coughed. "Here, meet my girlfriend, Jen."

"Well, it's very nice to meet you, Jen. Jack's really landed on his feet with you, hasn't he?" David leered, running his eyes over her in an overtly appraising way—his glassy gaze lingering on her bare legs for a moment longer than was acceptable.

Jen offered a hand to David which he accepted with both hands. "Nice to meet you, too, David."

Jack felt uneasy. He noticed David's sleazy stare and watched as his eyes slowly traced every curve of Jen's body. Anger and embarrassment rose in equal measure in his chest, and he could tell she wasn't comfortable either. She was a hugger. He couldn't remember her ever offering a handshake.

Before sitting down, David made a beeline for the bar, ignoring Rachel's protests about table service.

"I just want to see what they have with my own eyes, okay?" David snapped at Rachel.

"He's just a little wired, that's all," Rachel said—her words an announcement.

Always with the excuses.

"Don't worry, sis. I totally get it. I wouldn't mind having a scan either."

Jack joined David at the bar, leaving Jen and Rachel to talk. As he approached, David was already in deep discussion with the bartender.

"And another one of these please," said David, pointing to his already almost empty glass of scotch.

"They got anything good, mate?" asked Jack, as he leant on the bar beside David.

"Not a bad selection of scotch, to be fair. Want one?"

"Sure. Why not?"

"And another for my friend here, please, barkeep."

Who the fuck says 'barkeep'?

The bartender returned promptly with two glasses of scotch. David clinked his glass to Jack's while it still sat untouched on the bar and, without reciprocation, proceeded to knock it back.

"And another, if you would." David gasped.

"Steady on, pal," said Jack, his eyes wide. "Jesus. Are you okay?"

"Yeah. Fine. I'm playing catchup."

"Catchup?? We've only had *one*."

"Well you all need to raise your game, mate."

"We're doing just fine."

"Who are you to lecture me on drinking anyway, pal?"

"I'm not lecturing, just concerned, that's all."

"Well, you needn't be. I'm just fine. We're celebrating!" said David, his speech beginning to slur.

"What are we celebrating exactly?"

"We're celebrating you. And specifically, you managing to bag that absolute babe over there." David gestured over to Jen with his glass—another leery glance plastered over his face.

Jack knew there were no prizes for trying to steady David's inebriation. He felt there was something on David's mind, but didn't want to push it and decided to ease the tension by dropping it and keeping the conversation as casual as possible.

"Yeah well I'll drink to that, mate." Jack raised his glass just as the bartender returned with another scotch for David. They clinked glasses and Jack took a sip. David downed another.

"Shall we get some drinks for the girls, too?"

"I think they're still okay."

"Well, I'll order in some tequila shots then. You got this round, right, Jack?"

Something's definitely not right here.

With clear reluctance in his voice and raised eyebrows, Jack responded, "Yeah sure... I got this."

Jack and David returned to the table with a tray of shots and four glasses of scotch.

"Tequila shot, ladies?" David slurred.

"Ooh, I love tequila. Thanks," said Jen.

"Not for me, thanks, dear. I'm fine with the wine."

"More for me then," said David, as he sat two shots down next to his two glasses of scotch. "Salud."

Jen, Jack and David clinked glasses, licked salt off the back of their hands, downed the tequila shots and chewed on the lemon slices served with each. Jen winced slightly and let out a "whoop". Without pausing for breath, David proceeded straight onto his second shot.

The four of them stayed at the Roebuck for several hours and the evening continued like this. They drank—David more so than the rest of them, although he did slow his pace as time went on—ate, talked and laughed.

David continued to act inappropriately towards Jen—Jack catching him glancing lasciviously at Jen's body frequently throughout the evening. His lecherous stares lingering for longer than could go unnoticed; sweeping her legs all the way up to the seam of her skirt and resting on the pronounced extrusion of her breasts beneath her T-shirt. Jack became increasingly frustrated, which Rachel seemingly picked up on.

Leaning over, Rachel whispered in Jack's ear, "You know what he gets like after a couple of drinks."

Excuses, excuses.

His sister's comment only resulted in frustrating Jack even further. For the sake of his sister though he bit his tongue and managed to keep his shit together. He did worry about how Jen was taking this, but she appeared unfazed and blissfully oblivious.

When David wasn't leering over Jen, Jack noticed an edginess and distractedness in him. It unsettled Jack more than the sleaziness or the insatiable boozing—with which he could relate. David was usually the epitome of cool and collected, but this evening he was totally off his game; fidgeting in his chair and checking his phone at every given opportunity, maybe as a distraction tool or: *was there something else going on?* Jack thought.

Fortunately, David's behaviour didn't seem to upset the evening too much. Jen was on fire. Utterly charming and hilarious. She and Rachel were giggling away like school girls all evening and Jack's infatuation was growing stronger than ever.

Around 10:30 Jack leaned over to Jen and whispered in her ear, "Do you want to get out of here? I want to get you back home and do naughty things to you."

Jen pursed her lips. "Oh hell, yeah," she whispered back, looking deeply into his eyes with her sultry, green-eyed stare.

CHAPTER 11

Jack felt a stirring in his crotch.

Jen bit her lip, her fingers sliding over Jack's as she squeezed his hand under the table. "Let's go," she whispered, her breath warm against his ear.

Jack stood, stretching with a deliberate slowness, and opened his arms to his sister. "Sis. It's been a wonderful evening. Thanks for inviting us, but it's getting past our bedtime. Jen and I are gonna hit the hay."

Rachel's brow furrowed. "Oh, Jack, it *has* been a lovely evening. So glad you could make it over." She gave him a strong and warm hug. Breaking the embrace, she looked over at Jen, but still addressing Jack, she continued, "And this one. Wow. I bloody love her. Take care of her, won't you?" She leant in to give Jen a hug.

"I will. You know I will."

"Oh, God, it was so nice to meet you, too, Rachel. Hope we can do it again soon."

"Oh, we will. I'll be pestering my brother non-stop to line something up."

"See you next time, David," said Jack, as he reached out to shake David's hand.

David remained seated, shook Jack's hand and slurred, "Sh-shir thang, Jock."

Jen kept her distance from the inebriated David—simply waving in his direction to say goodnight.

Walking hand in hand towards the tube station, Jack looked sincerely at Jen and asked, "Did you have a good night, babe?"

"Yeah it was so much fun. Your sister is an absolute delight. But... I have to ask... what's the deal with that David character? Is he usually like that?"

Jack felt his chest tighten. "No... It's actually quite worrying.

He's usually so cool and suave. He's a bit of a ladies' man, or likes to think he is. Maybe... maybe he can be a little sleazy at times, but I've never seen him like that. Did it bother you?"

"It did make me feel a little uneasy at times, yeah." She shrugged. "But I've dealt with worse. It's a shame I didn't get to meet him when he's on better form then. Why do you think he was like that tonight?"

"My gut says... and I've learned to trust that instinct; he's either having serious financial trouble, or... or he's having an affair." Jack sighed. "Or both. But something's not right there, that's for sure."

Chapter 12

Forensic detectives arrived in their droves and were directed by Detective Raines to bag and tag all evidence at the murder scene in the derelict barn. It was a painstaking process that continued well into the early hours of the next morning. The atrocity and chaos at the site of the killing were so extensive that a thorough approach was necessary to document everything accurately and efficiently, requiring half a dozen highly skilled detectives.

Throughout the first few hours of this evidence-gathering process, Susan sat outside the barn on the grass. Motionless. She couldn't bear to stare at the horrific sight any longer and felt numb to her very core. Pictures raced through her mind like some kind of sadistic movie trailer, reliving what she'd seen in all its gory, sordid detail. A reel of highlights—or lowlights—played back in a waterfall of despicable images.

Usually she was able to put on a brave face in these circumstances and maintain the ideal of a strong, stern female officer that those in the force had become accustomed to. Right now, however, she couldn't care less about keeping up the image. She let the mask slide. Not by choice. She couldn't help it. This scene had rattled her completely, and the secretive, personal tip-off—along with the grotesque welcome note she had received—only worked to accentuate that effect.

As she sat, she wept uncontrollably. She felt an overwhelming sadness—for the victim, for his family, for all the victims, and ultimately, for herself, knowing that she hadn't been able to make a difference and stop this lunatic from killing again.

With each death, the scenes unfolding before her were becoming more and more depraved, and she still didn't have the faintest fucking clue who was responsible.

After hours of sitting on the ground, having sobbed herself into a stunned silence, Susan got to her feet and patted herself down. She felt the need to take action, but she couldn't stay at the site any longer. Approaching the barn, she made sure not to look inside and called for Detective Raines to join her. He made his excuses to his fellow detectives and stepped outside.

"You okay, ma'am?"

"Not really, to be honest with you, Detective." Susan's face dropped. "This has hit me like a ton of bricks. I think the fact that someone reached out to me directly gives an edge to it that seems personal. I... I can't shake it and it's hit me harder than usual. How are *you* doing?"

"Not gonna lie. It's fucking awful in there. Everyone is feeling..." Raines paused, his shoulders slumped, and his face fell in symmetry with Susan's. "I can't think of the words."

Susan looked at her feet, her shoes crusted with mud from sitting on the grass. "I understand. I'm not sure there are words to describe how a human should feel at the sight of this." She met Raines' eyes. "But how are *you*?"

"I'll be okay. It's the nature of the job."

"It's the nature of my job too, but this time it just feels too much... That poor man." She sighed. "Do we even know who he was?"

"Afraid not. He was naked—no clothes found at the scene and therefore no ID. We're gonna have to rely on DNA samples, fingerprints, or dental records at this point. Although dental records will be more difficult to validate since, uh... most of his teeth were removed."

Susan clenched her fists, nails digging into her palms. "The sadist fuck." She could feel the sadness transforming into anger. No, not anger—she was beyond anger. She felt rage.

"And it looks like that happened pre-mortem, too."

"Oh dear fucking God. I can't be here, Detective. I'm sorry to do this to you, but do you think you're okay to wrap things up here without me?"

Raines gave an assured nod. "Ma'am, I've got this. You go and get some rest, yeah?"

"Thank you, Detective. I really do owe you for this. And not just this, but for all of today. I won't forget it. It's hard in this job to know who you can truly trust and I really do feel that I can rely on you."

Raines flashed the faintest of smiles. "Thanks for saying so, ma'am. I'm happy to assist you in any way I can."

Holding a hand up to Detective Raines, Susan said, "Can we stop with this 'Ma'am' bullshit? Please... call me Susan. All this impersonal nonsense that comes with the force I really can't tolerate right now. It's so inhuman at times. And what really takes the piss is that I don't even know your fucking name!"

"Right you are, Susan. And it's Nick. My name's Nick."

"Nick... I like Nick. Quite funny for a police officer, don't you think?" said Susan. Her wet eyes glistened in the moonlight and there was a lightness to them that had been released from captivity for a moment. "Is it okay if I call you Nick?"

"Yeah I had that a lot when going through training," said Nick, with a smirk. "I was actually quite happy when people had to start addressing me by my surname. But, sure, you can call me Nick."

"Thanks, Nick," Susan smiled. "Okay, I'm gonna head home to try and get some sleep and get this out of my head. I have a feeling we're going to have a busy day tomorrow trying to piece this all together. Are you going to be able to get back okay whenever you're done here?"

"Yeah I can ride in one of the other cars here. No problem. Go and get some sleep, Susan. I hope you can. You're right… you're going to need it."

"Thanks again, Nick. Good luck with the rest of it and call me if you need anything. Otherwise, I'll see you back at HQ tomorrow."

Susan traipsed away from the scene, got back in her car and drove home, gripping the steering wheel so tight with rage that her bone white knuckles looked as though they might implode under the pressure.

She screamed.

Chapter 13

Sitting at her desk, Susan reviewed the field reports from yesterday's crime scene while clicking the top of her pen, rhythmically. Incessantly. She had barely managed a wink of sleep since she got home—couldn't help but replay the day over and over in her head. She was wracked with guilt. Guilt for leaving Nick at the scene while she went home and, most crucially, guilt for not having caught the depraved bastard who was behind this.

Could I have prevented this latest killing?

Susan had missed crucial pieces of evidence, failed to establish the links that pointed to a serial killer at play, and had spent the night berating herself over it.

Hindsight bullied her—screamed at her—as she realised she hadn't taken Jack seriously in his protestations.

I'm sorry, Jack.

I'm sorry for all of the victims' families.

I'm sorry.

Susan's desk phone rang; the sound bringing her crashing back to the present moment.

She grabbed the handset, but before she could speak, a voice on the other end cut in.

"Reeves?"

"Superintendent Hale. How are you, sir?"

Ignoring the question, Hale snapped, "I need to see you in my office. Right now."

"I'll be right there, sir."

Hale had already hung up.

* * *

Superintendent Hale made Susan wait outside his office. It was clearly some sort of power play, but she had more pressing concerns and refused to let it get to her.

Not wanting to give him the satisfaction, she sat and waited patiently, but an overriding thought occupied her mind:

He said he wanted to see me right now. And yet, here I am. Waiting. What an arrogant prick.

Ten minutes passed. Finally, Hale opened the door, beckoned Susan, and returned to his throne-like chair. She got up and strode into his office. It had the trite air of authority—plaques of merit, framed pictures of Hale glad-handing high-profile individuals, and, as the ultimate power play, a purposely small chair for visitors.

Refusing to take the bait, she remained standing.

"You wanted to see me, sir?"

"Yes, Reeves," said Hale. His brow furrowed, his expression dark with discontent. "What the hell were you thinking?"

"Excuse me, sir?"

"What did you think you were doing, going to a crime scene on your own, without backup and totally unsolicited?"

CHAPTER 13

"I'm sorry, sir, but I was contacted directly and—"

"By who?" Hale snapped, refusing to let Susan finish her sentence.

"I don't know. They never gave their name. They called anonymously and informed me about a murder having taken place. I have no idea if it was the perpetrator, a witness, or a random member of the public that had stumbled across the site."

"And you didn't think to run this past me?"

"Actually no, sir. Do you know how many hack jobs we get calling in, wasting our time? I figured that it would be most prudent to check it out myself. If it turned out to be nothing then no harm would be done and no resources wasted. If it did turn out to be something—"

"Then, what? You'd call it in? And risk having contaminated a crime scene?"

"No!"

"No, what?" Hale's eyes narrowed.

"No, sir." With her arms behind her back, Susan felt her hands turn to fists uncontrollably. "I had a forensic detective with me, for exactly this reason."

"Who?"

"I'd rather not say, sir."

"WHO!"

Susan took a moment; Hale's yell still ringing in her ears. She didn't want to bring Nick into this—she had promised to take the flak—but she concluded that he would clearly be on the reports, so mentioning his name wouldn't make any difference at this point.

"Detective Raines, sir," she said, a resignation in her voice. "But, it was under my orders to bring him in... He's not responsible for any deviation from procedure."

"Well, I'll be the judge of that."

"Please, sir. Really this has nothing to do with him. He was just doing his job."

"Hmmm." Hale tapped his fingers on his desk, rhythmically. "I'll think about it."

"Thank you. And, sir?"

"Yes?"

"I think it's time we make a statement to the press. People should be made aware of this. We're now talking about a serial killer in our midst."

"And tell them what, exactly? That we have a madman running around killing people. In increasingly sick and malevolent ways? That we have no idea who's doing this? And, most importantly, that we have no idea what the link is between the murders, or how he's selecting his victims?"

"People have a right to know, s—."

"No, they don't!"

"Sir?" Shaken by Hale's outburst, Susan's eyes widened.

"It's our job to protect the people of this city. With that responsibility also comes the need to exercise our best judgement and it's *my* judgement to not reveal any of this to the public for fear of creating any undue panic."

Is he for real?

"Or are you more concerned about our public image, sir?" Susan stared at Hale intensely, wondering how he would take to being challenged on this. She could see anger growing in his eyes—his face, reddening—but refused to relent. "Stating that we're no closer to catching this bastard than we were when he started this trail of horror wouldn't make us look good. Right? It would make us look incompetent. Isn't that

CHAPTER 13

the real concern?"

Hale got to his feet to meet Susan's stare, head on. His hands, in fists, rested on his desk as he leaned forward to address her. "You're overstepping the line, Reeves. You're on mighty thin ice. This is *my* call."

"I hope you don't *regret* making that call, sir."

"What did you say to me?" Hale said, as his fists pounded the desk. His brow furrowed and the tension made his eyes look as though they might burst out of their sockets. Before Susan could respond, he growled, "Right, I'm taking you off the case!"

What the fuck?

"But sir. You can't?!"

"I'm *sorry*? I think you'll find I can. Make no mistake. I can and I am. Your lack of respect for authority is making you a liability, Reeves."

"I'm just trying to do the right thing." Susan insisted.

"No you're not. You're becoming *obsessed*. You're obsessed with this fucking case."

"What do you mean obsessed? If only I *had* been obsessed, maybe I could have made the difference. Maybe I could have stopped that sick fuck in his tracks."

Hale shook his head. "I've made my mind up, Reeves. You're off the case. I'm gonna hand it to Jones."

"Jones?!"

Detective Jones was the laughing stock of the department. The growing consensus among Susan and her colleagues was that if you wanted a case to be well and truly fucked up, you gave it to Jones. A bumbling fool of a man. How he'd remained in a job at the force—and at a fairly high rank—was a complete mystery. He must be related to someone high up or, better yet, have some serious dirt on someone, Susan had always thought.

Maybe he has dirt on Hale?

"Yes. That's right. Jones," Hale responded, looking sternly at Susan.

"With all due respect, sir.... *Jones*? And you're calling *me* a liability? For Christ's sake!" Susan's eyes rolled. Her rage was building more and more with each breath. Her fists became tighter and tighter, like screws being turned to the point of splitting wood.

"He's a very decorated and dedicated officer."

"This is bullshit, sir."

"Like it or not, Detective, my decision is made. Get back to your desk. I'll have a new assignment for you soon."

Susan said nothing. She stood, motionless, continuing to look directly at Hale, striking him with an icy stare.

"And I'd appreciate you giving Jones access to all of your case notes in the meantime."

"Like fuck I will," Susan muttered under her breath as she stormed out of Hale's office.

***

Susan burst out of the building. Her blood was boiling and she needed to clear her head. She paced around the car park out in front of the headquarters trying to make some sense of what had just happened. Thoughts raced through her head:

Hale took me off the case. Just like that. Gave it to that fuckwit, Jones. Does he even realise how serious this is?

The killer will *strike again. When? How soon?*

CHAPTER 13

Who was the latest victim? What did he do to deserve such a brutal, humiliating death?

Susan continued to march around the car park, trying to shake the frustration and anger. A flash of movement caught her eye—another officer, cigarette in hand. She wandered over to them.

"Can I pinch a smoke?"

"Of course," the officer said, as she opened up her pack of cigarettes and handed one to Susan. "I didn't realise you smoked, ma'am," she added, as she passed Susan a lighter.

"I don't. But I do today," Susan replied. She didn't know the other officer, but it was clear that they knew *her*. Susan was in no mood to make conversation, though. She lit the cigarette, exhaled and passed the lighter back, all without saying a word. With purpose in her steps, she then walked a few yards away to sit on a nearby bench at the edge of the car park, facing out to the street beyond.

"**FFFUUUUUUCCCCCCKKKKKKKK**!!!!"

* * *

Susan finished her cigarette and extinguished it with the sole of her shoe in an act of rebellion. She was reminded why she didn't smoke anymore—the lingering taste in her mouth was awful, and she coughed and spluttered like a teenager trying cigarettes for the first time. She did enjoy the headrush though; it was a welcome distraction from the feelings of rage that she had been dealing with.

As she sat, Susan's anger subsided slightly, giving way to a feeling of determination. Hale could take her off the case, but he couldn't dampen her relentless tenacity in following the investigation's progress.

She couldn't do this alone, though. She needed some help.

Susan took her phone from her pocket and called Detective Raines.

"Hi, ma'am... Sorry. Susan," Nick said, as he answered the call.

"Hi, Nick. How's things with you? Did everything go okay at the site last night?"

"Yeah, we got everything squared away there. The body... and all its pieces... They're over at the morgue now for autopsy."

"Oh, God. What a sight that must be. Again, I'm sorry for having to leave you there last night."

"That's quite alright. Honestly. As SIO you don't need to be there for that process anyway."

"But I dragged you into it."

"Yeah you did. But. If you hadn't, I would have been called upon later to head over there with those other forensics."

"Fair point. I just want you to know I appreciate all that you did for me yesterday."

"I know you do."

"There's more news though, I'm afraid."

Raines said nothing.

"Hale's taking me off the case."

"What the fuck?!"

Raines wasn't usually one to drop the F-bomb and Susan sensed his shock.

"Yeah. And guess who he's giving the case to."

"Go on. Tell me. Not Jones, surely?"

CHAPTER 13

"Yeah, fucking Jones." Susan sighed.

"What the fucking fuck!"

Susan couldn't help but laugh at this moment. Hearing Nick's reaction to this news was really telling. He was usually the epitome of calm and even he was losing his shit at this revelation.

"I know. It's ridiculous. I don't know who he's screwing to get this. Probably the highest profile case for a decade and it's being given to the most useless detective of a generation."

"They can't do this."

Susan felt a sense of satisfaction in the level of respect that Nick clearly felt towards her. It gave her a strength that she really needed right now.

"They're doing it," said Susan. "But I'm not going to let this be the end for me in this case. I'm not going to let this case get fucked up just because it's in the hands of Jones. I'm going to need your help though, Nick."

"How can I help, ma'am?"

"Susan, remember?"

"Shit, yes, sorry. How can I help, Susan?"

"Is there a way you can keep me up to date on the autopsy findings? DNA sampling? Dental records, et cetera? I need to know who this man is."

"I'll do what I can to keep you in the loop."

"No official channels though. Just call me on my personal number if you have anything."

"Of course."

"Thanks, Nick. Really appreciate it."

"Don't mention it."

Susan hung up the call. She remained sitting on that bench facing the traffic outside for an hour, basking in the summer sun, with a renewed sense of determination.

Chapter 14

His nerves were jangling. His hands shook gently, a subtle undercurrent of vibration running through them. He popped a Valium and swallowed it with a hefty gulp of scotch. Not just a sip—he downed it, winced, then immediately followed-up with another pill. His doctor had prescribed them for a sleeping problem, but that wasn't why he needed them now. He had to escape the nerves. But he also needed focus.

Valium wouldn't sharpen the mind, but overwhelming anxiety would be a far bigger hurdle for him in completing his task. And for that, he had to take the edge off.

Tonight was the night.

He dressed in what *he* considered to be inconspicuous clothing: a black T-shirt, black jeans, black boots.

Too black? Who cares?

He fastened the boots tight, stood, straightened his T-shirt and tried to pull his shoulders back, but tension kept them hunched.

He took a minute to remind himself of all the reasons he was doing this. The thoughts gave him purpose, enough to force his shoulders back and stand tall.

He'd picked what seemed to be the perfect night. A night when he knew where the person he was looking for would be—and, just as important, a night when his wife would be out. He needed to be alone to prepare.

He grabbed his rucksack and did one final check. He turned the bag upside down, shook it, and emptied the contents onto the bed. Black gloves. A document. A black marker pen. A piano wire with handles at each end.

He picked up the document and unfolded it, revealing typed words and a picture of a man—someone entirely unknown to him.

The notes told him everything—who this man was, where he would be at certain times and on specific days.

Today was one of those days—and one of those times was very soon.

The name of the man in the picture: Alan Poulson.

He held the picture close, studying the face again. He'd stared at this visage many times, leading up to tonight. Etched it into his mind. He knew the face well—seemingly. But memory was fragile, and he needed his recollection to be razor-sharp for what came next.

There could be no mistakes.

He had to recognise this man instantly. Instinctively.

* * *

Alan poured another lager and set it down on the bar. The customer handed over a ten pound note and waited for his change. Alan returned promptly, dropping the coins into the his hand with a wild grin and electric eyes. A typical look from Alan.

"You know, you're far too happy for this gig?"

"What can I say? I love my job," Alan chimed.

"Good for you, mate. Cheers." The customer raised his pint in appreciation before returning to his table.

Alan, a rake of a man, was working the evening shift at the White Hart Hotel. A traditional country inn on the outskirts of a busy London suburb, which somehow exuded a rural charm.

Throughout the bar area there were a number of solid oak tables and, during the winter months, a roaring fireplace would warm the bones of the patrons. Out front was a sizeable beer garden, furnished with outdoor heaters and standard picnic tables. Traditional real ales were available on draft and they served typical pub grub. For those occupying one of the half dozen rooms that they offered, a hearty breakfast was thrown in.

Alan worked at the White Hart a few nights a week to help make ends meet. He enjoyed the job, and he'd struck up some good relations with the punters—especially the younger crowd, who he served alcohol to, knowing full well they were underage. He had a predilection for teens. Preferably female—although he wasn't fussy—and this job gave him the open opportunity to gawk at the youngsters. As an added bonus they showed him appreciation and brought their friends along too, giving him more and more eye candy to leer over.

A win-win for Alan.

A girl, probably fourteen years old, approached the bar with a spring in her step. She was made up. Lip gloss. Eyeliner. Mascara. She leaned provocatively at the bar as she spoke.

"Hi, Alan," she pouted. "You're looking good tonight."

"Well, hello there, missy. Might I say the same about you," Alan beamed, as he gave a lewd wink and a crooked smile.

She smirked. "Could you be a legend and get me another vodka, lime, and soda?"

"Why, of course. Anything for you, my dear."

Alan backed away to prepare the drink. He felt a stirring in his crotch and fidgeted to hide the burgeoning erection.

As he returned, she began to open her purse, but he stopped her in her tracks with a raised palm.

"No need."

"Huh?"

"This one's on me."

"Oh, Alan," she said, softly. "You're too good to me."

"I know," Alan said, with a lecherousness that couldn't be mistaken. "But how could I not treat the prettiest girl in the bar, eh?"

The girl giggled, picked up her drink, and wove her way back to a table where eight of her friends sat, giddy and inebriated. As she sat down, Alan watched, trying in vain to listen to their conversations as they snickered around the table.

He misguidedly believed that they were speaking fondly of him.

* * *

The sun had long since set.

The man sat on a park bench, a few minutes' walk from the White Hart. He had all the information he needed about his target and he fully expected that Alan would walk back through

CHAPTER 14

this park on his way home from his shift at the pub.

The park was quiet at night. Dog walkers and joggers had completed their duties much earlier in the evening and, as he sat here, the man felt comfortable that there would be no risk of witnesses. Comfortable was a strong word at this point, however. The Valium had kicked in long ago, taking the edge off, but his nerves still jangled.

He opened his rucksack and took out the gloves, sheathing his hands with a scrunch of leather.

He sat patiently.

And waited.

* * *

Alan rang the bell to signify last orders. There was an audible sigh from the teens over in the corner and one of the boys ran over to the bar to order a last round of drinks. Alan gladly obliged, served the drinks, flirted inappropriately with the boy and then started to tidy behind the bar while the punters finished their last drinks. He knew that he would need to stay open for longer if there were any hotel guests still at the bar, but fortunately for him, they'd all hit the sack already.

Thirty minutes later, the gaggling flock of teens vacated the pub, in a stumbling mess, like a drunken conga at a wedding, to a chorus of "see you next time, Alan." He waved and leered as they passed him. His thoughts were dark.

Alan locked up. The ceremonious act of a jangling of keys and sliding of bolts. For the hotel guests there was a door that used a keycard system that was locked, by default, and only unlocked to the swipe of an active card. He made his way out of the pub via the keycard door.

It was dark outside. It would be darker if it wasn't for the slight glow on the horizon; the light pollution spilling over from central London, like an urban Northern Lights. A thrum of activity could be heard in the distance, but at this time of night it was eerily quiet in this part of town.

Alan strode to the nearby park gates. He liked to cut through the park at night. It was quiet, atmospheric, and as dark as his thoughts.

Opening the gate to a *'squeak'*, he entered the park.

* * *

Squeak.

The sound of the park gate opening shook him. He sat up with a jolt, looked over to his left and squinted to sharpen his vision. It was hard to see anything in the darkness, but having sat on the bench in the dark for what felt like hours, his night vision was at its peak. He could make out signs of movement near the park gates, which were about a hundred yards from where he sat.

Could this be him?

He continued to sit; as still as possible, despite the adrenaline rampaging through his veins.

He watched as the ambling mass grew ever closer. About 20 yards away now and he could make out more detail.

It was definitely a man.

A thin man.

CHAPTER 14

With trembling hands, he reached into his rucksack, pulled out the piano wire, and fastened the bag. He slipped on the rucksack and wrapped his gloved fingers around the handles of the weapon.

Ten yards away.

Five yards away.

Despite the darkness, he could now make out the man's features.

The memory of the man's image was fresh in his mind.

This *was* him. No doubt.

He rose and crept towards the man.

"Alan?"

Alan stopped in his tracks. He turned to face the man—his eyes, wide with shock.

"Y-yes?"

"Alan Poulson?"

"Who... who's asking?" he said, taking a step back.

"I'm sorry to have to do this, Alan."

The man swung a fist—hard and fast—into Alan's stomach. Alan, winded, hunched over, coughing and spluttering. While he was incapacitated, the man wound one end of the piano wire around Alan's neck, moved behind him, and pulled the two handles tight.

Alan arched upright, his hands clawing at the wire around his neck.

As he writhed, the man pulled tighter. The wire—cutting into his neck now—caused blood to seep down onto Alan's collarbone and shoulders.

"Unngghhh," Alan gagged. His expression was a contradiction.

Is he smiling?

The assailant continued to pull tight and Alan continued to frantically tug at the wire. Clutching at straws. It was futile. The more he wrestled against it, the deeper the wire dug into Alan's neck.

He pulled tighter.

Blood ran harder.

Alan writhed more erratically.

He pulled tighter still.

Tighter still.

Alan twitched and groaned.

Tighter.

He sweated from the exertion and continued to pull tight until Alan's arms fell limply to his sides, his body becoming a dead weight.

The man didn't let go yet but dropped to his knees, Alan's lax body slumping to the ground with him.

He held on for what felt like an age. He had to be certain the job was done.

Finally, he released his grip and uncoiled the piano wire from Alan's loose body. It had etched a deep gash in his neck. He had pulled so hard and for so long that he was surprised he hadn't decapitated him. Alan's face was left contorted—a surreal mix of pleasure and pain was portrayed on his face. His wild, wide eyes gave an unflinching dead stare.

The man took off his rucksack and rummaged around the contents. He retrieved the marker pen and began to scribble on Alan's warped face.

On his forehead, with a shaky scrawl, he wrote the words:

'THE DEBT HAS BEEN PAID'

CHAPTER 14

Rummaging further, he salvaged the photograph of Alan and placed it with careful precision on his lifeless body that now lay sprawled on the grass.

He snapped a photograph on his phone and his breath hitched as the flash went off.

What if someone was alerted by the flash?

He glanced around. No one to be seen. He closed his eyes and listened carefully.

No sound.

He slung his rucksack over his shoulder and ran through the park. His chest heaved and his heart drummed against his ribcage.

A few hundred yards later, he spotted moonlight glinting off a nearby pond. He paused for the briefest moment, then stepped closer and launched the piano wire right into the heart of it.

Reaching the exit gates at the far end of the park, he slowed his pace.

Panting, he stepped onto the quiet suburban street beyond.

As he walked along the street the man caught a glimpse of himself in a window of a parked car.

He barely recognised himself.

What have I become?

David stared at himself for a solid minute.

Chapter 15

CLICK. CLICK. CLICK.

Another minute passed by. Susan sat at her desk, rhythmically clicking the end of her pen. The tempo, slow; the speed correlating with how busy she was at any given moment. Right now she was idle.

Since Hale had taken her off the case, Susan's workload had diminished dramatically. He had put her on the most inane and absurd assignments—assisting other departments with nonsense such as background checks and road traffic violations. Certainly nothing deserving of her skill-set or experience.

She felt she was being punished by the Superintendent, but she wouldn't let that dampen her resolve.

If anything, this treatment gave her more free time, further fuelling her desire to solve the serial killings, but she was left hamstrung and frustrated by her lack of access to key information. She now relied exclusively on Nick to surreptitiously provide her with any updates, and all she could do was practise patience until then.

Patience was not one of Susan's virtues—the inner resistance to it was palpable. She couldn't sit idly at her desk any longer. She needed to get out of the office to avoid her frustration growing to a point where it turned into rage again.

She got to her feet and marched to the office exit, descended a flight of stairs, and swiped her keycard to open the door to exit the building.

She wandered out into the city streets and headed to her favourite café situated on the bank of the river. She didn't often get a chance to visit this place but, considering her current workload, she could definitely afford the time for a visit. She grabbed an oat, iced latte and meandered casually along the riverbank. It was a glorious day and this moment provided the perfect antidote to her busy, rambling mind. A gentle breeze created waves in her blonde hair and the sun on her back gave her a therapeutic hug of warmth.

A rare moment of calm.

Susan connected her earphones to her mobile and started listening to a true crime podcast that she'd been following. It was a bit of a busman's holiday for her—listening to crime stories—but this was one of her guilty pleasures. She'd often listen to such podcasts to fall asleep to. Her equivalent of a child's bedtime story.

No sooner had the title music finished playing when her phone rang and interrupted the podcast's jingle. It was Nick. She answered without hesitation.

"Nick?"

"Hey, Susan. How's things?"

"Terribly dull. Hale's got me on all manner of useless shit right now, so I've taken a stroll."

"Are you sitting down?"

Susan's interest was piqued.

"Do you think I should be?"

"Perhaps. This is quite out there!" Nick exclaimed. He sounded excited, which wasn't like him at all.

"One second, Nick."

Susan scanned the area and found a bench on the riverbank just a few yards away. She rushed over to it and sat down. She took a sip of her iced latte and readied herself with a deep breath.

"Okay, I'm sitting. What have you got, Nick?"

"Right. So, we ran samples on the latest victim to try and determine who the man was. Although his teeth were in an atrocious state and many were removed we were able to get a match on the dental records."

Susan's pulse spiked, but she remained silent, waiting for Nick to provide more information.

"Susan... We have a name."

Susan gulped. "Amazing... What's the name?"

"Wilson Fensome."

"*Wilson Fensome*," Susan repeated, under her breath. "Doesn't mean anything to me. Not sure it should. Does the name sound familiar to you?"

"No, it doesn't, but that's not the most significant part."

Susan felt butterflies in her stomach.

If getting a name wasn't significant then what else could Nick have up his sleeve?

"Okay, you've got me on the edge of my seat now, Nick. What's the most significant part?"

"You ready for this?"

"Shit, Nick. I'm ready! What the hell have you found?"

"Well, before we got the results back from dental we were running tests on the victim's blood to see if we could get a DNA match in our system, to help identify him."

CHAPTER 15

"And did you get a match?"

"We sure did…" Nick paused.

"Fuck's sake. You're not hosting Big Brother, Nick. Tell me what you've got!"

"Sorry about building the suspense, but this is a big deal." Nick took a breath before continuing. "The blood. It matched the blood trail left at the killing of Brett Anderson."

Susan sat bolt upright.

She couldn't speak.

Chapter 16

"Susan?"

...

...

"Ma'am??"

Susan had remained quiet for at least a minute.

"I'm here," Susan said finally, breaking the silence that weighed heavily. Even this modest response felt like a struggle. The revelation that Nick had shared had shaken her. She wasn't ready to speak just yet and needed a few moments to collect her thoughts before continuing.

Eventually, she responded. "I can't believe it... This is crazy. In all my time, I've never... seen anything like this." She paused, before continuing, making sure she understood exactly what this meant. She continued, slowly and precisely. "So what you're saying is that this latest victim—Wilson Fensome—was actually at the scene of Brett Anderson's killing? A seemingly unrelated victim?"

"Exactly."

"And Mr Fensome was most likely the killer of Mr Anderson?"

"It looks like it, as bizarre as that sounds."

CHAPTER 16

"Fuck me." Susan had no better words.

"Are you glad you were sitting down now?"

Susan pursed her lips and exhaled sharply. "Absolutely. My head's spinning."

"So, where do we go from here?"

"I need to think. Let me give you a call back in a sec?"

"Okay, sure."

"And thanks, Nick. I really appreciate you keeping me in the loop on this. I know it's risky for you."

"Not at all. I know you'll do a better job than Jonesy... Even when you're not on the case." Nick laughed. "Speak soon."

"Yep. Bye for now."

Susan hung up the call and sat perplexed for a few minutes. Her head reeled. She slowly sipped at the remnants of her coffee. The ice had all but melted, diluting the remaining contents, and turning it into a very light shade of brown.

Susan's mind spun as she replayed her conversation with Nick. She knew not to attribute too much to one situation. It could just be a coincidence, albeit a very *bizarre* coincidence, that one victim was killed in the same way that they had killed someone else. It couldn't be considered a pattern based on this sole circumstance. She'd need more proof of association, to draw such a conclusion.

Suddenly a thought ignited.

A spark in her mind.

She called Nick immediately.

"Susan? That was quick!"

"I've had a thought."

"Hit me with it."

"I want you to look back at the other cases in this serial. I don't think you were on the investigation team at the time, but hopefully you can still get access to the old evidence?"

"I don't think I was. Which cases were they?"

"There were two other murders that we're aware of, but we didn't realise any links between them at the time of the investigations. If I'm right about this then we might be able to find another link, to help prove a pattern. The two other cases were of a Lisa Stevens and a Nathan Brown."

"You're right. I'm not familiar with them."

Susan scratched her head. Something lingered at the back of her mind, just out of reach. The more she tried to grasp it, the further it drifted away.

"There was something, but I can't quite remember what it was." Susan sighed.

"Hopefully it will come to you. I'll be here if you do remember. I can always review the evidence anyway and see if I can turn up any new threads."

Susan's eyes widened.

A lightbulb moment.

Nick's words pulled the distant memory from the dark recesses of Susan's mind like a fisherman reeling in a big catch.

"That's it, Nick. That's it! You're a genius!" Susan exclaimed.

"I am?"

"Threads! Fucking threads!"

"Huh?"

"On Nathan Brown's body there were some errant threads. We found... traces of DNA evidence on these threads, but they didn't match anything back then." Susan stood up with a surge of energy and started pacing back and forth. "I'm betting that if you check the DNA from those threads, you'll find a match to Brett Anderson!"

CHAPTER 16

"Wow. Okay, I'll check that out immediately and get back to you as soon as I've got any news."

"Thanks again, Nick. We're really onto something here. I can feel it."

Invigorated by this revelation, Susan hung up the call and continued to pace.

Now came the even harder part—once again, she had to practise patience.

* * *

Susan clocked off early. There was no need for her to hang around HQ. Her total lack of interest in the work that Hale had assigned to her was just a frustration, and she was unable to focus on anything while she waited anxiously for Nick to get back to her.

She was almost certain that she was going to be proven justified in her hunch, but she wouldn't let herself assume that. She needed proof.

But what would I do with such proof?
If my hunch is correct, does this mean there isn't a serial killer?
It's so ambiguous. It actually raises more questions.

* * *

The trees waved gently in the light summer breeze of the afternoon. Susan relaxed. No. She *tried* to relax; sitting in her garden and already halfway through a bottle of wine. The house was silent. For now. Her two daughters were still at school and there was a dearth of chaos.

Susan very rarely had quiet time to herself. Her work was typically all-consuming, and in the fleeting moments of reprieve she'd busy herself with that other responsibility. Parenthood. She wasn't used to this pause. Her life was usually unrelenting and this moment of peace and quiet wasn't helpful to her at a time when she was trying to exercise patience. She pined for distraction.

Susan's two daughters, Violet (14) and Evie (11), were from her past relationship with Scott. She'd only ever had one long term relationship and you'd be forgiven for assuming that Scott was the love of her life, but if you asked her to respond truthfully she would say that being a detective was her *true* passion. The job had always come first for her and she'd invariably put it above all else.

Susan had never found it in herself to take the next step into marriage and her relationship had crumbled over time due to her being somewhat emotionally unavailable. Her mind was always on other things and Scott had grown impatient. He'd sought intimacy and, in the end, had found it in the arms of another woman.

He remained a good father to their children and Susan never blamed him for leaving. She knew she only had herself to hold accountable for how things turned out. Her devotion to her work came at a price.

Susan rarely reflected on her thoughts, usually too busy to even be drawn to them. But all of a sudden, she was overcome with a wave of remorse—realising that she'd let her obsession with the obscene acts of the criminal underbelly of society take prime spot in her life.

And for what? Obfuscating the more primal needs of family and love. She'd neglected Scott. Was she neglecting Evie and Violet, too?

She needed to rebalance her life. She knew this instinctively. She felt it, weighing heavy on her shoulders. A dullness in the pit of her stomach. She had to find a way to put her family life *before* her work and somehow make the job a little less absorbing. This was going to require sacrifice on her part.

She pondered this for several minutes and came to the conclusion that, regardless of the need to rebalance her commitments, she would need to first see out this case.

What case?

She wasn't even assigned to it anymore.

She knew she couldn't think about focusing on stabilising things between her job and her personal life just yet. After witnessing what she had earlier this week, at the site of Wilson Fensome's murder, she had started to question her ability—and even her desire—to remain a police officer. It had broken her. Had, in some way, taken a piece of her.

Never in her twenty-five years with the force had she reacted like that to a crime scene, and she wondered if she could ever go back to her matter-of-fact, black-and-white thinking that she'd typically had when it came to investigating and solving crimes.

Things would need to change. But not yet.

She wouldn't rest until she had helped bring this case to a conclusion.

* * *

The afternoon drew to a close. Susan was clearing away dishes and wiping down the kitchen worktops, while listening to her true crime podcast when Evie came crashing through the door.

"Hey, Mum," Evie crowed, as she dumped her school bags on the floor in the hallway and came running into the kitchen.

"Hey, sweetie," Susan responded, taking her daughter in her arms.

"Are you home *early*?"

"I sure am, baby. I wanted to spend some time with my gorgeous girls."

Evie frowned. "Are you fibbing?"

"No!" She was. A little. Not that seeing her kids wasn't a joy, but it wasn't the prime reason for her being home early. A little white lie wouldn't hurt anyone though, she figured. "Where's your sister?"

"She's with her friends. The 'cool' gang." She huffed. "She'll be home for dinner though, I think. What *is* for dinner, mum?"

Oh shit. Even when I finish early I'm still not as prepared as I should be for my mum duties.

"I haven't decided yet. What would you like?"

"Fish fingers!" Evie shrieked.

Susan smiled. "Fish fingers it is. I'll wait for Violet to get home first then I'll put it on."

Susan's phone rang, interrupting the exchange between her and her daughter.

She darted to fetch it from the dining table, hoping and silently praying that it would be Nick calling with the news she craved to hear.

It was.

"I've got to get this, sweetie. Can you go and play on your

iPad?" said Susan, motioning with her head to the device that lay on the table in front of her.

Mum of the year, as always.

Without hesitation, Evie grabbed the iPad from the dining table and galloped to the living room.

"Hi, Nick," Susan chimed. There was an excitement to her tone that was palpable.

"Hey Susan. Hope I'm not disturbing you?"

"Oh, you know, I'm up to my eyeballs in it right now." She laughed.

"Welcoming the downtime, eh?"

"I wouldn't say that. Mum duties never cease. And besides, I'm not very good at doing nothing. You got any news for me?"

"I have."

"Always with the suspense, Nick. Come on, mate, hit me with it."

Mate? Since when have I ever referred to anyone as 'mate'?

"You were right."

Her pulse spiked.

"I was?"

"Yeah. The evidence from Mr Brown's case was still accessible. We ran the sample of Mr Anderson's DNA against those threads that were found on Mr Brown's body." Nick paused—no doubt for his newly found love of injecting drama into an already dramatic situation. "It was a match... One hundred percent. Brett Anderson was definitely present at Nathan Brown's murder."

"Fuck. Yes! I knew it!" Susan punched the air. "Whooo!"

"It's a great result, but now that we know this, what does it change? What do we do now, exactly?"

The question made Susan halt her celebration. Being right

was one thing—it gave her a decent hit of dopamine—but she hadn't exactly cracked the case.

Nick was correct. It didn't really change anything in terms of their progress towards solving the investigation. They still had no leads, no way of knowing who would strike next, or who the next victim might be.

"I guess the only thing it changes is that we've identified the pattern, right? As bizarre as it is. Although it's not one hundred percent damning, the evidence does seem to suggest that Brett Anderson killed Nathan Brown and Wilson Fensome killed Brett Anderson, right?"

"Right," Nick agreed.

"But we still don't know who killed Wilson Fensome."

"Right," Nick conceded.

"So we need to follow that up. Focus our efforts..." Susan paused. She was getting carried away and came face to face again with the harsh reality that she wasn't officially on the case anymore. She took a breath, then continued. "By *'our'* efforts I guess I mean you and that fuckwit Jonesy, with me being a silent partner. The collective *'we'* should focus all efforts on trying to find who killed Wilson Fensome."

"Agreed. But how do we do that? We still have nothing to go on."

Susan sighed. "No. I guess we don't." She lowered her head in dejection.

"Maybe something will turn up in the other forensics tests. We still have a lot to sift through."

"Okay, that makes the most sense. Keep me in the loop on anything you find though, will you?"

"You know I will."

"Thanks, Nick. Now there's someone I really need to call.

CHAPTER 16

They really need to know about this."

"Oh, yeah? Who's that?"

"It's probably better that you don't know."

"Understood. I won't pry. Have a good night, Susan and speak soon."

"Thanks. You, too."

Susan hung up the phone and took a moment to gather her thoughts, struggling to make sense of this link between the cases.

What 'debt' are these killings referring to?

Why is it a different killer each time?

Why are those that are committing the murders then being killed with the same message displayed?

Do I really want to share this information? Would it help?

I owe him.

Before she could second-guess herself, she made the call.

Chapter 17

The hum of fluorescent lights and the clacking of keys on a keyboard were all that could be heard this evening. Alone in the office, Jack was working late.

Fuelled by a wave of motivation and caffeine, he was pepped up enough to keep going late into the evening, pushing to finish a draft of an article.

He had no concept of time as he typed away like a man possessed. All he could focus on was his work—that, and the occasional glance over at a photo of Jen that took pride of place at his desk these days. Her striking green eyes stared back at him with a warm expression. An emerald hug.

The photo of Lisa still remained, but it was now pinned to the desk-divider partition, and received less attention these days. By contrast, the photo of Jen was placed directly under Jack's monitor and was never out of sight.

Jack's phone rang, shattering the silence and startling him, yanking him out of his flow state and back to the reality of the office. He took his phone from his pocket, fully expecting it would be Jen calling to tempt him over to her place.

He looked at the screen.

The time: *10:15 p.m.*

CHAPTER 17

The caller: not Jen—it was an unknown number.

Jack would rarely answer a call from a random number and certainly not when he was in flow. He decided to ignore it and get back to his work.

A minute passed and the phone rang again. The same number. Out of frustration more than anything, Jack decided to answer the call this time.

"Yep," Jack snapped.

"Jack?"

Caught off guard, his stomach knotted. "Who's this?"

"Sorry to call you out of the blue, and to disturb you this late in the evening, but there's been a significant update and I thought that you should know about it."

"*Okay...*" Jack's eyes rolled. "But who *is* this?"

"Oh, God, I'm sorry... It's Susan Reeves."

Jack jolted. This was the last person in the world he expected a call from.

Why the hell is Susan calling me?

"Susan? I never thought I'd hear from you again."

"I half expected you to say that, Jack..." There was a sharp intake of breath. "I know I've been dismissive of you in the past and I'm truly sorry about that, I really am. But you... you were right about things. Things that I missed." An audible exhale. "And I really need to share some news with you about the case."

Jack's eyes narrowed. "Right about what, exactly? And, *news*? Is it about..." he gulped, "Lisa's case?"

"Well, not directly." Susan paused for a moment before continuing. "You were right about this being a serial murder case and about there being a link between the murders. Things have changed though and I'm... not on the case anymore. I've been... taken off it. I shouldn't even be *talking* to you right now, but I'm trying to make things right and there are things that I think you should know."

Jack scoffed, a thin, smug grin creeping onto his face. "You've been taken off the case? Why's that? Ineffective police work?" He still harboured a lot of resentment towards Susan due to how she had treated him throughout Lisa's case, and this passive aggression that he was displaying spilled out of his mouth without hesitation. A wave of satisfaction surged as he vented at Susan.

"I deserve that," she said, in surrender. "It's a long story and it's not important right now. I'm still working on it, but... behind closed doors, so to speak."

Jack's chest was tight all of a sudden. An anxious feeling washed over him.

"So what's this update?" He tried to sound calm, but his words were rushed.

"Right, well, uhm, I'm trying to think of how best to explain this." Susan hesitated. "Bear with me... There's been another murder. A very *brutal* murder... We couldn't ID the body, so we carried out forensics tests to try and ascertain who the victim was and the blood sample matched something found at the site of another victim. Brett Anderson. You're probably not aware of this victim at all."

"Oh, I am."

"*Really?* How? We tried to keep this out of the press."

"I have contacts, Susan," Jack retorted—a dry tone to his voice.

"Okay. Never mind." Jack could almost hear the ruffling of feathers. "But you may not know that there was a blood trail leading away from the site of Brett Anderson's killing."

CHAPTER 17

My contacts aren't that good.

Jack stayed quiet and waited for Susan to fill in the blanks.

"This latest victim... their DNA matched that of the blood trail left at that site."

Jack's breath caught in his throat. He coughed to clear it. "What does this mean exactly? And who was this latest victim?"

"Wilson Fensome was his name. Does that mean anything to you?"

"No, never heard of him."

"Okay, but wait, there's more," said Susan. A deep breath and an audible exhale ensued. "So I came to the conclusion... as random as it sounds... that Wilson killed Brett Anderson and someone has now killed Wilson."

Jack rubbed his temples in an attempt to ease the flow of information into his brain.

"This killing you're referring to. Wilson. Did it have the same..." Jack couldn't think of the right word. "*Artefacts?*" It was the best he could do.

"The words? The photograph? Yeah."

Jack's face scrunched tight; the cogs turning behind his eyes. "So, let me get this straight... are you saying that this Wilson guy killed Brett, leaving a note saying 'the debt has been paid' and left a photograph on the body, just like in the other cases?"

"Uh-huh."

"And now this... Wilson has been killed in the same manner?"

"Exactly. But I didn't want to draw any conclusions based on that, so I had someone do some digging into the other cases."

"You mean Lisa and Nathan's cases, yeah?" His grip on the phone tightened.

"Yeah. As you know we didn't really have any other evidence to go on in those cases, but I remembered that there had been some DNA from an unknown person found on Nathan's body. It didn't match anything on record back then, so we dismissed it as irrelevant, but when we retested it... we got a match."

Jack's pulse spiked. "A match? A match to who?"

"Brett Anderson."

Jack's head spun. He took a breath to fight the wave of dizziness.

"Oh my God. So let me work this through..." He took another breath. "Wilson, this latest victim, killed Brett. And now you've found evidence that suggests that Brett killed Nathan."

"Yes."

"Which means that Nathan must have killed..."

Oh my God.

Jen's brother...

Lisa.

It felt like the ground had swallowed Jack. He dropped the phone onto his desk.

"Jack? Jack?" A distant, muffled sound echoed from the phone that lay on the wooden surface—its bright screen shining in Jack's wet, red eyes.

"I've got... I-I've got to go," Jack stammered.

He jabbed at his phone and hung up the call. He glared at Jen's picture. Seething, he grabbed the photo and hurled it across the office.

It landed with a crack as the glass frame smashed.

* * *

CHAPTER 17

Jen, dressed in tartan pyjama bottoms and a white T-shirt, opened the door in response to Jack's rhythmic pounding.

Her eyes were wide—clearly surprised by his presence—but she gave a warm smile as she greeted him.

"Hey gorgeous. I didn't expect to see you tonight!"

Jack's hands trembled and he gave Jen a cold stare.

Her smile faded and her brow furrowed. "Jack? Jack, what's wrong?"

Rage was simmering beneath the surface and Jack couldn't hide it. "Your brother killed my wife," Jack bellowed, storming into the house. "That's what's fucking wrong!"

"Excuse me?"

Jack went on to recount the news that Susan had told him about the links between the cases. Jen sat, her mouth open wide in bewilderment throughout most of this revelation, while Jack paced up and down the kitchen, trying to calm himself with action. He couldn't sit still.

"And that's when I realised that Nathan was responsible for Lisa's death."

"No, Jack." Jen blinked several times and shook her head in disbelief. "You must be mis—"

"I'm not mistaken, Jen... The police have evidence."

"I can't believe this," Jen cried. She sat with her head bowed, taking shallow, panting breaths. "I can't... I can't believe Nathan could kill someone... Why? Why would he?"

Seeing Jen's distress caused Jack's rage to simmer momentarily. The change in emotion made his knees buckle. He pulled up a chair next to Jen.

"I never knew Nathan. Maybe he was capable of doing this, but I don't know why. I can't take this, Jen. I can't. I-I fucking love you, but *this*? This changes everything. *Everything*... It's ripped a hole right through us. Tell me. How can we go on after learning this?" He started to weep.

He'd never told Jen that he loved her. Never let himself.

What a time to fucking say it.

Jen met Jack's eyes and reached out to embrace him.

"Don't fucking touch me!" he snapped.

She recoiled and started sobbing uncontrollably. Her head in her hands.

"I'm so sorry," Jen said, from behind her hands.

"I can't be here right now. I can't even *look* at you right now."

Jack got to his feet and marched to the door.

"I love you too, Jack," Jen whispered.

He didn't hear. He'd already left the house, leaving Jen weeping at the kitchen table.

He was broken. Again.

Chapter 18

Bitter. Cracked. Broken.

Jack stood on his balcony, staring out at the river beyond. He felt those dark thoughts coming back to him, flooding his mind with that black cloud. It had been a while.

Welcome back, dark visitor.

He considered what it would be like to jump from this 8th floor balcony. The feeling of letting go. For it all to be over. A part of his brain was screaming at him to do it and he knew that it wouldn't take much for him to give in to this command.

He'd been down this road before and managed to resist, but he feared that the more these thoughts arrived—the more he was tested by them—the weaker his resolve would become.

Jack felt dizzy. Weak. He was petrified that he might actually jump this time. He clutched onto the balcony rail with pure terror. His knuckles, white.

Taking a deep breath, he relinquished his grip.

A flash of Lisa's face...

Not this time.

He backed away, one step at a time, all the while still facing out towards the river. As his back made contact with the window his legs gave out. He collapsed to the floor, curled up in a ball and wept.

A buzz from his phone brought Jack back to the present. He wiped his eyes, reached into his pocket and retrieved his phone.

Another message from Jen.

Notifications littered the screen—3 missed calls and 14 messages—behind which lay the blurred image of Jen that he'd set as his wallpaper.

He took a look at the messages. They ranged from anger, to denial, to apology:

- *'Why did you walk out on me, Jack????? I'm hurting too, you know!!! FFS'*
- *'You fucking monster. How could you drop that news on me, give me shit, then leave!'*
- *'I didn't do this. Why are you blaming me?????'*
- *'Can you please call me back. I need to talk to you'*
- *'We don't know for sure that Nathan killed anyone, you know?! The evidence is flimsy at best.'*
- *'Why won't you call me back????'*
- *'Did you get home okay, babe? Just let me know that you're safe, won't you?'*
- *'Talk to me! For christ's sake, Jack!!'*
- *'I love you'*
- *'I've done some thinking. This hurts me, so much it's hard to describe. Nathan was my brother. I loved him, dearly. The thought that he might have killed someone is hard to accept. I think I understand why you're feeling and acting the way you are. To now have a name associated with who killed your wife must be really hard and for that person to be the brother*

of your girlfriend I can't imagine how conflicted you must feel. This is not my fault though, Jack. Please don't punish me.'
- *'You said you loved me. Did you mean it?'*
- *'I'm sure we can work through this, no matter what, Jack. Can't we?'*
- *'I'm sorry Jack.'*
- *'Let's just talk, yeah?'*

Jack felt numb reading most of these messages, apart from the first one. That hit him the hardest. Guilt swelled. Leaving Jen alone at a time like this was the most selfish act he could commit. The second most selfish? Killing himself.

In an attempt to nullify the guilt and ease Jen's sorrow, he sent a message back with trembling fingers:

- *'I'm sorry, Jen, for walking out on you. I just couldn't take it. I just need to be by myself right now. And yeah, I did mean it.'*

Jack knew that he wouldn't be able to sleep tonight. He also knew that he shouldn't be alone.

He called his sister.

* * *

Rachel opened the door to greet Jack; a sympathetic look in her eyes.

"Oh, Jack, come here." Rachel reached out for an embrace and Jack gratefully accepted, falling into her arms.

"Thanks, sis," Jack sniffled.

"Come on in. Let's get you a drink, yeah?"

Jack sat down at the kitchen table while Rachel prepared him a G&T. David also sat at the table, drinking a scotch—more casually and in a more civilised manner than the last time Jack had seen him.

"I'm so sorry for keeping you guys up. I just didn't know what else to do."

"Nonsense, Jack. This is what family is all about. I wouldn't want you to be alone. You know you can always talk to me, don't you?"

"I know, sis. I really appreciate it."

"That goes for me, too, big guy," said David.

"Thanks, pal," said Jack, giving David a nod of acknowledgement.

Rachel sat the drinks down on the table, took a seat next to Jack and placed a hand on his leg.

"Do you want to talk about things?"

Jack appreciated the warmth and affection of his sister's touch and placed his hand on top of hers for a moment.

"Yeah, I think it would do me good to talk."

Rachel gave Jack a sincere, sisterly look. "So what's happened tonight, with you and Jen?"

Jack took a moment before speaking. Took a sip of his G&T. Savoured it and then responded. "It's quite a long story, considering it's all happened in a couple of hours. It started with a call... from Susan Reeves."

Rachel's eyes were wild. "That shitty detective that worked Lisa's case? What's she doing, calling you?"

"That's the one. Turns out she's been taken off the case since this latest murder."

CHAPTER 18

"Wait? What? There's been *another* one?" said Rachel.

David gulped at his scotch. His eyes widened and he leaned in. He suddenly seemed very interested.

"Yeah, some guy called Wilson Fensome. Means nothing to me."

Rachel looked shocked. "Oh, Jesus."

"Yeah, well, this Wilson guy had the same markings as the previous killings."

David's brow furrowed. "Markings?" His face was losing colour.

"Yeah, each of these killings has had the words '*the debt has been paid*' displayed somewhere at the murder site," recounted Jack, addressing David directly.

"What the hell!" exclaimed David. His hands were noticeably trembling.

"You knew this, honey," Rachel interrupted.

"I fucking didn't, Rach. That's news to me!"

"Calm down, honey," said Rachel. She raised a hand to touch David's shoulder and he brushed it off. "Oh... maybe Jack just mentioned it to me when we were chatting on the phone... I can't believe I never told you about it. I'm sorry... Jack said he and Jen found those words on a tree near where Lisa was killed." Looking over to Jack, she continued. "It was the same as Jen's brother, right?"

David stood, grabbed the half-drunk bottle of scotch, and returned to his seat, gingerly.

"There's more, sis. Much more."

Rachel and David remained quiet, staring at Jack and silently willing him to continue.

"It turns out she wasn't just calling to let me know there was another killing and that she'd been taken off the case. She'd also found out about something that links the cases."

"Something other than the same method and the markings?" said Rachel, her eyes seeking answers.

"Yeah... Something very... bizarre."

David took a sharp inhale. His eyes narrowed. "What is it, Jack?" He was fidgeting in his chair and swirling his scotch around in his glass.

He never seemed this interested before in this stuff. What's up with him now?

"Susan told me that there was a blood trail left at the killing of a man named Brett Anderson—one of the victims from a few months ago. They never found out who that blood trail was related to, but they suspected that it was Brett's killer."

"Right," said Rachel, nodding as she followed Jack's story. Her brow, furrowed in concentration.

"Well, they never found out who the blood had come from until they investigated Wilson's death, last week... It matched this guy, Wilson. And Susan wanted to ensure there was a clear pattern before calling me to let me know about this. After she found this out she then got forensics to look back at the evidence from Nathan Brown's murder. Jen's... brother. Turns out there was some DNA evidence there that they were never able to get a match on, until they retested it. It... it matched... Brett Anderson."

"So you're saying that this Brett guy killed Nathan?"

Jack nodded.

Rachel rubbed her temples. Squinted. "So, each killer has later been targeted and killed in the same way?"

"Exactly. It's fucking ment—"

SMASH

Jack was interrupted. He looked over at David. He was bone

CHAPTER 18

white. Blood had drained from his face and his glass had smashed while he still held it in his hand. Glass and scotch were all over the table and shards were lodged in David's hand.

"Oh God, honey! What did you do?!" Rachel exclaimed, as she moved over to tend to David.

David winced in pain. Blood was starting to flow from his hand and drip onto the kitchen table.

"That weak fucking glass just crumbled in my hand."

What the fuck? That doesn't just happen.

David pulled a sizeable chunk of glass from his palm with a shaky hand and dropped it onto the kitchen table with a clatter. He stood up and wandered towards the hallway, dripping blood on the floor as he went.

"I'm j-just gonna c-clean myself up in the b-b-bathroom," David stammered.

"You're dripping blood everywhere, David. Be careful."

David darted upstairs to the bathroom and moments later Jack could hear him retching violently.

What was with him?

And why doesn't Rachel appear to be as uncomfortable with this as I am?

Is she just pretending not to notice?

Jack knew that Rachel always seemed to be making excuses for David, but actively ignoring what was going on was a whole other level of complacency and denial.

"I'm sorry about him, Jack. Carry on. What were you gonna say?"

Again with the excuses. For fuck's sake, Rachel, get a grip!
There's something really wrong with your husband.

Jack looked up to the ceiling in an attempt to ground himself back in the conversation. He was shaken by David's surreal moment of breakdown. He took a breath, sighed it out, and focused on Rachel. "The big realisation was that it... it seems that Nathan... Jen's fucking brother... killed my wife."

"Oh, fuck."

Rachel rarely swore, so it was clear that she understood the gravity of the situation.

"Yeah. Oh, fuck." Jack nodded. His eyes, wide. "How am I supposed to look her in the eye again, Rach? How do I do that?" Jack started to well up. Wrestling against the tears, he continued, "I really love that girl. I really do, but how do I get past this? How do *we* get past this?"

"I don't know, Jack. This must be really hard." Rachel took Jack by the hand and looked him in the eye. "But, she's not responsible. You know that, right? And she's probably really hurting, too. You know that too, right? She's just found out her brother may be a murderer and that he may have murdered your wife. She's a good person and doesn't deserve this any more than you do... Maybe you need each other now more than ever."

"Yeah I do know that, but my head is all over the place. I don't blame her, but I can't look at her right now."

"Just take some time, Jack. This is a crazy situation... The craziest that I can ever imagine. If you love her, and I think it's clear that you do, then you won't let this destroy the two of you."

Jack sniffed and wiped his eyes. "I guess you're right. Thanks for letting me come over. I didn't want to be alone tonight."

"Anytime, bro. I'm here for you, always. You know that... I think I should check on David, though, don't you think?" Rachel got to her feet. "Do you want to crash here?"

CHAPTER 18

"Yeah go and check on him. I don't know what's up with him. He seems to be a bit off at the mo, eh? And no, I'll get the train back... but, thanks. My head is clearer now. I'll be okay... I'll give you a buzz tomorrow, yeah?"

Jack made his way to the door as Rachel rushed up the stairs to the bathroom. As he shut the door he could hear David screaming 'Just leave me the fuck alone, would you?!'

What is up with him?

He started freaking out when I revealed the link...

This is a leap, but... he couldn't be involved in these murders... could *he?*

Jack dropped the question from his mind. It didn't bear thinking about.

Chapter 19

Tap. Tap. Tap. Tap.

You couldn't have done this, Nathan. Could you? How could you kill someone? Why? That's not you!

Tap. Tap. Tap. Tap.

"What's your fucking password, Nathan!"

Tap. Tap. Tap. Tap.

Since Jack had left Jen at that kitchen table all she could do was focus on trying to get into her brother's email. It was the only thing that was able to distract her from her thoughts. Whenever she stopped trying new password combinations the pain would come rushing straight back.

She'd only received one message from Jack since last night and had given up trying to reach him for now. She knew that he needed space at the moment and she understood why, but that didn't stop her from feeling rage towards him for his selfishness. She felt out of control with the whole situation and the only thing she *could* control was putting all of her efforts into trying to find out anything she could about Nathan potentially killing Lisa.

So she did what she could.

She continued to type relentlessly. Praying for answers.

CHAPTER 19

Jen was methodical in her approach. She had tried memorable place names first. Then the names of people who might be considered significant to Nathan, favourite films, favourite bands et cetera.

The options were endless.

Needle in a haystack was an understatement.

Each time she cycled through she would try alternatives with a lowercase first letter, then an uppercase first letter, followed by both combinations with a 1 at the end, or 89—Nathan's birth year.

Jen took a short break to make herself a coffee. Her fingers ached from the endless futility of typing unsuccessful passwords. She returned to the laptop, mug in hand, cracked her knuckles, and moved onto sports.

Nathan had been a diehard Liverpool fan, so she started with this. She needed to do a bit of research on the club to learn about some key statistics that might factor into a potential password.

liverpoolFC96 - The amount of people killed at the awful Hillsborough disaster. No.

LiverpoolFC96 - With uppercase 'L'. No joy.

"Fuck."

LiverpoolFC05 - The year of the famous Champions League win that Nathan was always banging on about. No. Not that one.

"Fuck. Fuck."

LiverpoolFC90 - The year of the last time they won the league. No not that one, either.

Jen had a moment of dawning realisation that Nathan would never get to see his beloved team win the league. It would have meant so much to him. She started to well up, just at the thought.

She cleared her throat and carried on.

LiverpoolFC89 – His birth year.

Something *happened...*

The spinning icon on the screen acted differently this time.

There wasn't an immediate error displayed.

Jen held her breath...

The screen... refreshed...

She was *in*.

JACKPOT!

She was actually *in*.

A feeling of elation surged through her veins and her eyes lit up like Christmas.

Jen couldn't quite believe that she'd managed this and felt a huge amount of satisfaction for successfully being able to get into her brother's emails. There was also an overwhelming sense of hope that it might actually help her uncover what led to his death—or, more importantly, whether his emails contained any evidence that he was truly responsible for *Lisa's* death.

She took a couple of deep breaths, centred herself and began the daunting task of sifting through her brother's emails.

Jen was faced with nearly a year's worth of unread and unfiltered spam emails. She trawled past all of these to reach the date that Nathan was killed and proceeded to work backwards from there.

Painfully, after an hour or so of scrolling back and forth, she came up short.

Maybe the email account won't actually be helpful.

Why did I build this up as so important?

I'm no detective. How did I think I was going to figure this out?

CHAPTER 19

Feeling dejected, Jen aimlessly waved her mouse cursor around the screen in frustration and disappointment. She paused for a second when the cursor landed on the sidebar where a number of separate folders were listed.

Her heart raced as she spotted one named '*Private*'—an ominous wave of anticipation at what might prove to be another chance to find something of importance.

She inhaled sharply and, after a moment's hesitation, clicked on the folder to reveal its contents.

Half a dozen emails sat in the folder, and as she scanned them, one in particular jumped out at her.

Could this be?...

Her stomach knotted as she read the subject line:

'THE CONTRACT'

She was conflicted—part of her was dying to open the email, but another part of her heavily resisted the urge.

She knew that if she opened it and her fears were confirmed, there would be no going back. But ignorance wasn't exactly bliss.

Jen took a break from the laptop. She needed to think things through before she opened Pandora's box.

She paced up and down the kitchen. A futile endeavour, as she couldn't pretend she wouldn't open the email. This was exactly why she'd hacked her way in, and now she had what she wanted. Now she just had to find the strength to face the fear of what lay within.

Jen recollected the myth of Pandora's box. *What was it that lay at the bottom?* Hope. A significant analogy. She very much hoped that there would be something positive that would come from taking the plunge into the unknown.

Hope. That had been slipping away.

Maybe hope could save me.
I need to see what's inside.

Jen returned to the laptop, exhaled sharply, and clicked on the email. She started reading the contents slowly and carefully.

As she read, goosebumps pricked her skin, and a visceral dread filled her soul. Each sentence sent a shiver down her spine.

Her mouth involuntarily gaped open. It remained in a jaw-dropped state for several minutes.

Frozen in disbelief.

Fucking hell.

She reached for her phone and, with shaking hands, sent a message to Jack. Her mouth still hung open as she typed:

'I know you're not talking to me right now and you need your space, but you need to know this. I hacked Nathan's email and I found something. Something huge. Really fucking huge.
He didn't kill Lisa.'

Chapter 20

Jogging bottoms on? Check. Bags under eyes? Check. Shirtless? Check. Hungover? Check.

Jack sat on his sofa feeling dejected and woeful. He hadn't been able to sleep since arriving back from his sister's and had just sat and drank himself into a stupor. His default coping mechanism.

On the coffee table in front of him, his phone buzzed again. *Another message from Jen, presumably.*

He'd been screening the messages, but hadn't been replying. He couldn't help but feel selfish about this, but he was too numb to be able to offer a response of any utility. Too bitter to be able to deal with his feelings towards her.

He shrugged it off, reluctantly picked up the phone, and took a look at the latest message.

It *was* from Jen.

Jack scoffed.

But then he read.

He sobered up with a jolt.

A wave of excitement, joy, regret, guilt and shame washed over him all at once. He instantly responded.

'*You're sure?*'

Within a minute, a response from Jen.

'Yes, Jack. I'm sure.'

Jack gulped. His shame erupting within him like a geyser. He replied. Tail between his legs.

'Can I come over? I'm so sorry about how I've acted, Jen. I'm sorry. Xx'

Jack watched impatiently as the three blinking dots were displayed at the bottom of the screen, indicating that Jen was typing a response.

They blinked then disappeared.

Then blinked again.

Then disappeared.

"Come on, for fuck's sake!" Jack said aloud, as frustration rose within him. Then he silently condemned himself upon realising how difficult it must have been for Jen with him shunning her.

The blinking dots reappeared and finally another message from Jen dropped.

'Okay, sure. Just get yourself out of your pit of self loathing and freshen up. You're gonna need a clear head for this. Xx'

Self loathing? She knows me too well.

Although relieved at the seemingly forgiving nature of Jen's message, his feelings of guilt rose. He jumped to his feet, took the quickest shower known to man, swallowed down a couple of paracetamol, threw on some jeans and a T-shirt, and left his flat, heading to his nearest tube station.

* * *

CHAPTER 20

As Jen opened the door Jack leaned in to give her a hug. She dismissed this, left the door ajar and retreated to the kitchen. Wordless.

I deserve this.

Jack followed Jen to where she now sat in the kitchen, her laptop aglow in front of her. His head hung low, and like a wounded dog, he gingerly took a seat next to her and could only muster, "I'm so sorry, Jen. I... reacted appallingly. I was in shock, that's all. This is all so fucking crazy and the pain was too much for me. I was... selfish. I should have stayed."

Jen looked up to meet his eyes, streaks of mascara tattooed her cheeks. "That's right, Jack. You shouldn't have left me... I know why you did, but it wasn't fair. It was awful being left alone like that. Left to think the most... horrible thoughts about my brother."

"I know. Can you forgive me?"

"Help me find the person behind all of this and you might have a shot."

"I *will* help. I'm not leaving your side again, Jen. I promise." Jack felt a wave of passion so strong it was undeniable. He truly loved Jen and it was time to let her know. And not over a fucking text message. He gazed into those mascara-streaked green eyes. "I love you, Jen."

Upon hearing these words, Jen welled up again. She leaned in and kissed Jack passionately and then, their foreheads touching, she looked up into Jack's eyes and whispered, "I love you too, Jack. So much."

A feeling of warmth washed over Jack. He squeezed Jen's hand and, as she reciprocated, felt a strength in this bond that couldn't be contextualised in words. It just felt right, in so many ways.

"So do you want to see what I've found?"

"Hit me with it, Jen. I'm ready," Jack lied. He wasn't ready, but knew he needed to see this. He took a sharp breath and blew it from his cheeks.

Jen pulled up the email and positioned the laptop so that Jack could see it clearly. He read aloud.

Nathan,

I'm here to save your skin, but I need you to do a job for me.

I will give you one million pounds.

This will get you out of that hole you've dug for yourself and allow you to start your life again.

I'm aware that you're on the hook for £350,000 of gambling debt and the people after you are no joke. They will kill your family if you don't pay them back and then once they're through they will kill you. Rest assured. I know these people.

What do you need to do for me?

I need you to kill someone. And in a very specific way.

The details of who I need you to kill, when and how are down below.

How can you trust me?

I know this might be a very hard thing for you to do, so to gain your trust I will be transferring you £250,000 up front, upon acceptance from yourself that you will undertake this contract for me.

If you take the £250,000 but don't follow through with the completion of the task I will have you killed. Make no mistake.

Who do I need you to kill?

CHAPTER 20

The name of the man that you will kill is Jacob Williamson, a 45 year old property developer from Highgate.

Where / when will I find him?

People are creatures of habit, Nathan.

Jacob walks through Highgate wood every afternoon at around 2p.m.

I've attached a copy of his typical route through the woods. Use this as your guide.

How will I recognise him?

I've attached a photo to this email.

How do I kill Jacob?

Use any method of your choosing, but make sure that he is in fact dead.

Two specifics though:

1. *You need to lay the attached photo on his dead body.*
2. *You must leave the following words at the crime scene –* **'THE DEBT HAS BEEN PAID'**. *Be as creative as you want with this.*

Once you have completed the killing you will need to send me a photo of the crime scene with the above criteria met.

If you fail to supply a photo as proof or fail to fulfil the above two criteria the contract will be voided.

Why do I want Jacob dead?

That's not for you to know.

What do the words 'THE DEBT HAS BEEN PAID' mean?
That's also not for you to know.

Other key criteria:

- *You cannot tell anyone about this. EVER. If you do, I WILL know and you WILL be killed.*
- *If you take the down payment and run you WILL be killed.*

In summary, you either do this, and follow the above criteria to a tee or you will be killed by either the loan sharks that are after you, or by my own resources.

You have a sister, if I'm not mistaken. Jennifer? If you fail, she will also be killed, but before you so you have a chance to witness this.

Do yourself and your sister a favour.

Kill Jacob, save yourselves, and I will reward you with £1m.

If you want to proceed just send me an email response with your bank details and I'll send over the £250,000 immediately.

MM

Jack sat for a minute, his jaw open wide in disbelief. Jen stared at him and waited for him to speak.

"What the *fuck* is going on, Jen?"

"I can't quite believe it either. Nathan. A killer? A *contract* killer??"

"But it seems like your life was at risk too, here."

"Yeah, that's shocked me. Completely. I honestly think that

if it wasn't for me being mentioned, Nathan wouldn't have done this... In a way, he saved me."

"And put your life in danger."

"Yeah, I guess." Jen mumbled, as she hung her head.

"This raises as many questions as it does answers, don't you think? Like, who the *fuck* is MM? I'm pretty sure it's not Marshall Mathers." Jack tried to smile at his terrible joke. He knew it was in poor taste but had wanted to break the tension. His stomach knotted as he realised he'd missed the mark by a huge margin.

"That's not funny, Jack."

"I know. I'm sorry. Stupid of me. But there *are* a lot of questions here." Jack thought aloud and reeled off a multitude of questions that were currently ravaging his mind. "How did Nathan hide such a huge gambling debt from you? How did this 'MM' know about it? Was this Jacob responsible for killing Lisa? Why... why has this case never come to light? Why would this 'MM' guy pay someone one million pounds to kill a person, and presumably, this... this is a bit of an assumption, but I expect each one of these killings has a *'contract'* where this 'MM' would offer the killer a million..."

Jack paused for a second. His eyes strained and his mouth faltered, as a thought overtook his mind that he couldn't initially articulate.

"Does this mean Lisa killed someone, too?" His words were a whisper. He caught Jen's stare, as he dropped this bombshell — her eyes, full of compassion. "Did she kill? It seems she was the first victim and... it had to start somewhere. Maybe she got caught up in this in a different way and didn't actually kill anyone."

No way. Lisa? A killer? No way.

Jack shook his head. He wouldn't allow himself to dwell on the possibility of his wife being a killer. Instead, he latched onto an alternate scenario—one where she was the first victim in the series of killings and might be entirely innocent.

He was surprised at how level-headed he was acting during these insane revelations. How had he managed to detach emotion from this? It was the journalist in him. The habits, on autopilot. Ask questions first. Deal with feelings second.

"You're right. It does raise a lot of questions. I'm not sure I'm ready to deal with the answers, though." Jen narrowed her eyes. "How are you reacting so calmly to this?"

"I don't know. I think it's maybe that investigating is my thing. I realise this must be really hard for you." Jack squeezed Jen's hand, trying to convey empathy and support. "Also, this won't have hit me as hard as you. When I left here last night I thought that Nathan had killed Lisa. I was distraught at this thought, as it affected the two of us, as a couple. Now all signs point to Nathan having killed Lisa's killer and that is, as stupid and insensitive as it sounds, a positive for me."

Jen snatched her hand away from Jack's and gave him an icy stare.

"Well, I'm glad that's a fucking positive for you, Jack! Jesus, Christ!"

Oh fuck.

"I didn't mean it like that. Sorry, that was really insensitive."

"Yes, it was. I understand we're on opposite ends of the spectrum here and emotions are high, but pick your fucking audience, Jack. Read the room, yeah?"

The guilt. Oh the guilt. Again.

"I'm sorry, Jen. Truly," Jack said, as he tried to grab hold of

Jen's hand again. She batted his hand away and he shifted his posture. "Can we try thinking about the questions this raises though?"

"Which one to start with?"

"The gambling debt?"

Just like an etch-a-sketch being shaken to clear the surface, Jen's look of anger was erased and quickly replaced by a more forlorn expression.

"I knew he had a bit of a gambling habit, but I didn't think it had ever gotten him into any trouble. He obviously hid that from me very well. No idea how this 'MM' would know about it, but we don't have the faintest clue who that bastard is, do we?"

"No."

"And next question. Was Jacob responsible for killing Lisa? There doesn't seem to be anything suggesting otherwise."

"Yeah, I think it's safe to assume that, given the pattern at play."

"So, Nathan is your fucking hero," said Jen, raising her eyebrows.

Jack remained silent. He knew he couldn't win this battle. Couldn't dig himself out of this hole, without further stirring things up. He concluded it was best to let Jen get the anger out.

She sighed and continued. "And what else was there? Oh yeah, why have we never heard about this killing?"

"I don't know. We should look this up and see what we can find."

Jen nodded and took a deep breath. "Yeah, good idea."

Jen dragged the laptop over to her, opened a new tab on the browser and launched Nethunt. Jack admired the determination on her face and in her actions as she clicked, scrolled and read.

He sensed she needed a few minutes of silence to do some digging, so he got up, meandered over to the kitchen worktop and prepared a coffee for each of them. Caffeine was greatly needed right now. Focus for her, easing of the hangover for him.

Jack returned with a coffee for Jen and set it down on the table next to her. She offered a nod in appreciation—still very much focused on the task in hand.

Jack sat pensively. He sipped his coffee and pondered the myriad questions rolling around in his head, while Jen tapped away at the keyboard.

"This is it!" Jen exclaimed, pointing at the screen of the laptop. She moved it round for Jack to see what she was referring to.

Jack downed his coffee, set the mug down, and shifted his attention to what was displayed on the screen:

MISSING PERSON - JACOB WILLIAMSON

My husband, Jacob Williamson has been missing since 05/08/18. I'm reaching out on here to see if anyone can shed any light on his whereabouts and help me bring him home or find out what has happened to him.
The last time I saw him was when he was going on his usual early afternoon walk through Highgate Wood.
He would typically go for a walk in the wood, which is close to our house every day, but on 05/08 he never returned.
I've attached a photo to this post.
Did anyone see him on this day?
Please, if you know anything, please reach out. I'm going out of

CHAPTER 20

my mind.

"Wow. Yeah this is it. Can you bring up the photo they mention?" said Jack.

Jen clicked on the attachment and brought up the picture of Jacob that was posted on Nethunt. They compared the photo to the one on the email that Nathan had received.

Jack's breath caught in his throat.

It was a match.

Clear as day.

"This is definitely him, Jack."

"Is that the only post on Nethunt, about Jacob?"

"It's the only one I could find."

"So does this mean the body was never found? If so, it would make sense why we wouldn't have known about it. And it would also explain why the police didn't find a link between the killings until much later."

"I guess so. Oh, what did my brother do, Jack? Did he bury the body or something?"

"Oh, babe. I don't know."

"Could you do something for me?"

"Of course. What is it?" Jack noticed that Jen had tears forming.

"If Nathan did do this..." She sniffed and a tear rolled down her cheek. "Th-then there's probably something in his sent mail. He would've had to send a photo of the dead body there, right? I-I can't look." Jen shuddered. "But... can you? Please?"

Jack felt a wave of anxiety. Beads of sweat formed on his brow and ran down his back. His chest tightened. He really didn't want to look at the evidence, but he understood that there was no way that he could expect Jen to.

He had to do this, no matter how difficult.

Feigning confidence, he said, "Of course... I'll look."

He accessed the email tab of the browser window and clicked on 'sent'.

Jen was right, there was an email dated 05/08: a reply to the email titled '**THE CONTRACT**'.

He took a breath, sighed, and opened the email.

The content of the email was brief and to the point. A few words from Nathan explaining that the contract was complete and the proof was attached. Jack hesitated for a moment, trying to prepare himself for what he might be about to see.

As if I can ever be prepared for this.

His hand hovered over the image icon, but he wasn't ready. He took a series of deep breaths to psych himself up and—as prepared as he could be—he clicked on the attached image.

A wave of nausea swelled in Jack's stomach. The similarities between this and Lisa's death were a knockout blow to him and brought back vivid memories of her case. So similar in fact, that, for a second, Jack believed he saw Lisa's face in the photo, in place of the victim's.

Not just believed.

He *did* see Lisa. It was her face.

He gagged, somehow keeping vomit from tracking up his throat. He knew he must just be imagining this, but it felt extremely real. He shuddered and shook his head in an attempt to rid his mind of the vision.

When he looked back, the photo had returned to its initial state.

The image depicted Jacob lying face up in a, seemingly secluded, woodland area—his throat clearly slit, with blood pooled around him. The photo that was attached to the initial email was laid on Jacob's chest. The most striking similarity to Lisa's case, however, was a tree in the foreground.

Etched crudely into the bark were the words that were becoming all too familiar:

'THE DEBT HAS BEEN PAID'

Jack took a photo on his phone of the crime scene and of the walking route that had been attached to the initial email.

"What are you doing, Jack? What have you seen? Is it awful?" Jen's eyes were pained.

"I'm glad that you didn't have to see it, babe." Jack sighed, as he exited the email and closed the laptop.

"Why are you taking a photo of it?"

"We're going to Highgate Wood. We need to see this for ourselves. We need to understand why the body was never found."

Chapter 21

"I can't do this."

Jen had taken some convincing. Quite rightly—she had no particular desire to journey across London to see the site where her brother had apparently killed someone. Jack knew it was unfair to even suggest that she come on this macabre field trip with him and offered to go alone.

"No, Jack. I don't want you to go alone. I made you take me to Lisa's site, remember? It's only right that I come with you." Jen looked up at Jack. A determined look in her tear-soaked eyes. "We're on this journey together, right? If it helps us find this 'MM' bastard then I need to be with you."

"You honestly don't have to. I'm not sure it will do anything to help us find 'MM' to be honest, and besides, when I took you to see Lisa's site it was very different. I hadn't just learnt about it that day and it wasn't a site where she had killed someone, but where she had been killed herself and I'd visited it many, many times... It wasn't new to me... I *have* to do this, but seriously, *you* don't have to."

"I'm coming," Jen insisted as she squeezed Jack's hand.

CHAPTER 21

* * *

The hum and rattle of the Northern line tube train was the only sound. Jack and Jen remained silent for almost the entirety of the journey; a sombre feeling weighing heavily between the two of them. They held onto each other for strength and fortitude and Jack felt all the reassurance that he needed, in the warmth and tight grip of Jen's hand.

After what felt like hours they arrived at Highgate, took a right out of the station and headed up the busy urban street, past the Woodman pub, and turned right again until they reached an entrance to Highgate Wood. It was at this point that Jack broke the silence.

"Okay, once we're in here we follow this route," Jack instructed, as he showed the route map on his phone to Jen.

"How will we know when we reach the right spot?"

"We'll know, Jen. We'll know." Jack paused. He hadn't shared the full detail with Jen yet, but now was the moment. "I didn't tell you this earlier. Didn't want to, as I thought it might be too much to—"

"What is it?" Jen said, interrupting Jack, a worried expression adorning her face.

"This site. It's eerily similar to that of Lisa's. We're... we're looking for a tree. A tree with the words etched into it. Sound familiar?"

"R-really?" Jen said, shuddering.

"I'm afraid so."

"Oh, God. You were right not to tell me earlier. It *would* have been too much for me. In fact, it *still* is. I might not have been able to come with you if you had told me, but I know I *had* to.

I'm really fucking spooked, right now."

"I'm sorry."

"Don't apologise." Jen looked down at her feet. "This is just all too surreal," she muttered to herself.

A few seconds of silence passed and Jen looked up at Jack with a defiant expression, cracked her knuckles and declared, "Let's get in there. Let's just get this over with, okay?"

"Are you sure? Are you sure you're *ready*?"

"Don't make me second-guess it, Jack. Let's go."

The two of them entered the park. Jack acted as navigator and led them along the tree-lined pathways and into a deeper section of the woods, shielded from the throng of dog walkers, runners and idle chit-chatters.

Steadily, Jack kept his steely gaze on both the route map and the surrounding trees. He was fuelled by his determination and maintained an acute attention to detail as he and Jen marched along the route, as laid out by 'MM'.

Despite Jack's spirited attempt to find the site of Jacob's killing, he and Jen soon reached the end of the route and had come up short.

"We're not going to find anything, Jack. Let's just go home, yeah?" said Jen, dejected.

"I'm not giving up so soon. It's here. I know it's here. We just must have missed it the first time round. Let's try one more time and go round clockwise this time."

"Okay, one more then I'm done, okay?" Jen sighed.

"Okay," Jack agreed, knowing that even if they didn't find it the second time around, he'd be going for a third attempt. He had no intention of yielding. With or without Jen by his side he would not give up on this.

They backtracked. Things looked different this time. Venturing through from the other direction it was clear that the perspective was altered and it looked like a different woodland altogether. Jack made sure to keep his pace slow, even though Jen seemed to be wanting to rush through and get back home as soon as possible. He knew that if he slowed his pace dramatically she would subconsciously slow her pace, too.

In the final third of the route, even Jack was starting to lose hope, but he tried his best to avoid letting his ebbing determination show. Surprisingly, as *his* motivation waned, it seemed that Jen, if anything, was becoming *more* resolute. She had taken to surveying things in more detail and with Jack slowing down she was taking the opportunity to dip in and out of the woods for a deeper scan.

Jen had disappeared from Jack's eyeline. Even so, he continued to amble along the path, casting half glances at the trees as he passed them, hoping to spot those ill-fated words etched into the bark. It was proving to be a futile endeavour.

Hope was evaporating.

"Jack!"

"Jack! Here!!"

Jen had strayed from the route by a good ten yards and was screaming over to Jack to come join her, her voice cracking. The words tore through the eerie quiet of the woods.

She's found something?

Jack hurried over to find Jen staring at a tree. She was starting to weep.

"This is it, isn't it, Jack? This is where Nathan killed this man? I can't believe this is true."

Jack grabbed Jen, pulled her in towards him and held her tight, while she continued to cry. Her head nuzzled into his neck. Her tears, dropping down onto his shoulder.

Jack looked beyond Jen and focused on the tree that she had been staring at.

She was right.

There were etchings carved into the bark. Rudimentary etchings. Just about legible:

'THE DEBT HAS BEEN PAID'

A flashback to his moment of discovery at the site of Lisa's death, struck Jack. His body shook. Trembled.

He could have easily lost his focus at that moment, but holding onto Jen he found the strength within to shift into a higher gear. He needed to be strong right now. For her.

"You're right. This is it. I'm so sorry."

Jen broke the embrace and looked up at Jack with her wet, green eyes. "He did it to save me, didn't he?"

Jack knew this wasn't exactly true. Knew that Nathan had got himself into this mess. He did concede, however, that Nathan probably wouldn't have gone through with the killing if Jen's life wasn't also at risk.

But saved her? No.

He couldn't afford to take his time in responding. Every second that passed would have cast doubt into Jen's mind. No matter how deluded he believed Jen to be at this moment, he knew that she *needed* to hear that this was the reason behind the killing. He swiftly weighed this up and responded.

"Yeah. He did, Jen. He had to do this... to... save you." He hated the hesitation in his voice. He brought her back in and hugged her tighter. She wept, profusely.

Jack averted his gaze. His attention, drawn to the ground beyond the tree.

Staring at the undergrowth—transfixed—he became aware of something inconsistent with the surroundings. His eyes widened and he loosened his grip on Jen.

"Jen, look at this."

She raised her head, wiped her eyes, and strained to look over at what Jack was pointing to.

"What is it? I-I don't see anything."

"You see that patch of ground there."

"Yeah. What about it?"

"Don't you think it looks a bit different from the rest?"

"Just looks like soil, twigs and grass to me."

"Of course. But, it's newer. Younger than the rest. Don't you see?"

"Perhaps. I'm not an agriculturalist, Jack. What are you getting at?"

"I think you were right... before."

"*Right?* Right about what?"

"I think the reason Jacob's body was never found was that Nathan buried him."

"*Seriously?*"

"Yeah." Jack's finger stabbed in the direction of the young undergrowth. "And he did it right *there*."

* * *

Shaken to the core, Jen was withdrawn. Her brow, furrowed. Her mouth, frozen open.

A heavy silence echoed between her and Jack, broken only by sporadic birdsong.

A couple of minutes passed like this until Jen blew air from her cheeks and took a couple of staggered steps backwards.

She dropped to her knees, her wide, watery eyes maintaining her focus on the spot that Jack had pointed out.

"Are you okay?" said Jack. His eyes followed Jen's gaze to the spot where he believed Jacob to be buried. His chest ached from the worry about what effect this revelation might be having on her.

"I'll be okay... I think. This is all just so hard to accept right now." She hung her head. "It's becoming more and more real and I'm struggling to process it. It's just gonna take some time," she said, in a whisper.

"Of course. I'm here for you, you know that? We're a team on this, right?"

Jen raised her head and met his eyes. "You betcha," she said, as she forced a narrow smile. A comforting sign that her spirit would not be broken. "Now that we're here though, what do we do? I don't think I want to know if anything is actually buried there. I'm definitely not... digging."

Me neither. I'm not digging up bones in a public park. Or anywhere for that matter!

"I wasn't going to suggest that," said Jack, shaking his head.

"Good. There's only so far I'm willing to go with all this," Jen uttered, shifting her focus from Jack to the undergrowth. "The question remains though. Now that you have your theory, what do we do with it? Where do we go from here?"

"I think we have to call the police."

Jen's head whipped round to face Jack. Her eyes narrowed. Her stare, icy. "No, Jack," she snapped. "I don't want the police involved. I can't handle Nathan's name being associated with this. I don't want him to be... branded as a killer."

Jack sighed. "I'd be exactly the same if this was Lisa. And you *know* I don't hold the police in very high regard." He gazed

CHAPTER 21

up to the sky, as if searching for answers. "I could call Susan."

"Susan? *Really?*"

"Yeah, I have her direct number now and after I last spoke to her I feel I've built a certain level of trust with her. I'm sure she would be discreet with the details."

"I'm not sure about that. I trust you, of course, but I don't trust her. She wouldn't be able to keep the details quiet."

"I guess you're right. And even if I didn't give her the details, she'd no doubt figure it out for herself now that she knows the pattern behind the killings. We do have to get the police involved though." Jack looked down at Jen as she remained on her knees looking up at him. She had a pained, desperate expression. "If only so that the victim's family can find out what happened to Jacob. I imagine they're going out of their minds with the uncertainty. As awful as it is, it's probably better that they know the truth about what happened to him, rather than go on not knowing... Don't you think?"

"Yeah I guess so," Jen conceded, "But I don't want Nathan's name to be mentioned when you talk to Susan, okay?"

"Okay, I'll tell you what, I'll let her know my theory without giving away the details of how I know this. She may still come to the conclusion that Nathan was responsible, but I promise it won't come from me."

"Okay, Jack. I trust you. I don't want to be dragged into the conversation though, okay?"

"Of course. Leave it to me."

Jack helped Jen to her feet, reached for his phone and dialled Susan's number. Two rings and she picked up. Jack put the call on speaker, so that Jen could listen in.

"Jack?"

"Yeah, it's me. Hi, Susan."

"Are you okay? I was worried about you after the last time we spoke."

Susan Reeves? Worried about me? Is this the same person?

"Yeah, I'm sorry I had to hang up. I was a bit shaken by the news, that's all... I'm fine."

"Okay. Glad to hear you're doing okay. What can I do for you?"

"I've got some news for you."

"Interesting timing. I've got some news for you, too."

Jack's chest tightened. "Really? What news?"

"You first."

"Okay." Jack took a breath. He hadn't really considered how he was going to break this news to Susan. He spoke slowly, relaying the information, making sure he didn't make any direct indications of Nathan's involvement. "We—" Jen poked Jack in the ribs. *Fuck!* "Sorry... I've found evidence of another killing."

Well played, Jack. Well played.

"Who's we?"

You had one job.

"I didn't mean we. I meant I. Anyway, that's not important."

"Okay... Another killing, you say? Recent?"

"No, I believe this was the person who killed my wife, so it would've been about a year ago now."

There was an audible exhale on the line, before Susan spoke. "Oh, wow. Go on, Jack."

"I think the reason it was never picked up by the police was that the body was never found and it was just considered a missing person's case. A man named Jacob Williamson."

"The body was never found? How come you know about the victim then?"

CHAPTER 21

"I'd rather not go into detail about that right now if it's all the same to you. This is why I'm calling you directly and not the police. I'm hoping this conversation can be kept off the record?"

Jack was using his journalistic tendencies to try and build trust with Susan and also testing the waters to see to what length she could be trusted.

"Happy to speak off the record. You know I'm not on the case anymore."

"Yeah I know. That's why I feel I can trust you more than anyone else." Again, building the rapport by suggesting that it's only her that he can trust.

"You *can* trust me, Jack. And besides, I owe you for how I treated you during your wife's case."

Jack chose not to respond to this directly and instead just carry on with his train of thought.

"There's a reason this body was never found, Susan... I think it was buried."

"Buried?" Susan sounded shocked. "That's new for these murders."

"Yeah it does seem to be a first, but, as we now know, each murder has been committed by a different killer, so it stands to reason that there wouldn't be a clear pattern in terms of MO."

"You're starting to sound like a detective, Jack."

"Must be the journalist in me."

Susan laughed, which Jack thought not only seemed out of character for her, but also not really in keeping with the sombre theme of the discussion. Was his comment funny? He certainly hadn't meant it that way. He allowed Susan to continue without questioning the nature of her response.

"Where do you think the body is buried then, Jack?" said Susan, her tone switching back to her professional default.

"I can ping you over the coordinates. I'm at the site right now."

"I didn't expect that!" Susan exclaimed.

"Yeah I thought that might come as a bit of a surprise, but we've." *Fuck. Again with the we.* Jen gave Jack a stare that he knew to mean '*doghouse*'. He continued. Carefully. "*I've* been made aware of this other case and it's pointed me to a place in Highgate Wood. There's the usual words etched on a tree at the site."

"The debt—"

Susan attempted to interrupt, but Jack spoke over her. "The ground looks younger than the surroundings which makes me believe the body's buried there. I won't tell you how I got this info. At least, not yet... but if I'm right I want the victim's family to know about it. I'm sure they're struggling to come to terms with Jacob being missing all this time and knowing what's actually happened to him might allow them to grieve properly. That's all I'm concerned about... Can you get the police involved in this, but leave me out of it?"

"I see... okay, Jack, I'll honour your request for secrecy. No problem. I'll say we got an anonymous call about it and relay the information to those who are now on the case."

Jen's look softened slightly. He interpreted this as less '*doghouse*' to more '*on the sofa*'. Progress.

"Thanks, Susan. I really appreciate it. So, what was your news?"

"My news?"

"Yeah, you said you had news for me as well."

"Oh damn, I almost forgot. Your revelation totally threw me

CHAPTER 21

off."

Jack waited patiently for Susan to continue.

"There's been another one," Susan said plainly.

"Another debt has been paid murder?" He noticed Jen's expression change to that of shock. He reached out to grab her hand. It was trembling. He squeezed it in an act of reassurance and mouthed the words '*it's okay*'.

"Yeah certainly seems that way. The body was found in Bushy Park. The team is over there now, analysing the scene."

"Jesus..." Jack sighed. "Do you know who the victim is?"

"Not yet. This is hot off the press. I'll keep you posted on anything that's useful though."

"Thanks Susan. I appreciate it. Speak soon."

"No problem, Jack. Stay safe out there."

"You, too."

* * *

Jen was still shaken and Jack walked her over to the Pavillion café, so that she could have a much-needed sit down.

The Pavillion was a quaint little spot, situated in the centre of the wood, that served all manner of baked goods and brunch favourites. Outdoor seating, bordered with hanging wisteria gave the place a traditional English summer vibe.

Being a weekday, the Pavillion garden was quiet. Jack sat Jen down at a table as far away as possible from other customers, to maintain privacy and went inside to grab a couple of cappuccinos. As he walked back to the table, cradling the coffees, it dawned on him that he'd first met Jen *in* a café and there was some kind of nightmarish symmetry to the situation.

He set a coffee in front of Jen and took a seat, opposite.

"Thanks, Jack." Jen sighed.

"You're welcome, babe. You know it just occurred to me that we met at a café."

"We must stop going to cafés," Jen responded with an eyeroll. "They always seem to be associated with death."

"Sad, but true."

"Thank you for how you handled things with Susan. It *was* the right thing to do."

"I'm glad you think so and I'm glad you're okay with it."

"I am... I think... Except when you mentioned '*we*'." She pursed her lips. "You slipped up there, big time. Bad move, journo."

"Sorry about that. I deserved the prod in the ribs."

"You did."

"And I deserved the doghouse stare."

Jen's brow furrowed. "How do *you* know my doghouse stare?"

"I know when I'm in the doghouse with you, Jen. I know you better than you realise."

"Well, just so you know, you're out of the doghouse now." Jen laughed.

Interrupting their shared moment, Jack's phone rang.

It was David.

"David? Everything okay?"

"Jack, I need to talk to you. Can we meet?"

Chapter 22

A bar.

Of course, a bar.

David had suggested meeting up with Jack at a wine bar in the City—one that they'd often frequented in the past and one that Jack now knew well. He'd only ever been here with David though, as it wasn't really to Jack's taste; he was more of a spit and sawdust man. He must have been here on at least half a dozen occasions, sharing those nights of drunken debauchery where David typically flaunted his wealth and flirted, unashamedly, with the female clientele.

Jack entered and felt a wave of nostalgia. A rush of familiarity. *How times had changed though,* he thought. So much had happened to him since he'd last set foot in here. It must have been at least two years. *He* had certainly changed, but here everything seemed just as he'd remembered it. The film and music quotes, in purple and pink neon, mounted on the exposed brickwork throughout the bar area gave the place a sleazy cyberpunk feel.

The place was relatively quiet at this time in the evening, but still had a buzz about it. Jack wandered through and propped himself up against the bar. A few moments later a bartender appeared, wearing a bow tie and looking eerily similar to the illusory barkeep, Lloyd, in Stanley Kubrick's, The Shining. He stood beneath a neon sign emblazoned with the immortal quote from Taxi Driver *'you talking to me?'*

"What'll it be, sir?"

He even sounded like the bartender in The Shining.

Am I dreaming right now?

"Two bourbons, please. Straight up."

"Very good, sir."

Maybe this was just a character the guy was playing?

Maybe some things have changed here.

Letting go of the surreal encounter, Jack grabbed the two glasses and navigated through the bar until he found David, sitting alone in a quiet corner, under a neon sign that read *'Let's Dance'*. He placed one of the glasses under David's nose, which shocked him out of his clear obliviousness to Jack's presence.

David got up with a start and hugged Jack. There was a kind of desperation in his embrace.

"Oh, Jack. Thanks for coming."

"No problem. I remember this place... Lots of memories."

Jack sat down opposite David, noticing that he already had two drinks on the go.

"Yeah. Halcyon days, eh?" David murmured, as he picked up one of his three drinks and looked away, dismissively.

"So what's going on, David?"

There was silence on both sides of the table for what felt like an age. David swilled his drink, took serial sips and then looked Jack squarely in the eye.

"I'm fucked, Jack."

Jack remained silent. He knew there was more that David wanted to get off his chest, and if his time in journalism

CHAPTER 22

had taught him anything, it was that silence was your most powerful weapon. People would open up like a tin of beans if you remained silent.

"I killed a man."

WHAT THE FUCK! Please, David, don't tell me this was part of the MM killings. The killing that Susan was referring to, earlier. You're not a part of this, are you?

Now was the time to speak.

"I'm sorry. You what?!!"

"I killed a man, Jack."

Jack knew where this was heading. His instincts were usually right, but he hadn't let himself believe that David was involved in these killings. It was too awful to bear, but here they were. Now the doubts were washed away. All it took were four words from David's mouth.

"MM?" Jack's voice was surprisingly calm.

David recoiled.

"What?! How do you know that name?" His face, white, under the neon sign.

"Am I right?"

"Yeah, but—"

"Nothing surprises me nowadays," said Jack, with a shake of the head. "I saw how you reacted the last time I was over at your place... It all makes sense now, but... how could you?"

"He had things on me, Jack. He knew everything." David's eyes were wild. "He knew what I'd been doing and how much shit I was in. I don't know how, but he *knew* it. Knew fucking all of it!"

Jack took a sip of his drink and kept his gaze on David. He spoke clearly. Direct. His tone, low. A harsh whisper. "As far as I know, you're the only person alive who has knowledge of who this 'MM' character is, so you need to tell me what you know about him... Now."

David's eyebrows raised and he gave a dramatic shrug. "I don't know *anything* about him."

"You must know more than me. How did he contact you? What did he ask of you?"

"It's like this, Jack..." David downed his scotch and moved onto the bourbon that Jack had bought him. With his spare hand he fingered a black paper napkin. "I'm in a lot of financial shit right now. The markets are fucked and I lost a lot on leverage. I'm personally about five hundred k in the hole."

Jack nodded, took a sip of his bourbon and raised an eyebrow, prompting David to continue.

"I got an email... From some random guy. Called himself MM. He seemed to know everything about me. Knew exactly how much I was in debt and he knew..." David lowered his head. "He knew other things, too."

"What other things?"

"Does it matter?"

"Yes. Of course it fucking matters! The details matter right now. You came to *me*, remember. I'm here. Tell me what you know."

"You're not going to like what you hear, mate."

"I think we're already in that territory. You killed a man. You think I like hearing that?"

"Okay, Jack. Okay." David ran a hand across his forehead and rubbed his eyes. He looked up to meet Jack's stare. "He knew about all of my affairs, too."

Jack shook his head, almost imperceptibly. He wasn't surprised to hear this, but was greatly disappointed and saddened to know that his sister had been duped for so long

CHAPTER 22

by this man, all the while continuing to make excuses for his detestable and reprehensible behaviour.

No words from Jack. He sat still. Quiet. Judging. His hand tensed around his glass.

"What, you're not going to say anything about that?! I've just told you I was cheating on your sister."

Still no words, but Jack shot David an icy stare that clearly conveyed his feelings about the matter.

"He knew all of them," David continued. "Six of them, to be precise. He knew them by name. Where we'd met. Where I'd taken them for dirty weekends. Everything. He even had photos of me with them... He also knew about the prostitutes."

"Oh there were prostitutes, too? Of course, there were. You're a fucking disgrace, David," Jack snarled, finally breaking his silence.

"I know. I know. I'm not proud of any of this, mate. I've been a total and utter wanker."

"Your words, but yeah, that's putting it mildly."

"And this 'MM' guy was going to expose all of this stuff to Rachel if I didn't do what he wanted. I was going to lose everything."

A wry smile washed over Jack's face. "Ah, so that's what this is about? You were scared my sister was going to find out how much of a scumbag you were, so you killed a man? Very noble, David."

David hung his head. Buried himself in his glass of bourbon. "I've not treated her well. I know that. It was only when I was threatened with losing her that I realised how much I love her... How she's the most important thing in my life." He met Jack's eyes. "She's a fucking angel, Jack! I can't lose her."

"She *is* an angel. You don't deserve her." Jack's jaw

tightened.

"And it wasn't just the risk of her finding out. This guy offered me a million to kill this guy. A *million*! That would get me out of the hole I'd dug for myself and he *knew* it. I didn't believe it though. I mean, who would? He said, if I accepted, that he'd transfer a quarter mil over to prove he was legit. So I did. I accepted. I was calling his bluff. I never figured that he'd actually send the cash."

"And, did he?"

"Yeah, he did... The next day, two hundred and fifty k landed in my bank."

Fuck. He actually sent it.

Jack felt a shiver go down his spine. "He actually sent it," whispered Jack, as he stared into his drink—his inner thought spilling out.

"Yeah I never imagined that would actually happen, but he said in the email that if I didn't go through with killing this guy, after receiving that money, then he'd have me killed. So I'd... backed myself into a corner. And then, he also went on to say that if I mentioned any of this to anyone. *Ever.* He'd have me killed, too."

"So, why are you talking to *me* about it?" Jack knew the answer, but asked anyway.

"Because, when you came over the other night." David paused, had a drink, squinted, presumably in thought, and then continued. "Man, it was just yesterday, wasn't it? It feels like a long time ago now. Anyway, when you came over and explained about the links between these killings, I realised that I was involved in this fucking chain and that if you were right I was going to be killed next. I didn't even know there was a serial set of killings going on, until you mentioned this

CHAPTER 22

'the debt has been paid' thing." He took another drink and gasped. "I've got a fucking target on my back, Jack. I'm going to be killed next, aren't I? I-I need you to help me."

"*Me*, help *you*? How can *I* help you?"

"I don't know. Fuck. I don't know, but you're the only one I can talk to about this. You've got to find a way to help me!" David punched the table.

"Okay, calm down. Let me think for a minute."

"Okay. You have a think. Don't know about you, but I need another scotch. I'll go get another round."

As David staggered over to the bar Jack had a few moments to reflect on the conversation. His mind was wracked with a swamp of thoughts:

How could David do this to my sister? How could he kill a man? Does he deserve my help after how he's treated Rachel?

How could I help him... even if I wanted to?

David returned with a couple of glasses and set them down on the table. Before David could even sit back down, Jack piped up.

"I've got four questions for you, David... and you'd better answer every single one."

"Okay."

Jack took a deep breath and exhaled sharply. "One. What was the name of the guy you killed?"

"His name was Alan Poulson... Mean anything to you?"

"No. Never heard of him." Jack was direct and matter of fact about his speech. He purposely kept his response short to avoid getting sidetracked and continued with his questions. "Two. Presumably when Jen and I met with you and Rachel at the Roebuck it was *after* you'd received this email, but *before* you killed this Alan guy, yeah?"

"Yeah. That's right." David sat down and pulled his glass of scotch over.

"Makes sense why you were so on edge that night. And presumably why you were checking your phone frequently. Reading through the email again, I guess?"

"Was that one of your four questions?"

"No. Just trying to find out a little more detail about the previous question."

"Yeah, you're right, I was re-reading the email. I actually sent the response that I would accept the request to kill Alan that evening, too. The booze was a loosener... but I honestly did think I was calling his bluff."

"You called it alright," Jack derided, rolling his eyes. "Three. When I came over to yours last night, that was *after* you'd killed Alan?"

David took a sip of his scotch and hung his head. "Yes," he muttered. "I did it the night before."

"How did you do it? Again, this isn't one of my four questions."

"I strangled him," David murmured. His voice was barely a whisper.

"I can't hear you."

"I fucking strangled him!" David shouted, glaring at Jack.

Jack looked around and noticed a man at the bar, peering over with a shocked expression.

"You've got to stay cool, David. You can't go shouting these things, for Christ's sake."

Jack couldn't quite rationalise this conversation. It was all too surreal. How was he remaining so calm while discussing the finer points of a murder? Somehow, keeping his cool, he went on to his final question.

CHAPTER 22

"Four... Did you actually receive the million?"

"Yeah... Today. He actually came through with it." David's eyes were pained. Red. Bloodshot. Watery.

"I think I finally know what 'the debt has been paid' means."

"Huh?"

"It's blood money."

"How do you mean?"

"So, I'm thinking this 'MM' guy... he reaches out to people in desperate situations. That's clear. He lures them into killing someone by offering them a way out of their situation, whether that's debt or threat of exposing dirty secrets. Or in your case, both." Jack gave a pity stare and could see David's face coloured with regret and shame. He continued. "He also reaches out without them knowing that the person they're being asked to kill has already done the exact same thing to someone else. They'd killed someone and taken the money. That's blood money and that's what MM is considering to be debt... They've then paid with their lives."

"Why is he doing this to me?"

"Because you took the bait?" Jack shrugged and took a sip of his scotch. "I don't know what his motives are, but he didn't force you to do this. You accepted the offer, remember. And now... now you're at risk."

"I don't want to die, Jack," said David, as he grabbed hold of Jack's hand. "Please help me," he pleaded.

Jack felt David's desperation. He was disgusted—by the murder, by his betrayal of Rachel—but still, he hesitated.

His loyalty was to his sister. Not David. Even if he *could* help—*should* he? Could David change?

Jack always saw the best in people. To a fault.

I don't know if David can change, but I have to believe he can.

Regardless, I can't bear seeing my sister become a widow.

He would do what he could.

Jack shook his hand free of David's desperate grip. "Here's what you're going to do. Listen very carefully."

David looked up at Jack—a hopeful expression plastered over his pitiful face.

"First, you're going to go home. You're going to tell Rachel that you love her and you're going to be the husband you should have been all along. You're not going to contact any of these other women. Ever again." Jack stared hard at David. "And I do mean *ever*. You got that?"

Tears formed in David's eyes. "Of course, Jack. All I want is Rachel."

"Second, you're going to send me a copy of the email thread from 'MM'. If I'm going to have any chance of helping, I need to see that."

"Third, and most importantly, you're going to stay home unless absolutely necessary. If I'm right, 'MM' is right now looking to recruit someone to kill you as soon as possible." Jack's eyes narrowed. "He'll know your habits just as he knew the habits of this Alan guy. Do *NOT* act like you would usually, okay. Stay hidden away."

"I can do that," said David, as he wept.

"Listen up. This MM fucker is the reason Lisa's dead and I want to find the bastard and avenge her. If I can also save your pathetic existence in the process then that makes it even more worthwhile, but I'd be doing that for my sister. Not for you." David hung his head again. "But you have to buy yourself time and the only way I can think that you could do that is by staying hidden."

"How am I going to explain this all to Rachel?" David's eyes, pained and puppy-dogged. He cradled his scotch with both hands as if it held answers.

"That's up to you. I'm sure she'll be pleased that you're around more and not '*working late*' all the time. Or…" Jack rolled his eyes. "You could do the honest thing and tell her the truth about all of this."

"I can't tell her the truth." David looked down at his drink. "You know that."

"Well, that's your call. I certainly won't be the one to do your dirty work, but you *should* tell her. No more secrets. That's what's got you into this mess in the first place."

"I'll think about it, mate. I will. Thank you. Honestly, I mean it. Thank you, so much."

David wiped his eyes and held out a hand for Jack to shake. Jack stood up, downed the remainder of his scotch and ignored David's offering.

Walking away, Jack hollered, "Now go home, David. And forward me that fucking email."

Chapter 23

Autumn 2017

His arms wrapped around her. A kiss on her neck. She roused and rolled over to face him.

She could see the love in Jack's eyes. Still. After over ten years together he still showcased that glint, that unmistakable dance in his eyes that told her everything she needed to know.

"Morning, you," Lisa yawned.

"Morning, gorgeous. Sleep okay?"

"I always sleep well with your arms wrapped around me. Well, at least when you're not snoring."

"That's typically only when I've been drinking though, right?" Jack gave Lisa a nudge in the ribs in response to her tease. "Which is a rare occurrence these days and you know it," he scoffed.

"Yeah, I know. Only really when you get out on the town with Ralph and those other lads. They really do know how to get you in a state."

"Well, what can I say, boys *will* be boys." Jack got out of bed and threw on a T-shirt. "Breakfast?"

"Oh, yes please, babe." Lisa yawned once more, stretched and squinted, still adjusting to the morning light. "You're a star."

"Don't I know it."

Lisa got dressed. The distinct smell of smoked bacon wafted through the one bedroom flat. She followed the scent to the kitchen to see Jack squirrelling away at the hob, scrambling eggs in a pan and frequently flipping the bacon to ensure it wasn't burning. Lisa didn't like her bacon crispy and Jack knew that all too well. She went over to him and cuddled him warmly from behind.

"You treat me so well, gorgeous one. I'll make the coffees, okay?"

Jack said nothing in response—just squeezed one of Lisa's arms with a warm touch. They knew each other's body language so well that it often transcended the need for words.

Lisa and Jack sat down to eat breakfast on the sofa in the living room. Not having enough room for a dining table they tended to eat on their laps.

"When are we going to get our own place, Jack?"

The two of them lived in a poky, one bed, rented flat, above a shop along Clapham high street, just fifty yards away from the infamous 'Infernos' nightclub. They'd lived there together for six years, but had long since outgrown it. They'd shared some great memories and had grown as a couple during their time here together, but Lisa was starting to become impatient and hankered after a bigger place and, more importantly, a place they could call their own.

Properties in London were prohibitively expensive and way beyond their means, but this wouldn't stop Lisa daydreaming about one day being able to move out of this place and into a more lavish place of her own.

"I'm working on it, Lise."

"How much have we got put aside now?"

"About twelve grand, I think." Jack grimaced.

"We're never gonna get there, are we?" Lisa groaned. Forlorn.

"Why are you in such a rush to get out of here, anyway? We're never going to find anywhere as cool as Inferno's to live by," Jack teased with a thin smile.

"Jack. I know you're just joking, but we're not twenty-one anymore. Infernos was okay when we were younger and just going out on the piss all the time." Lisa paused and started laughing at what was coming out of her mouth. "What am I *saying*? Infernos always *was* shit and always *will* be shit. We deserve better. We both work hard. Why can't we afford somewhere better?"

"Because. London. Is. A. Bastard."

Lisa laughed out loud and nearly choked on her mouthful of bacon and eggs.

"Isn't it just?! Fuck's sake. Well, we'll just have to keep on grinding, I guess. Maybe something will come up, to help us out."

"Get manifesting, Lise."

"I'll try." Lisa finished off the rest of her breakfast and took her plate out to the kitchen. She yelled back, "I've gotta get off to work in a mo. I'll just do the dishes, grab a shower and get out of here, babe. I've got to bring home the bread to keep that savings pot well and truly stocked now, haven't I?"

CHAPTER 23

* * *

Lisa hadn't been able to shake the frustration all day, about still living in that one bedroom flat.

What can I do to save more money?

She reasoned that the only realistic way to do so would be to earn more money—she couldn't imagine *spending* less.

It's not that she was thrifty, but there were certain habits that she knew she wouldn't be able to let slide. She enjoyed eating out at nice restaurants, but she and Jack only did that occasionally. It wasn't as if they were flamboyant and excessive about it. Surely they deserved this rare treat, instead of always eating on the sofa.

Monthly binges on buying clothes could maybe take a bit of a cut, but nothing too substantial. She prided herself on looking on trend, but her ever growing credit card debt wasn't going to right itself.

She kept her debt a secret from Jack, as she didn't want him to know quite how bad her shopping habit had become. She must have been about thirty grand in debt across half a dozen credit cards by now, but the excess never felt real—just numbers on a screen that were shown on her monthly statements. Monopoly money.

Until now.

Now she was starting to feel the strain.

The interest free periods were evaporating and, with them, so was her expendable cash. Each month she had less and less disposable income to call upon, but her spending habits never dwindled.

Something would have to give.

Maybe I could get another job?

Maybe I could start taking my current job seriously and push for a promotion?

Who am I kidding? I'm not worthy of a promotion and even if I did get one, that wouldn't magically take care of these problems.

These financial issues were starting to feel significant and she was realising that *she* was going to prove to be the real problem behind her and Jack not being able to afford a place of their own.

She *had* to tell him about it. Had to figure out a solution.

There was no way she was going to get through this alone and for that she would have to swallow her pride.

Fucking pride.

* * *

5:30 p.m. on the dot and, as per usual, Lisa was itching to get away. She'd done her hours and was ready to clock off.

Always being an advocate for prioritising a healthy work-life balance, Lisa wasn't the sort of person who would take her work home with her and always favoured a motto of '*work to live*', rather than '*live to work*'. It had served her well, generally, but there was always a hint of resentment, mostly towards herself, that she had never been particularly successful in her professional life. She was realising more and more that this mindset might need to shift if she was going to get what she wanted in life, but it was always met with huge internal resistance.

Lisa really didn't want to sacrifice what was most important

CHAPTER 23

to her. Freedom.

Packing away her things for the day, Lisa paused to quickly check her personal emails. Taken aback, she noticed a new email had arrived in her inbox that stood out amongst the usual spam-worthy contenders—those which promised varying degrees of offers, discounts and incentives for revitalising her already over-subscribed wardrobe.

Her breath hitched at the sight of the email.

The subject line read: '**Probate of Mr Richard Wainwright**' and seemed to warrant her direct and immediate attention.

Wainwright was Lisa's maiden name and, as such, the email sparked both her intrigue and concern; she wasn't aware of anyone in her family that was named Richard, but that didn't mean there wasn't someone in her extended family that she'd previously known nothing about.

She had maybe a dozen cousins whom she was scarcely aware of and would barely be able to name or pick out of a random line-up. Her nuclear family was all she really knew well enough to consider family. Anyone beyond that core group was basically a stranger to her.

Lisa's hand hovered above the trackpad on her laptop—hesitant for a moment.

She took a breath and, with curiosity getting the better of her, clicked on the email.

Her jaw dropped.

She blinked several times in disbelief and then furrowed her brow, squinting to make sure she was paying full attention to the detail laid out in the email.

The contents succinctly detailed how a distant relative of hers, recently deceased, had left her a substantial sum in their will.

Four hundred thousand pounds, to be precise.

Lisa's head spun.

How can this be? I've never even heard of Richard Wainwright?

A conflicted mess of confusion and exhilaration, Lisa was overwhelmed by the potentially colossal impact this email could have on her life. She continued to read slowly and carefully, making sure she was fully understanding of the content held within.

The email went on to explain that the sum of four hundred thousand pounds—*four hundred thousand fucking pounds!*—was the total remaining after inheritance taxes and would be delivered to a bank account of her choosing by her simply digitally signing the linked document.

There was one condition, however: she could never tell anyone where she got the funds.

Richard apparently didn't want his family members to know how his wealth was shared; worried that it could cause a rift between his relatives and that his legacy would be tarnished as a result.

Lisa rolled her eyes. It all sounded too good to be true.

She re-read the contents, and from what little she knew about legal matters, it did sound very official.

How absurdly coincidental, Lisa thought. Here she was driving herself crazy, wondering how she was going to get herself out of debt and one day being able to get out of that mediocre one bedroom flat, and this had landed in her lap the very same day.

Surely manifesting and asking the universe for answers isn't this easy?

She laughed to herself at the surreal moment.

This has got to be a scam.

Lisa leaned back in her chair, stomach tight. She wasn't

stupid. She'd seen enough dodgy emails to know when something reeked of fraud.

She weighed up the risks and narrowed it down to two key factors.

Firstly, she was using her work laptop rather than her own. If, as a result of clicking on this link, she opened herself up to a computer virus then it wouldn't be her personal items that were affected. Selfish, but sometimes it pays to be.

Second, and most importantly, this whole interaction didn't seem to be requesting funds—just the opposite, in fact.

Just check. If they ask for money, you walk away, Lisa. Okay?

But if they don't. If this is legit, then just imagine how much this could change your life, Lisa.

She clicked on the link.

The webpage was sleek, professional. A formal document outlined the terms again with two highlighted areas for her to fill in—her chosen bank details and a digital signature.

That was it. Seemingly this was all she had to do.

Her fingers floated above the keyboard.

Just use the prepaid debit card details. If it's a scam, they won't get a penny.

Her heart thudded in her chest as she typed.

Name.

Account details.

This is all too good to be true.

She held her breath and clicked 'submit'.

The click echoed louder than it should have. Her stomach twisted, anticipation coiling through her like a tightened spring. Then—silence. No immediate explosion, no flashing warnings, just... a new screen.

Transaction complete.

Her eyes widened, she exhaled sharply, and with her hands trembling, she refreshed her inbox.

A new email.

A succinct message, from the same sender as before, explained that the transaction was approved and that the funds would be available in her nominated bank account within twenty four hours.

Lisa could barely contain her excitement. She was confused and overwhelmed by what had just happened to her in the last few moments and how monumentally her life could be about to change.

She remained seated as dizziness swelled in her head.

She knew she would find it hard not to tell Jack about where this money had come from, but for the sake of how hugely this money could improve their lives she would keep that secret from him as best she could. She wouldn't risk having the money taken back due to her not obeying the sole condition.

Lisa read through the email one more time to make sure she wasn't imagining the whole thing.

There was no denying the detail.

It was very simple.

Very specific.

This was real. Or at least, it seemed to be.

And now, she had a secret worth £400,000.

Her eyes travelled down to the bottom of the email.

'Yours, sincerely, MM Solicitors'.

24th March, 2018

An orb of pure energy. Lisa burst from the doors of her gym after an intense body pump session. Her body felt tight and strong and her spirits were buoyant. Her world was in order, the stars were aligning and she had an almighty spring in her step.

On her way home she decided to stop off at the mini supermarket near her gym. Jack was out with his friends and she thought it would be a nice surprise if she made him dinner on his return, so she picked up: a couple of steaks, potatoes, some assorted vegetables and the pièce de résistance, a bottle of his favourite bourbon.

What an impeccable wife I am.

Stuffing the shopping into her gym bag, Lisa entered the gates into Battersea park, just opposite the Prince Albert pub. This was her typical route back from work, to the nearest tube station and she enjoyed the shortcut. Not only was it quicker, but she also appreciated the change of scenery to the calming environment of nature that was in stark contrast to the urban city streets.

Taking her usual route, Lisa drifted away from the main drag and into a more densely wooded part of the park. British Summer Time had yet to take hold, and at 8 p.m., the sun had long since set, leaving the park drenched in darkness. There was a dearth of lighting, and even the trees were now barely visible. Ghostly silhouettes.

Lisa stopped in her tracks to rummage through her gym bag and retrieve her head torch. Holding it in her hand she switched it on, piercing the oppressive darkness.

Continuing her steps along the wooded path, the light cast shadows of the trees into the distance, which swayed spookily as her hand bobbed along in concert with her stride.

With each step she took further from the park's thoroughfare, Lisa felt more on edge. Not quite scared, but certainly on the verge. Her nerves were frayed. Her stomach, tight. Her palms, moist.

She knew this route well enough for it not to have that extreme an impact on her, but for some reason, tonight felt more eerie than other nights; a sense of foreboding filled the air, and along with it, her soul.

Her chest tightened.

Her mouth felt dry.

Primal instincts kicked into a higher gear, heightening her senses.

In the distance she heard something.

Trees rustling.

What was that?

Was it the wind? Was it an animal?

Did I imagine it?

Dismissing these thoughts, Lisa continued on down the trail, further through the tenebrous woodland landscape and turned a corner, just a hundred yards from where she would exit the park and arrive at the tube station.

As she rounded the corner, her ears pricked.

Another rustling.

Closer this time.

Shadows of branches looked like spindly arms that could reach out and grab her at any second. Oppressive and ominous. Her hand that was holding the head torch shook, animating the sinister shapes before her.

CHAPTER 23

Foliage parted.

Lisa squinted to see more clearly.

A man?

A tall, hooded man had slipped out from the trees in front of her.

He approached.

Lisa stood still—her mind, unable to make a decision about fight or flight. She instinctively froze. Rooted to the spot.

Useless thoughts flashed through Lisa's mind, quicker than she was able to process them:

Why do I come this way? I always hear horror stories about what happens to women walking alone. Why aren't I more careful? Why do I never think it will happen to me?

"Lisa Stevens?" the man asked in a hauntingly hushed voice.

"Y-yes." Lisa gulped.

"I'm sorry."

As the man leapt towards her, the flash of Lisa's head torch glinted off a blade he clasped in his right hand.

It was too late.

Before she knew it, in a split second, he had grabbed her, spun her round, and restrained her from behind. As he raised his right hand, she felt the icy coolness of the blade's metal press against her neck.

Before she could say anything or scream, Lisa felt the knife plunge deep into her neck and slide smoothly across her throat. The pressure vanished as quickly as it had come.

The man turned to face her and she saw blood spurt across his face. Rhythmically.

Once.

Twice.

Is that...

Three times.

My blood?

Her head torch hit the ground as she clutched at her throat in a futile attempt to stem the bleeding. The relentless blood flow oozed effortlessly through gaps in her fingers, soaking her T-shirt in a torrent-like stream.

Feeling weak, her legs failed her and she dropped to the floor.

A thousand flashes erupted in her mind—perceptual snapshots of things she would never experience. Things she had planned for her life with Jack. That road trip around Iceland. That road trip across the US. The two babies they would have—a boy and a girl. Seeing them grow up—all of it lived in seconds within her imagination.

The triumphs.

The tragedies.

The love.

The loss.

"J... J... Jack," Lisa gurgled.

Her hand fell away from her throat. The blood, no longer a jet, but a tame trickle.

"I-I'm so sorry."

And then.

The lights went out.

Chapter 24

"Jack! You crazy bastard," said Ralph as he answered the phone. "How goes it?"

"Ralph, you daft twat," said Jack. He wasn't feeling particularly jovial and didn't have time for banter right now, but he played along regardless. He needed a favour, and the best way to negotiating it was to play into Ralph's hands. "All good on this end, mate."

"Glad to hear it. What do you need? Or are you just calling for a catch-up?"

"Actually... I need a favour." Jack grimaced as the words fell from his mouth.

"A favour, eh? And when exactly are you gonna start *repaying* these favours?"

Jack noted the sarcasm in Ralph's tone but also detected a slight seriousness.

I guess he's right. I have been heavily accruing favour tokens from Ralph over the last year.

"I know, mate. You've been very patient with me, and I certainly do owe you one... or two. I'll come good... in time. Scout's honour." Jack lifted his right hand, three fingers raised in the scout's honour sign—a pointless gesture that wouldn't be seen.

"You were never a scout, Jack," Ralph scoffed. "I'll put it on the slate. Now, what do you need?"

"Thanks. It's only a minor one this time. Do you still have that contact who works in cybersecurity?"

"Vinny?"

"Yeah, that's it. Vinny." Jack cringed, hearing the name. He didn't have the best of memories from his past interactions with Vinny—he'd found him a very strange man and far too eccentric for his tastes. But he needed someone with his skills right now and had to push past his own prejudices.

"Yeah I think I've still got his number. I'd totally forgotten about that guy. What a character." Ralph laughed.

"Isn't he just. Can you share the details with me?"

"Yeah, of course. I'll forward it over." There was a slight pause on the line before Ralph continued. "What do you want with him anyway? Is this for work?"

"Cheers, mate. I appreciate it. No... not for work." Jack took a breath and waited for Ralph's unwanted—yet expected—questioning.

"What's going on, fella? Don't tell me this is something to do with you wanting to hunt down this serial killer? Please, God, don't tell me that."

Jack's stomach knotted. "It might have, but I don't want to talk about it, really, mate."

"Damn. You should leave this well alone. Let the police do their job."

"Like I say, I don't want to talk about it. Just ping me Vinny's number, will you? I'm... I'm asking as a friend."

"Okay, fine. I'll send it over in a sec."

Jack could tell that Ralph was far from impressed with his

focus on playing detective rather than concentrating on work, but he was beyond caring at this point. Since meeting up with David, he had had time to ruminate on things and piece it all together in his mind.

A kaleidoscope of emotion.

First Lisa, and then the brother of the woman he now loved.

He wanted vengeance. No. He *needed* vengeance for the pain that had been caused. Pain that could still be caused.

His blood was boiling, and yet he retained focus. He needed to try and somehow save his sister from having to live without a husband.

Nothing would shake his resolve.

* * *

"Bury it. I won't let you bury it. I won't let you smother it. I won't let you murder it. And our time is running out. And our time is running out!" Vinny screamed, mimicking playing drums as he drove his beaten-up Saab through the country lanes of Surrey. The car windows were open wide, the wind blowing his long, greying hair back with gale-like force.

He wore camouflage-print cargo shorts and a white T-shirt adorned with multiple curry stains down the front. The T-shirt was at least one size too small and, as such, showcased his bloated gut, which seeped out below the hem. A sprouting crop of hair was clearly on display, leading up to his belly button, which was buried beneath the many surrounding layers of fat. His pallid complexion was saturated by a redness of broken capillaries on his nose and cheeks.

Vinny's faux drum solo was interrupted by a call. His mobile, which was streaming the music, switched from the song to an annoying ringtone. Frustrated, he answered abruptly.

"What?"

"Vinny?"

"Who's asking?"

"Sorry to interrupt you. I'm Jack... I work with Ralph at *The Weekly Reporter*. He gave me your details."

"Ah, *The Weekly Reporter* jam. I get you bro! Awesome sauce. What's the dealio?"

Dealio? Awesome sauce? Jack was quickly reminded of what it was like to speak with Vinny and was taken aback by his eccentricity.

Can I ever get used to this guy?

"Well, the dealio," Jack cringed, "is, I could maybe do with your help?"

"Sure thing amigo. What's a-boggling your mind, brother?"

"I don't know if this is anything you might be able to help with, or even if it's possible for that matter, but... how do I say this? Is there a way you can track the location of someone based on an email they sent?"

"Does the pope shit in the Vatican?!" *That's a yes, presumably.* "You're damn right it's possible! Depends on how cyber-savvy the sender of the e-to-the-m-to-the-a-i-l is, though."

"That's amazing," said Jack, his eyes lighting up.

"Gotta tell ya, there's not much in the world of transistors and CPUs that I can't help with."

"No idea how savvy the sender is, though. How can I check?"

"One way is to check the original source code of the email and look for the sender's IP address. Plug that into an IP trace, and it'll tell you the approximate location. If the sender is sending from their own mail server then you might even be able to get something a bit more specific than that."

"I have no idea what you just said to me."

"Mucho apologies, señor. How about you ship the mail over to me, and I'll take a goosey."

"That would be great. Could really do with your expertise," Jack praised, playing into Vinny's ego. "What's your email address?"

"Vinny, the monster slayer at gmail dot com."

Of course it is.

"Awesome sauce," Jack mimicked. "I've got two separate mails from the same sender, so I'll send them both over. Thanks again."

"No problem. I'm driving right now, but I'll take a look and give you a holla. Peace out, my G."

Vinny went back to singing.

* * *

Jack sat at Jen's kitchen table with her by his side.

Following his conversation with Vinny he'd immediately sent both Nathan and David's emails over for him to review and had headed over to see Jen while he waited for a response.

"So what did this Vinny guy have to say, exactly?" asked Jen, as she got up from the table and wandered over to the counter to make a coffee for the two of them.

"He's quite a sort." Jack laughed. "He would refer to me as 'G' and referred to email as 'e-to-the-m-to-the-a-i-l'… You really have to meet him."

"I think I can live without, babe," said Jen. "Or should I say 'my G'?"

"You can call me that if you like. I think it suits me, don't you?" Jack smiled. "He reckons he might potentially be able to track the location that an email was sent from. How huge would that be?"

Jen walked over, placed the two coffees down on the table and took a seat next to Jack once again, a forlorn expression gracing her face.

"Pretty huge, I guess."

Jack, picking up on Jen's expression, questioned the reason for the worried look. "What is it?"

"What do you mean?"

"Why so morose?"

Jen took a moment, seemingly lost for words. Before she managed to express herself she shifted in her seat, inhaled sharply, shrugged her shoulders, and looked Jack in the eye.

"It's David," she whispered, and lowered her eyes to focus on the floor. It seemed she couldn't maintain the focus on Jack while she divulged her concerns.

After Jack had left David at the wine bar, he'd thought long and hard about whether to tell Jen about the revelation, but concluded that he needed to be one hundred percent honest with her about this. If they were going to work together on finding this MM character, then there could be no secrets between them.

He'd filled her in on everything and shared the full detail of David's indiscretions: his affairs, his interaction with MM, the murder he'd committed.

Upon hearing all of this, Jen had remained quiet. She'd not said a word about it since Jack had revealed the details and he was surprised that she'd seemed so placid about the revelation. Maybe she *had* been shaken by it, but she certainly hadn't shown that to him. Jack had fully expected that Jen *would* open up and want to talk about this at some point.

Now seemed to be that moment.

"What about him?"

"It's just too close to home," said Jen. She rubbed her temples. "You and I have known... very *closely* known... victims of these killings. But now we both know someone who has actually carried out one of these killings and is still around to tell the tale. I just... I... I can't quite believe it. It's... surreal. I'm still processing it, I think."

Jack squeezed Jen's hand and she looked up to meet his eyes once again.

"Obviously I don't know him like you do, Jack. Did you ever think he was capable of something like this?"

"No." Jack felt a tightness in his chest as he responded. "In his heart, David is a good guy, you know? I know you haven't seen the best of him. In fact, I'd say you've seen him at his very *worst*. At his most desperate. MM has somehow known what a tight spot David is in and has exploited that knowledge."

"Should we tell the police about this?" Jen muttered, biting her lip.

"Jesus. No!" Jack exclaimed. "We can't do that to him. He's *family*. He's at risk now of becoming a victim himself and he knows it. As much as he's behaved abhorrently, he needs our support right now. We need to find this MM before David's killed, too." His eyes narrowed. "I can't have my sister paying the price and going through the grief of losing her husband, no matter what he's done. MM is the true villain here. Not David."

"Fair enough. I agree MM is the *true* villain, like you say. But David is still a villain in his own right." Jen paused and bit her finger—presumably realising that in saying this she was saying that her brother was also a villain to some extent, and potentially Lisa, too, for all they knew. She moved her hand away from her mouth and continued. "Obviously I'm not as loyal to him as you are, but I'm with you on this. You know that, right?"

"I do. Thanks. I don't know what I'd do without you."

"Is there anything I can do to help?"

Jack shook his head. "I don't think so. Not right now. I just need to see what Vinny comes up with, really. I don't have any other angles right now—"

As Jack was speaking he was interrupted by his phone ringing. He let go of Jen's hand to fumble into his back pocket and retrieve his phone.

It was Vinny.

"Vinny. Thanks for calling me back. Have you got anything for me?"

"J man! I sure have," came the exuberant voice from the other end of the line.

"Hit me with it, V man!" said Jack, cringing at the words he uttered.

"So the most recent message shows that the sender is a bit more cyber savvay."

Jack's brow furrowed. "Savvay?" he muttered.

"Sorry, man. My bad. Savvy. I like to embellish my words a little, you know?"

I've noticed.

"No worries. So what do you mean exactly?"

"I mean he's covered his tracks a little on this recent one.

CHAPTER 24

Probably used a VPN and some mail routing tech to obscure where he's sending from. You with me?"

"A little, yeah. I know what a VPN is. It hides your IP address, doesn't it? So, we've got nothing to go on?" He hung his head and reached out for Jen's hand again.

"That's right, my man. But wait... there's more to this yarn, J Dog."

Jack's eyes lit up in anticipation. "Oh yeah? Tell me more."

"Well, in the first mail it seems he was less secure in his approach. I've got the IP address."

"Sounds promising. So, what does that tell us, exactly?"

"It gives us a rough approximation of where the email was sent from. Nothing too specific, but we know it was sent from a certain borough in London."

"Wow, that's clever. We can't narrow it down any more than that though, I guess?"

Vinny laughed maniacally. "Oh, you're doubting me, Jacky boy. We *diddly* can and I *diddly* have narrowed it down."

"What? How? Wh-what have you got Vinny?" Jack—energised by the potential of this revelation—stood up and paced around the kitchen.

"In the first email, it seems he routed it through his very own mail server. From a company of his own, I reckon. A schoolboy error, sending this sort of shit, if I've ever seen one."

"What does this mean, Vinny? You've lost me."

"Badda, fucking bing! Hold onto your seat, J Dog." Jack's eyes widened. "I have an address. That's what it means."

"You're kidding."

"I kid you, not."

Jack's jaw dropped.

Chapter 25

A barrage of computer monitors created an aura around him. An array of data from countless sources streamed past on the displays as he actively sifted through them, searching for the next participant in his sordid game.

Meditatively cutting the end from a Montecristo cigar, he wafted it under his nose, taking in the oaky, sweet aroma. Holding it to his mouth, he lit it with a long match and puffed fervently, bringing it to life in a bright blaze.

Savouring the cigar smoke, he took occasional sips from a fine scotch while he perused the data in front of him. As the smoke billowed, it created a haze above him, stretching far into the warehouse-like setting where he held court as a solitary man.

Behind him—and stretched from one side of the room to the other on a thread—a clothesline of photographs hung on display.

It exhibited the faces of those ensnared by his macabre obsession: before-and-after shots of his 'players.' First, in a state of blissful ignorance, unaware of what awaited them; then, in stark contrast, their lifeless husks—painfully wrecked as a result of his game.

CHAPTER 25

A shrine to all who had met their end.

A depraved bunting.

Frozen snapshots.

Lisa Stevens, Jacob Williamson, Nathan Brown, Brett Anderson, Wilson Fensome, Alan Poulson, and lastly, David—yet to meet his demise.

But the man sitting here was working on it—meticulously searching for the ideal candidate to take part in his game next and lay David to rest.

Leaning forward and paying close attention to the data on display in front of him, 'MM'—or so he referred to himself as—puffed on his cigar enthusiastically while he sifted through debt records, police records, social media sites and myriad other sources of data.

His scrawny, ashen skin stretched over an aged face, riddled with wrinkles so deep they resembled tyre tread. His thin, wispy, balding, grey hair waved gently in the subtle breeze created by the incessant whirring of his computer's fan.

"Kat Jenkins," MM muttered to himself, his eyes narrowing as he squinted to focus on the information in front of him.

He spent several minutes analysing correlating information before concluding that she wasn't appropriate. Didn't have enough at stake. She wouldn't take the bait. His experience of manipulation had taught him how to more efficiently sift through information to easily eliminate inappropriate participants.

Frustration nagged at him. He took a mindful sip of scotch, inhaled deeply, and was dragged back to his sense of purpose and focus.

MM's obsessive trawling continued. His eagle eyes, tucked behind steel-rimmed reading glasses, hunted through reams of data—dissecting, eliminating. Searching for his next disciple.

His next pawn.

After an hour or so of 'hunting', as he considered it, he stumbled across an interesting prospect. "Kendrick Gleason? Mmm, you could be my man," he whispered to himself.

MM's lips curled and his eyes widened with excitement. His pupils narrowed. This could be a prime participant, he determined. Just the man. On first glance it would appear he had enough to lose.

This one warrants further investigation.

Oh, how he enjoyed the chase.

There was one thing he enjoyed more than the chase though—manipulation and exerting his power over people. With that in mind, he paused his investigation into the finer details of Kendrick and made a call that he'd been wanting to make for some time.

* * *

Sun, obscured by clouds, mirrored Jack's mental state as he sat out on his balcony. Since his conversation with Vinny—and the revelation that he had potentially obtained an address for MM—Jack had headed home.

He needed to be alone to consider his next move.

In some self-destructive way, part of Jack had hoped Vinny's investigation would turn up nothing. Rather than excitement, his first instinct was a wave of fear and dread at Vinny's discovery—he worried what it might actually mean for him.

CHAPTER 25

If Vinny hadn't found MM's address, at least Jack wouldn't feel compelled to take action. There would be simplicity in failure.

But that choice was gone. He *had* to pursue this—he had no excuse for not doing everything he could to bring MM to justice and, if possible, save David.

He breathed deeply and gazed out at the river below, watching the calming ripples as he sifted through his storm of thoughts:

Should I give the police this information?
Should I go to this address and confront MM?
How would I even go about confronting him?
Would this put Jen in danger? I can't do that.
What if Vinny's wrong? What if MM isn't even there?

RING!

The shrill tone of a call on his phone cut through Jack's thoughts, snapping him back to the moment.

He raised the screen to his eyes.

No caller ID.

Typically, Jack was resistant to answering such calls, but his mental chatter was getting him nowhere and he welcomed a distraction.

He answered.

* * *

"Hello." Jack's voice rang out from the other end of the line.

He's answered.

Oh, this is going to be such fun. I've waited a long time for this and now feels like the right time.

"Jack?" the man questioned. His voice was low and gravelly—it rasped.

"Who's this?"

"Jack Stevens?"

"Who *is* this?!"

In an even huskier tone—a harsh whisper—he said, "You're looking for me, Jack."

A silence hung on the end of the line for what felt like an eternity.

I've surprised him. He knows it's me, and he's shaken.

Just as I'd hoped.

I'm enjoying this already.

"Cat got your tongue, Jack?" MM quizzed, after nearly a minute of deafening silence.

"*MM?*"

"Ah, there you are, Jack. Did I surprise you?" he taunted.

"*MM?* Yeah, I guess you can call me that."

"How did you get this number?"

"I know how to get things, Jack... This was one of the simplest."

"What the fuck are you calling me for?"

"Language, Jack," MM heckled.

"Wh-who the fuck are you to tell me to watch my language? You had my wife killed, you fucking bastard!" The words screamed through the earpiece.

"She got herself killed, Jack. Wasn't at my hand. You must know that by now."

"I know about your sick game, you maniac."

CHAPTER 25

"You must have many questions for me, Jack," said MM, a snarl to his voice. "I'm here to give you a chance to ask them."

This was, in truth, part of the reason MM decided to call Jack. He wanted to give him the chance to ask questions and to leave him with a clear picture in his mind of exactly how all the murders had taken place, and specifically, why Lisa was the one to start it all off.

He wanted Jack to know that *he* was in full control, and he wanted to toy with Jack. Ultimately, he wanted to hear his pain.

"Oh, I have questions," Jack said, dryly. "First off, why did you have my wife killed? Did *she* kill anyone because of your '*game*'?"

Here we go.

Thank you, Jack. Thank you for indulging me.

"Oh, no, no, no, Jack... Lisa didn't kill anyone." His eyes narrowed. "I thought that might be the first question on your mind, actually. You must have been wrestling with that thought, eh?" Out of sheer satisfaction that Jack was performing exactly as he expected, MM chuckled to himself as he puffed gently on his fat cigar.

"Then why the fuck would you have her killed? You sick fuck!"

"She was the first, Jack. I wanted someone pure to begin my work. She was a pure soul." MM paused, knowing this would hit Jack hard. He considered what else he could say to make the blow land even harder. "Bless her."

"Bless her?!" Jack screamed. "If she was so pure, then what had she done to deserve that fate?"

MM grinned—his wrinkled face, crinkling. "She took the bait. That was all."

"What bait?"

"Oh, the questions are coming thick and fast now, Jack. This is nice, isn't it? Nice to have some quality time, getting to know each other," MM goaded.

Jack didn't respond. Despite only being a phone call, MM could feel the tension arising from Jack. These moments of silence said all he needed to hear.

Ooh, you're hating this, aren't you, Jack?

On the contrary, I'm loving it.

"You see, Jack, I posed as a solicitor. I reached out to Lisa informing her that she was due an inheritance of nearly half a million pounds. She took the bait, under the proviso that she would never tell anyone about how she received the f—"

"What the hell?" The level of shock and confusion came through loud and clear.

"How do you think you were able to afford that apartment you're sitting in? Did she ever tell you how she was able to get the money to buy it?"

"How do you know about our home?"

"I've told you, Jack. I know things. I have access to lots of information. I know… everything about you."

Again there was a lengthy silence on the other end. MM considered that Jack's only play at this moment was keeping quiet. It was the only way for him to have some semblance of control.

Let's goad him some more, shall we?

"I know about your romance with the lovely Jennifer Brown, too. Isn't it poetic how the two of you have found solace in each other."

"Don't you dare mention her name!" Jack shouted.

MM remained unperturbed. If anything, Jack's anger fuelled his satisfaction. A warmth spread through his body, deepened by another sip of scotch. Unrelenting, he continued. "The widower finds love in the arms of a vulnerable woman whose brother has been killed in the same manner." He closed his eyes and pursed his lips. "Beautiful... Just, beautiful."

"You sadistic fuck—"

"It was blood money, you see, Jack. Lisa took it and that started the cycle. And it would seem that your brother-in-law is going to be the next to go. He shouldn't have told anyone about this, but I'm pretty sure you're aware. The debt must be paid. There's no such thing as a free lunch."

"Blood money? It's not blood money. It's a sick game! You prey upon people, for Christ's sake. What had these others done to deserve this?"

"Well, this is an interesting subject and one that has a common theme in most cases. Let's talk through the history, shall we?"

MM stood up from his desk and wandered over to his shrine of photographs, hanging on a thread. His gallery of sin.

Starting from the left, he perused his display—an exhibition of imagery he knew only too well—the memories deeply etched in his mind from many months of obsessive voyeurism.

"So first there was Lisa and we both know all about that now," MM said, as he stroked the images of Lisa, adoringly; his cigar gripped firmly between his teeth.

He held a special place in his heart for Lisa. Admired her. He felt grateful—beholden to her—for taking the first step and allowing him to begin his 'work'.

Moving onto the next of his participants, he continued. "She was killed by a man named Jacob Williamson. He was a property developer whose portfolio of properties had taken quite the hit during a market downturn. He was up to his eyeballs in debt and his company was at risk of going under. He was easily swayed, let me tell you. A fine candidate, indeed."

MM could hear the flaky, crispness of a cigarette burning from Jack's end of the line, followed by the sound of Jack spluttering.

"You shouldn't smoke, Jack. It's bad for your health," MM taunted. A wry smile crossed his face, contorted by the grasp of his cigar between his teeth. "And then there was Nathan... I'm assuming you know all there is to know about him... given you're nailing his sister." MM laughed to himself.

"Of course, I know about him," said Jack. The anger, palpable.

"He'd got himself in a right state, the poor lad. A total gambler-holic. He'd got in with some really shady loan sharks. Not the sort that you mess with. They would have killed his sister if he didn't find the money to pay them and that was the key that motivated him to go ahead and kill Jacob. I gave him a way out and he took—"

"Gave him a way out, only to put him in harm's way," Jack sniped.

"He'd already put himself in harm's way, Jack... Like I say... the debt needs to be paid... And then there was the third," MM continued, as he strafed to his right, admiring the next set of photographs. "Brett Anderson." He stroked the picture of Brett's dead body. "A highly functioning drug addict. A serious cocaine abuser. Another man with a serious debt problem. There's almost nothing that addicts won't do to fuel their habits, you know, Jack?"

"Like murder, right?"

Bingo.

"That's right, Jack. Even murder. He was easily swayed,

too."

"And then it was Wilson Fensome, wasn't it?"

MM was taken aback by Jack's forthrightness. "I'm impressed, Jack. You seem to know the whole trail. Well done."

"I'm an investigative—"

"Journalist," MM interrupted. "I know, Jack. You're very smart... Not as smart as me, of course, but still, pretty smart," MM teased, as he wandered over to the next adornment in his display. "Yeah, you're totally correct, it was Wilson Fensome next. He worked as a recruitment consultant. Was a family man and therefore had a lot to lose. He'd wracked up so much credit card debt. He was up to his eyeballs, too. Status was a big thing for him and he liked to impress people with his faux wealth." MM raised his eyes to the ceiling. "What a foolish obsession wealth can be. Wilson's poor wife believed he earned more than he actually did, and to keep up appearances he couldn't help but keep applying for more and more credit to keep up this charade."

MM stared at the grotesque image of Wilson's disembowelled and dismembered corpse. Still, to this day, amazed by the hideous scene. Rather than be repulsed or horrified by the state Wilson was left in, however, he felt admiration—in some way, proud. Proud that his personal game could result in something quite as sordid.

"So you exploited this knowledge to get him to take part in your sick game, eh?"

"I never forced anyone, Jack. They chose to be involved." MM took a deep breath and puffed on his cigar. "Greed is a terrible thing, isn't it?"

"Greed may be a bad thing, but the coercion you've employed is worse and you're on a whole other level, you depraved bastard. You've exploited these people and blackmailed them into a corner."

Oh, you're trying to goad me *now, Jack?*

Nice try.

Refusing to get drawn into a discussion on this, MM continued with his monologue. "And then there's Alan Poulson. He was the oddball in the mix. He wasn't motivated by money. Wasn't in debt. What I did have on him was arguably the worst of the bunch, though. He was a paedophile, by nature. I don't think he'd ever exploited these fantasies, but he was an avid voyeur of child pornography and I simply threatened to expose him. He didn't take much convincing though. If anything he seemed *keen*. He was a bizarre soul."

MM looked on at Alan's photo with a fond attachment. Reliving in his mind the journey of finding him, investigating him, and being privy to the outcome of his nefarious efforts. He remembered that he had given Alan an instruction to directly reach out to detective Susan Reeves, so that she was the first one on the scene and got to see the untainted work of Alan, set proudly on display for her.

A vision that almost sent her over the edge.

"It wasn't just his predilection for the underaged, though," MM continued. "He was into snuff films and torture porn. Makes sense now, when you see what he did." He chuckled. "He had one hell of a dark mind and it seemed that he was excited by the prospect of having a reason to kill someone. You should have seen what he did to poor old Wilson. Alan was a seriously sick individual. He *enjoyed* torturing that man."

"And most recently you've had David kill Alan."

"That's right, Jack. David shouldn't really lose any sleep over that one. That man was very sick."

CHAPTER 25

"And you're not?! Tell me, what does MM stand for?"

"Oh, I wondered when you were going to ask that. And I'm glad you did." He paused to savoured this moment. He puffed on his cigar and blew clouds up towards the ceiling, before placing it back between his toothy grip. He raised his eyebrows. "Master Mind. That's what it stands for."

"*Master Mind?* You arrogant prick! Who the fuck do you think you are?" Jack shouted.

Rather than feel insulted, MM felt his ego inflate with Jack's outburst. He did consider himself a master mind. He was proud of his work. He took a glancing look at David's photo on the line—the only '*player*' with just the one photo. A victim in waiting.

He returned to his desk and picked up his scotch, savoured the aroma and took a short sip, before responding—the welcome burn in the back of his throat. "I'm a man that is able to control people's will and get them to act out my desires. That's who."

"You're deluded. That's what you are. Sick in the head. You prey upon the vulnerable."

I sure do.

And that's what makes them such easy and willing targets.

Sensing that Jack had more to get off his plate, MM took a seat and, in a zen-like state, quietly puffed on his cigar—smoke billowing above him—waiting for Jack to pipe up.

"How do you find people to play in your *game*? Where do you get the information?"

"Oh, I'm a very wealthy and powerful man, Jack," MM gloated, as he reclined his chair. "I own a lot of companies and have control over many. I have access to a *lot* of information." He removed the cigar from his mouth to take another gentle sip of scotch. "Just like you, you *do* realise that the police know there's a link between the cases now, yeah? Have you ever stopped to question why the police haven't issued a statement about that? If they did, my game would be over, wouldn't it?"

"Okay, I'll bite. Why haven't they?"

"You see, I have control over the police. You wonder why they never pursued your case harder, Jack? That's why... Also, that detective... Susan Reeves. She's a real go-getter and she was really pushing this case hard. I had her... removed. She thought it was her superintendent's call. It wasn't... It was mine."

"I know about corruption in the police force. Nothing surprises me there. And this wealth and power is the reason you're able to offer people one million pounds to do your dirty work?" said Jack—his tone, full of anger and detest. "Has it always been one million?"

MM's eyes flitted up, as if accessing past memories. He sighed with pleasure. "I tried different sums. There have been a lot of people that wouldn't go for the bait. One million seems to be the sweet spot. There's something about that number that gets people all in a tiz." He smiled. "Anything less and their scruples seem to hold up. I realised that I was able to tip the scales in my favour and get people to do the unthinkable when offering them a million. It's a small sum to me... but it seems it's huge to the everyman."

"You're a lunatic. If you're so rich and powerful, isn't there something better you can do with your money?"

MM shrugged. "Like what, Jack? When you get to my age it's not uncommon to be filled with bitterness and resentment."

MM recognized this all too well about himself. Attaining power and opulence had not brought him the satisfaction or

CHAPTER 25

happiness he'd expected. On the contrary, he had become reclusive and depressed. Having always believed this was what he sought in life, he discovered that upon achieving it, instead of feeling content, he was left hollow and unfulfilled.

A couple of years ago—just before starting his 'game'—MM had become suicidal. He found salvation in his 'work'; it gave him a deluded sense of purpose.

"And become malevolent?"

"This game is my entertainment, Jack. Everyone needs their passion in life."

"*Passion?* Jesus Christ, you're fucking insane. Why the hell did you call me?"

"Oh, Jack. Haven't you realised that yet?" MM teased. "To taunt you. That's why... This is all part of my entertainment. I wanted to mess with you. Wanted you to have my voice in your head when you hear the news that your brother-in-law is dead. When you realise that your sister is now a widow. And to know that I'm the reason your wife is dead and your new lover no longer has a brother."

MM heard the sound of a glass smashing on the other end of the line.

"Spill your drink, Jack? Clumsy."

"Listen to me, you depraved mother fucker. I'm going to find you and I'm going to fucking kill you!" Jack screamed.

Good luck with that, Jack.

"Oh no, you won't, Jack. You won't find me."

The line went dead.

Chapter 26

A mismatched pair sat side by side. Still and poised, their eyes sharp. One had a look of excitement, salivating at the prospect of what was to come. The other—apprehensive, yet composed and self assured—focused on the task ahead but not entirely confident that he would find the man that he sought.

Jack and Vinny were seated in a van that Jack had rented. He had been specific in his requirements. It must have blacked-out windows. That was a deal breaker. If they were going to be successful in staking out the location that they believed MM occupied then Jack couldn't risk being seen. Given the resources clearly available to this man, he must know all too well what Jack looked like.

Despite having blacked-out windows the van itself appeared fairly inconspicuous parked out on the urban street.

Vinny was the first to break the silence. "Those emails you shared with me are dark, Jack! Damn! Are they for real?"

Jack stared through the windscreen, his eyes narrowing. "Sadly, yes. The less you know about all of this the better, though... What I shared with you was necessary, but I really shouldn't tell you any more." Jack turned his head to face

CHAPTER 26

Vinny, who sat in the passenger seat. He met his eyes. "And like I said, you can't tell anyone about any of this."

"I totally get you, amigo. You kidding? My lips are well and truly sealed. Those emails make me realise you're dealing with a totally deranged and *de-rangerous* geezer. And, hey, I get to play detective. That's a childhood dream come true, right there. Bucket list? Tick! I can't believe I'm on a stakeout!" Vinny beamed, holding his hands out—palms up, fingers curled towards the sky—as if grasping something tightly, a tangible display of excitement. "So what's your POA, muchacho?"

"Plan of action?"

"Yeah, that's the one, guv'nor."

"I'm not entirely sure," said Jack, a look of dejection plastered his face. "I have no idea what this man looks like, nor can I be one hundred percent sure that this address is correct. And... not that I doubt your talents, but even if it is the right address we can't be sure that he's here." His stomach knotted. He took a breath and sighed it out. "Even if someone is there, we don't know that it's him. I have to be sure. I can't risk getting this wrong."

"That's a whole lot of doubt, friend."

"Doubtful until proven right, Vinny. What about you? Do you have any thoughts on how we should play this?"

"Of course, I do, Jacky boy." Vinny looked down at the laptop he had positioned upon his legs. "I've found a wifi connection that appears to be coming from there. It's a faint signal from here, but strong enough to pick up on. If I could just get into that, then I could wreak all kinds of havoc."

Jack's dejection vanished, his eyebrows lifting. "Havoc? Really?"

"Absolument, amigo."

"What would you need to get into it?"

"Just the WPA2 key."

"The password?"

"Yeah, the password, to get me into the WIFI network."

Jack clenched his jaw. "I wouldn't know where to start." He scratched his head and redirected his attention to the urban setting in front of him, hoping MM would reveal himself.

The van was parked across the street from the modest warehouse, situated at the exact address Vinny had obtained. On their side of the road, there was an artisan café, a bakery, and a barber shop. It was a seemingly quiet street with limited footfall—a cloying mix of urban and suburban environments, typical of a small borough in West London.

"The guy's an egomaniac," continued Jack. "Calls himself the Mastermind. Wouldn't surprise me at all if his password wasn't a play on—"

Jack was distracted by the warehouse side door opening.

Out stepped an elderly man, balding, with grey wispy hair. He looked both ways to check for traffic—there was none—then walked confidently into the street, crossing toward the café.

Jack sprang to life. He reached into the back seat to grab his SLR camera, which had an almighty telescopic lens attached. One of the perks of being a journalist was having access to highly sophisticated photographic equipment.

He took several shots of the man as he neared the van and breezed past toward the café. The photos didn't need to be perfect. Just good enough to be able to identify the man and for his features to be clear. Jack quickly reviewed the snaps he'd taken and—little by little—zoomed in on the face of the man.

The face came into sharp focus.

Jack's jaw dropped.

His palms began to sweat.

His chest tightened.

I know this face.

Is this MM?

"I know this guy," said Jack. His voice, a whisper.

"Huh? You know him?"

"I think so."

"Holy fuck knuckles. Really? Who is he?"

Jack's memories came flooding back. The hours spent investigating. The interviews with those who had been privy to clandestine conversations. The dirty secrets kept buried, ensuring favours were carried out. The bribes that were accepted.

"He's someone I exposed. A real shady piece of shit."

"Exposed? Was this to do with your *Weekly Reporter* gig, my man?"

"Yeah. The guy's a billionaire property tycoon. Michael... something. Matthews?" Jack scratched his head, as if digging up the man's name that eluded him. His eyes widened. "Matherson?" That felt right. "Matherson! That's it. Michael fucking Matherson. That's the guy."

MM.

"Fuck. MM! It's not just Mastermind. It's his initials," Jack whispered.

"What did this dodgy dingo do, exactly?" Vinny asked, his eyes transfixed on his laptop screen as his fingers tapped away at the keyboard

"He was bribing politicians. If I remember correctly, he was lobbying for the abolishment of capital gains tax on property. It would have saved him millions."

"And you put the mockers on it?"

"I had a hand in it, yeah."

"And you think you poked the hornet's nest?"

"What do you mean?"

"I mean, muchacho, do you think he knows that you messed with his plan and he's got it in for you?"

Jack was silenced. The thought had never crossed his mind that MM could actually be someone that he had known. Someone that he had aggrieved. Someone that was seeking revenge. Someone that might want to bring harm to Jack by...

Fuck.

It's my fault.

I'd led him to Lisa.

"Bingo baby!" Vinny exclaimed.

Vinny's voice brought Jack back to the present moment. He buried his thoughts. For now.

"Bingo? You in?"

"You betcha, bitch!"

"No way!" Jack stared; stunned. "What was the password?"

"You were right, man. It *was* Mastermind, but with a 4 for the 'a' and a 1 for the 'i'. So, so simple. This guy is no match for me, Jack. He needs to raise his game."

"I can't believe it. So what now?"

"Now we have some fun, Jack. I've got a nice little tool that I created that'll be just the thing for this occasion."

"You're a legend, Vinny. What does it do, exactly?"

"What *doesn't* it do, mon ami? I can watch. I can see everything that's going on in the network. I can see what *he* sees. I can intercept his web traffic and..."

CHAPTER 26

Vinny paused for what Jack interpreted as an attempt at dramatic effect.

"*And??*"

"And I can see him, too! Assuming he has a webcam, of course. And the best part? He won't know that any of this is going on." A smug, animated grin spread across Vinny's face.

"Oh my God."

Jack's heart hammered in his chest. He couldn't believe what he was hearing. If Vinny was right, it meant that Jack could not only confirm, beyond all doubt, the true identity of MM—a fact he was still hesitant to accept, fearing the pain of the truth—but also potentially observe the data MM used to find participants for his sick game.

Vinny reached into the left pocket of his army jacket and retrieved a bag of sweets.

"Tangfastic, Jack?"

"No thanks, mate."

"You're missing out, man. These things keep me sharp at times like this. Plus, they taste *delilally-lightful*."

Jack looked away from Vinny and out of his driver's side window, where the café stood adjacent to him. The man he now suspected to be MM was exiting the café, cup in hand. Jack took the opportunity to snap a couple more photos while the man was close, capturing the clearest and most detailed shot of his face yet. The man passed the van, seemingly unaware of Jack and Vinny's presence, and continued towards the warehouse.

A minute later, Vinny's laptop lit up like Christmas, multiple windows popping up on the screen.

"Here we go, my friend. Here we go. Buckle up!"

"What have we got, V man?" Jack couldn't help but play up to his partner's vernacular. He was a mix of elation and visceral guilt at the revelation of the identity of MM. Could it just be chance that he had chosen Lisa and David to be a part of his game? Potentially, but that seemed highly unlikely. Denial can be a powerful thing, but Jack knew better than to put this down to chance. He was certain that MM had actively targeted him and the guilt that welled within threatened to consume him.

The only thing that Jack could do now was focus on avenging Lisa and saving David's life. He couldn't allow himself to wallow in his own culpability. After all, he had only been responsible for outing a crook. It was this fucker who had implemented a sick game of murder to exact revenge on Jack and he couldn't consider himself responsible for that level of malevolence.

MM had to be stopped.

"You see all these windows here, Jack?" said Vinny, pointing at his laptop screen. A cherry-shaped sweet clasped between his thumb and forefinger.

"Yeah. What am I looking at exactly?"

"Well each of these is coming from the same user. In fact, there's only one user on the network. Disregarding little old me, of course. Each one of these windows is one of his monitors. Looks like he's got four monitors on the go.

"There's a lot of info on display here." Vinny stuffed the cherry sweet in his mouth and proceeded to chew like a camel. "And this one here." He pointed at another window in the top corner of his screen, his speech a little slurred from the wet-mouthed munching. "This is the feed from his webcam."

"Can you enlarge that for me?"

"Sure can. Here you go."

A face filled the screen. Aged. Gaunt. Thin, grey, wispy hair.

CHAPTER 26

Cracked, thin lips. A cigar held firmly in his mouth.

It was, without a doubt, the man Jack feared it might be.

Michael Matherson.

MM.

"This is the same guy, alright," said Jack, a level of surrender in his voice. "Can you take a screenshot of this?"

"Sure can."

Jack reached out and grabbed Vinny's hand, before he could take action.

"Without him knowing?"

"I'm not a rookie, Jack. He will never know."

"Okay... do it." Jack let go of Vinny's hand.

"Smile. You're on CCTV," Vinny proclaimed, taking the snap while still chewing on his sweet. "Done, Jack."

"Thanks. So what is he looking at exactly?"

"Let's look through the screens shall we? This is great, Jack, you know? I feel like a modern day Starsky to your Hutch. You're the man, Hutch!"

Jack laughed to himself at this ridiculous analogy. "No, you're the man, Vinny. Or should I say Starsky?"

"Yeah, partner. Call me Starsky!"

Jack was revelling in the excitement exuded from Vinny. His excessive jubilance was contagious and created an effervescence in Jack, nullifying his guilty thoughts for a moment.

He leant close to the laptop screen, seduced into looking at the array of information on display on Vinny's screen—salivating at the prospect of what they might find out.

"You know what? I will take a Tangfastic."

"Any preference?"

"Fizzy cola bottle."

"Nice choice. Here you go, Hutch," said Vinny, as he reached into his bag of sweets, extracted a cola bottle and passed it to Jack who gratefully accepted the sweet, popped it in his mouth and chewed with enthusiasm.

"So what can we see, Starsky?" Jack cringed as the words spilt from his mouth.

"Seems to me like a load of records related to a guy named Kendrick Gleason."

"What records, exactly?"

Vinny's eyes squinted as he flicked between windows, assessing the information.

"He's got his Facebook page up, what looks like some kind of back end to a banking site, and some hospital records from what I can tell."

"Can I see?"

"Of course, amigo." Vinny rotated the laptop so that Jack could see the information more clearly.

"Oh wow. Looks like this guy is in a lot of debt. That's a bit of a trademark of this MM guy's victims... This is definitely our man. You're amazing, Vinny."

"Good to flex my skills," Vinny beamed. "What do we do now?"

"Keep looking."

Vinny pulled up the window displaying the hospital records. He and Jack sat in silence for a few minutes as they sifted through the information.

"These aren't Kendrick's hospital records." Jack shook his head and furrowed his brow. "They're for a woman named Veronica Gleason."

"His wife? Sister?"

"Or mother," Jack posited.

"Yeah could be, eh? And it looks like whoever she is has a

serious health condition that they're treating privately, rather than on the NHS. That's gotta be some serious dollar."

Jack exhaled slowly. The pattern was all too clear. MM's twisted game always preyed on desperation.

"This is the angle MM is going to play. I'm sure of it. That sick mother fuc—"

As Jack was uttering these words another window popped up. MM was composing an email.

To Kendrick.

Jack and Vinny looked on with fascination as words were typed and displayed on the screen in front of them. The structure of the email looked all too familiar to Jack.

There was a pause in the typing as MM opened a folder and selected an image file to attach to the email.

"Can we see that file he just attached?" asked Jack.

"Yeah, just give me a second. I'll download it here."

Clickity-clack.

Vinny's fingers moved like lightning as he worked on the task. Jack's eyes darted between Vinny's rapidly moving digits and the laptop screen. The typing had resumed.

"Here you go, Jack."

Jack double clicked on the file to open it. An image of a man filled the screen.

Oh, fuck.

Jack exhaled sharply and he hung his head. What he saw didn't surprise him. He was expecting this, but naively he hoped somehow he'd be wrong.

Vinny's brow furrowed. "Do you know this guy?"

"Yeah I know him," said Jack. A throbbing of dread coursed through his veins.

"Who is he?"

"He's my brother-in-law."

Chapter 27

Brown eyes. Brown skin. The smoothest of complexions. Perfect. Yet, at this moment, made *imperfect* by the furrowed brow.

Tainted.

The weight on his shoulders was clearly taking its toll; bags had formed under his eyes from the strain of the burden he carried, adding years to his otherwise youthful visage.

Kendrick wasn't a killer.

It wasn't in his nature, but he was backed into a corner.

This was something he was convinced he now *had* to do. He'd fallen into a trap; tangled within the intricate weavings of a spider's web.

A man known only as '*MM*' had reached out with an indecent proposal.

Kendrick was convinced the approach was phoney but, given his desperate predicament, saw no harm in calling MM's bluff—accepting the offer in order to vindicate himself in his belief that the proposal was false.

It wasn't false—minutes after responding to MM and stating his acceptance, Kendrick had received a payment of £250k.

The '*contract*', as MM had put it, meant that Kendrick now

needed to go through with a despicable deed: killing someone.

Not just anyone. He had to kill someone in particular—or be killed himself.

In return for completing this killing, Kendrick would, according to this contract, be paid a remaining £750k, bringing the total sum to one million.

He didn't need one million.

£250k was enough to resolve his problems. And he did have *significant* problems. He was eighty thousand pounds in debt, with interest accruing—falling deeper and deeper into the hole he'd dug for himself.

On top of the existing debt, his mother was receiving experimental cancer treatment. This treatment wasn't available on the NHS and without giving it a shot she would almost certainly die.

The costs of private healthcare were mounting and this was where the majority of Kendrick's debt had come from. It was wholly unsustainable, but he refused to let his mother worry about this.

He would carry the load himself—do all he could to save her.

To give her a chance to live.

Kendrick regarded his mother not only as a parent but also as his closest confidante and dearest friend. Their bond was unbreakable.

He would do anything for her.

He couldn't bear to lose her.

But would he kill for her?

To give her a fighting chance?

He was about to find out.

Tonight was the night.

CHAPTER 27

Kendrick stared blankly in the mirror. He barely recognised himself. His eyes—usually bright and vibrant—were dull and scared. Deadened.

Anxiety filled his soul. Fearful; not only about the act that he was yet to commit, but that upon doing so he would lose a part of himself that he could never retrieve.

He feared a sense of existential loss. He wished he could turn back time and ignore MM's proposal, but knew that he couldn't.

It was too late for that.

The contract was written in blood. His. Or someone else's.

He must go through with this now and hope that his soul wouldn't be irreversibly shattered.

Making his final preparations, Kendrick stuffed a rucksack with the essential items he needed to carry out this task. The first item to enter the bag was a butcher's knife. Kendrick—a chef by trade—had an array of sharp knives on hand. Never had he intended to use them on anything animate, however. He choked on some stomach acid that crept up his throat at the sheer thought of this. Repulsed.

The second item: a photo. A photo of a man. *The* man. His intended victim. Not someone he recognised and he was at least grateful for this, however, he did harbour a feeling of prescient guilt towards what was intended for this poor soul.

He grasped the photo and took in the image of the man; wondered what he had done to deserve this fate.

The third item: a change of clothes. Kendrick had the foresight to determine that he'd need to take with him fresh clothing, fully expecting that in committing this deed his clothes would become heavily soiled.

There would be blood.

The fourth, and final item: a paintbrush. Kendrick pushed away the thoughts that rose in his mind about the necessity for this item.

Dressed in dark jeans and a hoodie, Kendrick donned the rucksack and left his house.

There was no going back. This had to be done. N*ow*.

Unlocking his car, the sound of the *beep* made Kendrick jump. He got in, mounted his phone on the dock on the dashboard and entered an address in his navigation app.

This address, the exact location where the man he should kill would be, according to the '*contract*'.

The expected duration of the trip, given current traffic—which was light—was approximately thirty minutes.

Kendrick started the engine and made his way.

Steadily.

Feeling extreme anguish at the task ahead, Kendrick wrestled with the steering wheel. He punched at it with the heel of his hand, channelling his unease.

His mind was screaming at him to stop the car and turn around. To give up on this. He could still retain his purity.

What are you doing, Kendrick?

You can't do this.

You're not a killer!

Contrary thinking entered his head to even the equation.

Think about your mum.

If you don't do this, you're going to be killed.

What would she do without you?

The anguish ebbed. Replaced by focus.

His eyes narrowed and sharpened.

He sped up.

CHAPTER 27

* * *

Arriving at his destination, Kendrick parked up about a hundred yards away, not wanting his car to be recognised as being nearby the scene.

He opened his rucksack, retrieved the butcher's knife and stuffed it up the sleeve of his hoodie.

He took a couple of sharp, deep breaths, exited the car and walked towards the address given to him in the contract's instructions. His legs were like jelly, but he remained steadfast on the task in hand.

He was focused, yet strangely unaware of his surroundings. It was as though he had a kind of tunnel vision. The destination was in clear focus and vibrant. Everything surrounding, blurred and colourless. His peripheral vision, almost non-existent.

He stood.

The door in front of his face.

Took another deep breath.

Then another.

One more.

Then knocked.

Chapter 28

Wide-eyed and pepped up with caffeine, MM sat at his desk, experiencing a wave of childlike excitement. He got like this every time a participant of his game had accepted his proposal—a sense of impatience and jubilant expectation at the thought of receiving confirmation that the deed had been done.

He felt the warm, tickling sensation of butterflies. A palpable exuberance at the prospect of being able to view the outcome of the killing of David, and salivated at the thought of being able to add the new work of art to his hanging gallery.

Another one to fall by the wayside.

This never got old for him. After half a dozen of these killings that he'd contrived, he still relished the result. Couldn't wait to see how Kendrick had carried out this murder. Couldn't wait to see the state of David's body.

And the pièce de résistance—once it was done—he couldn't wait to taunt Jack even further.

To drive him crazy.

To MM, the money he spent on this '*hobby*' of his was irrelevant to him. Silencing the voices in his head, however, *was* relevant. His mother's overbearing tongue, telling him he was worthless. That he was vile. That he was a burden. That he was responsible for his father leaving.

He would give away all of his money in a second if it would permanently silence the echoes in his head that taunted him relentlessly. He'd spent a fortune on therapy, trying to overcome the pain he suffered on a daily basis, brought about by his insufferable childhood.

To no avail.

The only thing he'd found to be successful in quieting the voice was his focus on his 'game'. The control that he was able to exert over people and their behaviours gave him a sense of empowerment and purpose. This was priceless to him. This sense of power fuelled him and was the driving force that kept him going.

Despite MM having created this outlet that gave him a feeling of power, the noises couldn't always be stifled. They still fought back and found their way into his mind at times.

This moment was one of those.

As he waited patiently, hoping to hear from Kendrick, his mother's words erupted in his head.

'Mikey.'

'Oh, Mikey.'

'Mikey, you vile snob.'

"Shut up, mother! Get the fuck out of my head!"

'You snivelling little urchin.'

'You worthless, weak child.'

"Shut up. Shut up. Shut UP!!!!!!"

Against his will he was forced to return to memories of his younger years. Those paralysing memories.

MM's childhood had been anything but perfect. His parents were wealthy. Very wealthy. Materially he grew up with everything a child could want.

But paternal love? Now that was severely lacking.

His father had split when the boy was around five years old and his mother was left to take care of him.

She'd taken it very hard. The infidelity. The deceit. The abandonment. She took this grief out on her son by becoming overbearing and abusive—forever knocking his self-confidence before he was even aware it was a thing. She would put him down constantly and limit his contact with other children.

As a result, he grew up without friends.

Was not socialised effectively.

Grew up to be defective.

Damaged.

Later in life, MM was able to understand why his father had been driven to leave his mother. He could rationalise it. Make sense of it.

Believing it would help him deal with his childhood trauma, he badly wanted to seek out his father and get to know him—only to be left further devastated upon finding out that his father had committed suicide a few years after leaving him and his mother.

Broken, he'd found solace the only way he knew how. In making others suffer.

Projecting his own suffering.

A depraved coping mechanism born from the depths of his unresolved trauma.

MM shook his head and screamed to push the voices away.

They relented.

For now.

CHAPTER 28

How long would they stay away this time? He may need to raise his game to new heights to satiate them.

* * *

Jack sat at his dining table, his laptop in front of him. After his time with Vinny staking out MM's location, Vinny had taught Jack how to access MM's webcam at will.

Jack tapped away, and seconds later, a live image streamed directly from MM's camera to Jack's laptop.

Despite being a dozen miles away, the image of the man stared back at Jack. Face-to-face. He felt repulsion. Angered by the sight of him. He wanted so badly to cause MM the same level of pain and torment that he had endured.

You're gonna pay for this, you son of a bitch.

Jack picked up his phone.

* * *

MM was shaken by the sound of his phone vibrating on his desk. His phone was on silent, and he rarely received calls, so he was caught off guard.

He checked the screen. No caller ID.

Out of sheer curiosity, he answered.

"Hello."

"You're looking for *me*."

"Who's this?"

"Don't you recognise my voice?"

"Jack??"

"That's right. Your good old friend, Jack."

MM was shaken. Dizzy. His head spun and he felt off balance. Teetering.

"How did you get my number?"

How did he get my number?

"I've got more than that, MM. Or should I say... Michael Matherson?"

What the hell??

"You're not the only one who's been watching, you know?" Jack taunted.

He knows my name? How could he know my name?

What is this?

MM was lost for words. He sat rooted to the spot, eyes wide. His caffeine-fuelled state twisted into anxiety as a tightness gripped his chest. His palms turned moist.

"Cat got *your* tongue, Michael?"

Chapter 29

Alone. Listless.

David sat in his living room, twiddling his thumbs. A futile attempt to alleviate his anxiety.

Rachel was out with the girls this evening and he couldn't stand these nights alone—not under his recent circumstances. Ever since he'd learnt that he had a target on his back, he'd become withdrawn and desperately on edge. He felt—quite understandably—that any day could be his last, and there was nothing he could do about it. The only control he had was in heeding Jack's advice by keeping himself hidden away and David was driving himself crazy with the idle lifestyle that he was now forcibly becoming accustomed to.

With any day potentially being your last you'd hope that you'd go out of your way to enjoy each one, rather than while away your time under some form of house arrest.

One positive that had come out of all of this, however, was that he and Rachel were in a much better place than they had been in years. David had been far more attentive and affectionate towards her; had put her on a pedestal and finally given her the love she deserved.

He hadn't been able to bring himself to share with Rachel

the reasons for his recent hibernation and obvious change of attitude, but had made some excuses that seemed to be accepted by her as rational.

Somehow, when he was with her, his anxiety had been quelled somewhat. He'd put his efforts and attention into her and that had helped shift his focus from his internal dread into something that he perceived as salvation.

Her.

She was more important to him now than ever. The errors of his ways had come to light in a shocking twist of fate, as he realised that he may pay with his life for his misdemeanours.

He would do good from now on.

He must.

He was steadfast and resolute in that belief. So long as he got that chance.

He prayed he would get that chance.

David hadn't whispered a thing about his debt, his indiscretions, the murder he'd committed, or the fact that he now could be at risk of becoming a victim in the same way as Lisa and Nathan. He couldn't imagine what it would do to her, or to *them*, if he revealed that truth.

Thoughts flashed through his mind as he sat, idly waiting.

How long am I going to have to live in isolation?

I can't keep making excuses to Rachel as to why I never leave the house, why I can't go out anywhere with her, or why I can't even do the simplest of things to assist her, like help out with the shopping.

Do I need to come clean?

Should I?

No. I can't. That would destroy us.

David couldn't contain these ruminations. He brought his

hands up to his head and ruffled his hair out of anguish.

KNOCK

An assertive tap at the door brought David back to the present moment.

Who could this be?

I'm not expecting anyone.

David got to his feet.

He felt a wave of dizziness that nearly caused him to collapse then and there. Was it a headrush from getting up too quick, or anxiety induced? He wasn't sure.

He steadied himself by placing one hand on the wall behind the sofa and, after taking a second to stabilise, traipsed towards the front door.

His fingers hovered over the safety latch. His pulse rattled in his ears.

Slowly, he cracked the door open.

Chapter 30

Cat got my tongue?

Has Jack really been watching me?

KNOCK

MM sat bolt upright—his train of thought, interrupted by a rap on the warehouse door.

"Oh, is that a knock at your door? I think you'd better get that, Michael," Jack taunted.

MM was still cradling the phone to his cheek, but didn't respond. Couldn't think of anything to say. This was all too surreal.

He had no words, just a barrage of thoughts that raced through his mind.

Who was knocking?

Was this Jack?

He said he'd find me, but how could he?

Uneasy and anxious, MM picked up a baseball bat from under his desk and crept towards the warehouse door, leaving the phone upon the desk—the line still open.

He flung the door open. Ready to face whoever was on the other side.

What he came face to face with shocked him to the very core.

CHAPTER 30

His mouth hung open.

Chapter 31

"What are *you* doing here???" exclaimed MM.

Chapter 32

"Wh-what are you *doing* here???" spluttered David, stumbling over his words.

Chapter 33

As the door opened, Kendrick immediately recognised the man standing before him. It was him—the target he sought. The very man pictured in the *'contract'* email and he *was* here, as it was promised he would be.

The man's expression caught him off guard. He looked surprised to see him. Kendrick hadn't expected such an emotion from his target.

But what did I expect?

There was no time for hesitation.

This is my moment.

I must act now.

"I'm sorry."

Before the man could respond, Kendrick unsheathed the butcher's knife from his sleeve and drove it deep into his chest with incredible force.

The man's face contorted in horror.

Kendrick shoved him further inside his abode and kicked the door shut, all while maintaining a firm grip on the knife, still buried deeply in his chest.

With a sickening wrench, he pulled the blade free and struck again—plunging it once more into the man's chest, causing him to stumble and fall to his knees.

The man gurgled, blood spilling from his mouth.

Through the choking, he spat out a few wet, broken words.

"B-but I-I-I sent *y-y-you!*"

The clatter of a wooden item being dropped resounded, as a baseball bat fell from the man's hand and rolled along the concrete floor.

"I'm sorry, Michael. I had no choice."

* * *

A sudden *slam* echoed through the speaker. Jack's breath caught as MM stumbled back into view—a male shoving him inside, a knife buried deep in his chest.

Jack's eyes widened, his jaw slack.

That's Kendrick.

Oh shit. It worked.

He watched as Kendrick wrenched the blade free and drove it in again.

He saw MM fall to his knees.

Heard him utter the faintest of words:

"B-but I-I-I sent *y-y-you!*"

Jack smirked, his fingers curling into a fist.

Oh, Michael, you must be so confused by this turn of events.

MM's desperate words were followed closely by Kendrick's.

"I'm sorry, Michael. I had no choice."

Jack continued to look on as MM fell onto his back, writhing and spasming, while Kendrick struck again. Once. Then twice.

He heard Kendrick let out a wailing scream as he landed the

fatal blow and saw him cover his mouth with a gloved hand, as if to stifle it.

Jack exhaled sharply, then punched the table.

"It's over for you, MM, you sack of shit."

* * *

Kendrick straddled MM's body, sitting at his waist. His hand moved away from his mouth, trembling, as he gripped the knife—still buried in his victim's chest—with both hands.

He held it there, pushing down, until MM finally stopped writhing.

He realised that he'd been acting almost instinctively until this point.

On autopilot.

He'd prepared himself by playing out this scenario in his head countless times, so that when it came to the reality of the situation, he was ready—or as ready as he could be given the unscrupulous nature of the scenario.

Now, as he sat on top of MM's dead body, his conscious mind finally caught up with him. As it kicked into gear, a wave of guilt, remorse and horror crashed over him.

What have I done?

Blood pooled below the now quiet body, seeping from the chest, stomach and mouth. Kendrick slowly got to his feet. Trembling. The pool of blood bore two circular voids where his knees had been planted—voids that were quickly swallowed by the thick red tide surrounding them.

He stepped to the side. An unease to his steps, as his knees

CHAPTER 33

leaked tiny droplets of blood onto the concrete surface.

He shrugged off his rucksack, rummaged around and retrieved the paintbrush.

Gingerly, he stepped back towards the body, dipped the brush into the warm pool of blood, and began making brushstrokes to the right hand side of the corpse. A few sweeping arches, then back to the pool to top up the brush with the thick, red, viscous fluid.

Detaching himself from the gruesome nature of the task, Kendrick carried out the deed in as mindful a way as possible. He breathed deeply, and focused on the intricacies of the brushstrokes, without allowing his mind to wander onto thoughts of how deeply sadistic this was.

Once finished, Kendrick placed the photograph of MM on the body, pulled his phone from the front pocket of his jeans, and took a snapshot of the scene.

MM's body, still, lifeless, and shrouded in a bloody aura, lay next to Kendrick's other handiwork—a crimson message smeared onto the concrete:

'THE DEBT HAS BEEN PAID'.

Turning away from the body, Kendrick shook himself violently in a futile attempt to rid himself of the repulsion he felt towards what he'd just done.

He removed the change of clothes from his rucksack, swiftly undressed and stashed his blood stained clothes, the knife and the paintbrush back in his bag.

He changed into clean clothes and forced himself not to look back at the scene he'd created.

A moment of headspace.

Not peace. Not even close—but at least, a miniscule moment of clarity.

He shouldered the rucksack, pulled up his hood, and headed towards the door.

He bundled his hand in his sleeve and, as he reached for the handle, a thought popped into his head.

He froze.

What did Michael say to me?
But I sent you?
Is that what he said?
What the hell did he mean?
Oh, God.
What have I done?
But... he was *the man in the photo.*
He couldn't *have sent me.*

* * *

Jack stared at the screen for several minutes, his gaze fixed on MM's lifeless corpse. The sense of triumph—the elation of seeing his arch nemesis dead—was short lived. It didn't bring with it the feeling of completeness that he'd expected.

Instead, a surprising emptiness filled him.

He had won.

He had beaten MM.

And not only that, he had beaten him at his own game.

There was a kind of poetic justice in watching MM die in the same way that he had orchestrated others to kill.

A righteousness.

But it wasn't enough. Jack had convinced himself that seeing MM's demise would finally mend the hole inside him—the one

CHAPTER 33

Lisa's death had left behind.

Naive.

Now, in hindsight, he saw the truth. Nothing could fill that void. Revenge, while briefly satisfying, was fleeting. It couldn't bring her back. Couldn't heal his wound. Nothing could.

Jack closed his laptop and let out a sharp exhale. He had seen enough. Had lived enough of this gruesome, horrific journey.

It was over.

It was finished.

Emotion took hold.

He wept.

For Lisa. For Nathan. For Kendrick. For all of the other victims and their families.

He wept for himself, and for Jen.

As the tears fell, tiredness washed over him. The journey into the dark depths of MM's game—his search for retribution and vengeance—had drained him. And now, with the release of emotion, his body was telling him something his mind hadn't let him hear.

He could rest now.

He *needed* to rest.

But not yet.

Not yet.

There was somewhere he needed to be.

Chapter 34

"Wh-what are you *doing* here???" spluttered David, stumbling over his words.

Relief.

The emerald green eyes of the person who stood in the doorway filled him with a sense of safety. At this moment there were only three people in this world that David felt he could trust, and he was comforted that—during a time when he feared for his life with every waking second—he'd opened the door to one of them.

A very welcome reprieve.

Comforted, yet also surprised. His eyes, wide.

She spoke first.

"Hey David. Is Rachel here?" asked Jen.

"N-no. She's out tonight," said David. His jangling nerves were clearly on show, but they were beginning to ease at the sight of Jen. He could see a warmth in her eyes that was calming. She offered him an embrace, which he gratefully accepted with an awkward shakiness. "Boy, am I glad to see you."

David gestured for Jen to come in, and she entered, walking through to the kitchen with David traipsing behind her after

CHAPTER 34

having securely bolted the door.

Jen took a seat at the kitchen table, with David pulling up a chair opposite. His puppy-dog eyes looked up at her, filled with a mix of hope and despair.

"How are you doing, David?"

"I've been better," he said, his hands visibly shaking. "Not being able to get out of the house is sending me stir-crazy and I'm sure Rach is starting to guess that something's up. I'm trying to hold it together, though… for her sake."

"Yeah, I'm sure that's not been easy. I don't think you'll need to wait much longer, though." She smiled.

More hope filled David's eyes. Still a hint of despair, but the shift was noticeable.

"You think? Why'd you say that? What brings you here? And… where's Jack?"

Focusing solely on the last of David's many questions but not going into detail, Jen said, "He'll be on his way soon. He had something to take care of first."

David's brow furrowed, clearly bemused by what Jen was saying.

"Take care of what? Is he okay?"

"Yeah, yeah, he's fine. I'll let him explain when he gets here. I promised I'd come and check in on you in the meantime… Looks like you need a drink, David. I know I could do with one."

He let out a sigh and nodded towards the kitchen worktop. "There's some scotch over there if that works for you. You're right… I could definitely do with a drop."

Jen got to her feet, poured a couple of glasses, and set them down on the table. Without a clinking of glasses, David took a hefty gulp.

Jen sipped.

The two of them sat in silence and drank at their polar opposite paces. An unease lingered in the air. Jen checked her watch at regular intervals and eyeballed David as his hands shook and sweat glistened on his brow, reaching out every so often to touch his hand and settle him.

No further words were shared.

The silence was broken with a series of taps on the door. The abruptness of the knocking made David shudder. His grip on his glass slipped, the sound of it hitting the kitchen table echoing through the room.

"I'll get this," Jen said, as she rose to her feet. "Don't worry," she added, noticing the look of terror in David's eyes.

Jen wandered over to the front door, unbolted it and opened it to reveal Jack standing in front of her. His hair, ruffled, but his expression jubilant.

"Where's David?"

"Through here," said Jen, ushering Jack inside.

David jerked upright at Jack's voice, shoving his chair back to see the hallway.

"David," said Jack as he made his way through to the kitchen. He took a seat opposite. "I'm glad you're sitting down. I've got some news."

"What is it, Jack?" said David, righting his glass of scotch.

Jen had followed Jack into the kitchen and had taken a seat alongside him. They both looked intently at David, as his eyes flitted between the two of them.

"We got him, David," announced Jack.

"What?"

"He's gone."

CHAPTER 34

"Who?... MM?" David's eyes narrowed. "Don't fuck with me, Jack."

David was taken aback. He didn't want to let himself read between the lines here. He was on edge—on the verge of breakdown—and wasn't thinking clearly. He knew only too well that he couldn't rely on his thoughts at this time.

"Yeah." Jack smiled. "It's over, pal."

"Wh-what?"

"He's dead," said Jack, a finality to his voice.

How powerful words can be.

Those two words that leaked from Jack's mouth made all the difference.

'*He's dead*'.

That's all it took.

In an instant, the weight of them shattering the fear and dread that had consumed David.

It was fortunate that he was sitting down, as he could no longer feel his legs. He dropped the glass again. The weight of the stress, worry and anxiety that David had been experiencing for the last few weeks was a heavier load than he'd consciously realised.

At that moment—and upon hearing those words from Jack—there was a sense of relief of gargantuan proportions and his body gave out. The floodgates in his eyes released and he sobbed uncontrollably. Quivered. Convulsed—rhythmically in concert with his sobbing.

He held his head in his hands as his elbows rested on the table.

"It-it's o-o-over? Really?" David mumbled, looking over at Jack with a puppy dog expression, tears dripping from his chin and splashing onto the wooden surface of the table.

"Yes, David. Really."

"Really. You're safe now," Jen added, placing a hand on David's.

"D-d-did... *you?*"

"Kill him?" said Jack, his eyebrows raised. "No, it's better than that... There's no blood on *my* hands. I found him *and* the man who he was recruiting to kill *you*... Poetically, *he* killed MM—he died in the same way he intended for you."

David was dazed and confused, unable to unravel all that Jack was telling him.

"B-but how d-did you do this?" David stammered, tears still streaming.

"Let's have a cuppa. It's a long story."

Chapter 35

Detective Nick Raines looked on in disbelief as SIO Rupert Jones manhandled evidence without gloves on.

"Sir?" Nick quizzed.

"What is it, Detective?" said Jones.

"Gloves? Sir?" Nick sighed. The bewilderment that Nick was feeling caused his eyebrows to raise so high that worry lines in his forehead became heavily pronounced, intertwined like a network of peaks and valleys.

"What do you mean?"

Nick shook his head, rolled his eyes. "You're messing with evidence? Tainting it."

"Right you are. Pass me some gloves would you?"

Nick obliged. He wandered over to his forensic kit, grabbed a pair of latex gloves and handed them to Jones.

"Thanks, Detective."

Jones proceeded to put the gloves on, while trying to maintain a grip on his cup. His bumbling attempt sent coffee spilling onto his shoes and the concrete floor.

Nick sighed, again. Incredulous. "Excuse me for a moment, sir." He made his way outside of the warehouse, stripped off his gloves and took his phone out of his pocket.

***

"Nick?" Susan's voice, full of surprise, as she answered the call.

"Hey, Susan."

"What's up? You sound troubled."

"You're not wrong. Yeah, I am... troubled." He rolled his eyes.

"Where are you? What's going on?"

"There's been another one. I'm at the—"

"Another one? Fuck, I hate being out of the loop on this. But I appreciate you calling me... So that's what's troubling you? It's not as grotesque as the last one we saw together is it?"

"Actually, no. That's not really troubling me. That's par for the course these days, it seems."

"Oh, so what is it?"

"Jonesy." The frustration in Nick's voice was palpable.

"Oh, Jonesy." Susan sighed. "What's that idiot doing now?"

"It's more what he's *not* doing. He's an absolute moron. He's fucking the crime scene up completely."

Nick's usual reluctance to swear impressed upon Susan the gravity of the situation.

"Why doesn't that surprise me?!"

"Can you come down here?"

"You know I'm not on the case anymore, Nick."

"I know, but I could really do with you here. There's something different about this one and I can't just stand here and watch Jonesy fuck it up."

Susan wanted more than anything to be involved in this case. To help bring it to a conclusion. She hated having her hands tied, but she couldn't just rock up at a crime scene, unsolicited. Sadly, it wasn't her case anymore.

Fuck it.

"Ping me the address. I'll be right there. Oh, and I didn't hear about this from you."

***

Susan flashed her badge to the officers guarding the perimeter of the crime scene outside the warehouse. Without question, they let her under the tape and she proceeded to the closed door, presumably where she'd be greeted with the bloody site of another grisly murder.

She took a breath and barged into the scene.

Upon entering, Susan shared a subtle, yet knowing glance with Nick and wandered over to SIO Jones.

"Ma'am."

"Jones," Susan replied.

"Sir, don't you mean?"

"Jones," Susan repeated, not entertaining any pleasantries. Jones didn't deserve her respect and she wasn't going to give him the pleasure.

"What are you doing here?" Jones questioned. He was dressed, as expected, in full police get-up. His uniform, too tight for his sprawling gut. His hat was the only item of clothing that seemed to fit appropriately and he was never without it. The world didn't need to see his diabolical comb-over.

"I'd heard there'd been a murder. I thought I'd check it out."

"This isn't your case anymore, ma'am."

"Oh, is this another part of the serial? I had no idea." Susan shrugged, her eyes flitting around the scene. "As I've come all the way here it can't hurt for me to have a look around."

Before Jones could challenge Susan she'd already turned away from him and approached the epicentre of the crime scene. The body of an elderly gentleman lay face up near evidence marker '1' and was surrounded by a murky dark red pool.

Alongside the body the recurring motif was present. Written in blood.

Susan shuddered.

I've seen too many of these. If I never see another one it'll be too soon.

Nick took a pause from bagging and tagging evidence, got to his feet and crept towards Susan.

"Thanks for coming. I, I know you're not supposed to be here. So glad you came."

Susan gave a wry smile. "I wish I could say the same. I hoped I'd never see another one of these scenes."

"You may not after this one." Nick raised an eyebrow.

"What are you saying, Nick?"

"You see that string of photos over there?" he said, as he pointed to the clothesline of photographs at the end of the warehouse.

"I haven't looked over there yet." Susan squinted. "What is that?"

"Go. Take a look. Let me know what you think." Nick's eyes darted to Detective Jones. "Jonesy has no idea... But *I* have a theory." He met Susan's gaze. "I'm pretty sure you'll come to the same conclusion."

CHAPTER 35

Intrigued, Susan bounded over to the string of photos. As she perused them her eyes grew wider and wider in disbelief.

She blinked rapidly as she struggled to contemplate what she was seeing. A series of photos were on display, showing highly contrasting photos of people at peace and then, in tandem, brutally murdered.

Both sets of photos she knew all too well.

As she scanned from left to right—her index finger tracing her line of sight—Susan muttered under her breath, slowly, "Lisa Stevens... Jacob Williamson. Nathan Brown. Brett Anderson... W-Wilson F-Fensome. Alan Poulson and..."

Susan was taken aback. She stalled. Her jaw, slack.

The face portrayed in the photo at the end of the line she didn't recognise.

With a gloved hand she unpegged the image and brought it closer to her eyes.

Thoughts rushed through her mind.

Who is this guy?

This one... How come he *doesn't have a matching death photo?*

Her eyes glanced over to the body laying on the cold, concrete floor.

And who is that dead guy over there? He certainly doesn't match this *picture.*

A sharp inhale caught in her throat.

Is he THE guy?

Her eyes widened.

Jack?

Did you figure it out?

You did, didn't you?

"Good for you, Jack."

She smiled.

Epilogue

Snowfall imposed its magic on the dark days of winter, adding a sense of mystery and intrigue to the monotony. Jack lay on the sofa in Jen's flat, a blanket draped across his legs, cradling a mug of hot chocolate while his feet rested snugly in a pair of fleece-lined slippers.

"God, I feel like an old man, Jen. Look at me!" Jack hollered through to Jen, who was pottering around in the kitchen.

Jen walked into the living room, took one look at Jack, and burst into laughter, doubling over.

"Oh my word, get a grip. It's not that cold in here. You're only in your forties, you know?! Do you need me to get you a pipe to go with those slippers?"

"That would be comforting, but I gave up smoking."

"I know, babe, but if you want to carry off this old man persona, you may have to take it up again."

"I need some sun. Some vitamin D. I'm tired of these dark days, babe. They *make* me tired. I need some *action*."

"Let's book somewhere then. Where do you want to go?"

"Shall we?" Jack set his mug down on a side table. "Yeah, let's do that. How about the Maldives?"

Jen scoffed. "If only. I don't think we can afford that."

Jack raised his eyebrows. "I know someone with money who owes us a favour."

"You mean David."

"Yeah, I'm sure he'd be more than happy to help. Let's at least take a look, eh? We'd only have to pay a deposit for now."

Jen's eyes lit up. "Sod it. Why not? I'd love to go somewhere like that. It looks like absolute paradise… Not sure you'd get *'action'* there, though, as you put it."

"Maybe I don't need action. Just some sun and some snorkelling. A few cocktails… A couple of weeks away from this London dreariness will do us both the world of good."

"And our first holiday away together. How grown up! I'll get my laptop… Let's do this."

Jen left the room with a spring in her step. She fetched her laptop and sat beside Jack on the sofa. They rifled through a number of sites trying to find the perfect deal for a trip to the Maldives, and after half an hour of searching they found just the thing. They looked at each other, nodded in unison, and, without words, booked their holiday.

"How exciting!" Jen exclaimed, leaning over to give Jack a quick kiss.

"Yeah. Pack your bags, baby! Can you just check that you've got a confirmation email?"

"Sure."

Jen opened her email, frowning when she didn't see a confirmation.

In fact, she didn't seem to have received any emails recently at all—except for one that stood out from the rest.

"This is weird, Jack."

"What is it?"

"I don't seem to have a confirmation here, but I do have an

EPILOGUE

email from Metro bank."

"You don't *have* an account with Metro bank... do you?"

"That's right. I don't. That's what's weird... It says something about a safety deposit box at their branch on Tottenham Court Road."

"Huh?"

"It says my subscription is about to lapse and that if I don't renew it then the contents will be disposed of. I don't have a safety deposit b—"

"What are you thinking, Jen?"

She fumbled around on the laptop for a few seconds.

"It's Nathan's!"

"What?"

"It's Nathan's box. I'm still logged into his email account and I didn't even realise. I never knew he had a safety deposit box."

Jack's eyes widened. "What are you going to do about it?"

"Well, I need to see what's in it, but I don't know how I'd do that... I doubt they'd just let me access it on the basis of being his sister."

"Definitely not, and I think with those things, the banks don't necessarily keep spare keys."

"Keys?" Her eyes narrowed. Her brow furrowed.

"Yeah, keys. How else do you think they open them?"

"Keys!" Jen exclaimed and jumped up out of her seat, leaving the room in a hurry.

What's going on here? She's gone wild.

A few seconds later, Jen returned, and waved her set of keys in Jack's face.

"There was a *key*. After Nathan died and we packed up his belongings, I found a key. I never knew what it was for, but I added it to my keyring, to always have something of his with me."

"Let me see."

Jen handed the keys over to Jack. He took an inquisitive look.

"You're right. This might actually be the key for the bank's box."

"We need to go and take a look, Jack."

Jack could tell by the look in Jen's eyes that she wasn't playing around. There was an immediacy in her emerald stare.

"What? Now?"

"Yes, Jack. Now! Put your shoes on."

***

Jack and Jen exited the Goodge Street station and made their way down Tottenham Court Road—braving the incessant snowfall—to the Metro Bank branch on the corner of Store Street.

They entered, shook themselves off, and approached the cashier's desk.

"I'm here to access my safety deposit box," said Jen, an assertiveness to her voice.

"Do you have your key, ma'am?"

"Yes. Right here," Jen said, as she waved the key at the man behind the perspex divider.

"Okay, right this way."

The cashier led the two of them down a corridor and into a room with wall-to-wall anonymous deposit boxes.

Jack stared in awe at the imposing room.

EPILOGUE

I wonder what kind of random curiosities are stored in here. More importantly, what was Nathan hiding?

"I'll leave you to it. If you need anything, please just let me know."

The cashier returned to his desk, leaving Jack and Jen alone to stand and look on at the array of boxes in amazement.

"Four-oh-three," Jen muttered to herself, scanning the columns.

"There it is, Jack," she proclaimed, pointing up towards a large box marked '403'.

Before she could insert the key, Jack reached out and grabbed her hand. He could feel it trembling beneath his grip.

Looking Jen in the eye with a deep, unwavering sincerity, he said, "Whatever's in there. Whatever it is. Just know... just know that I've got you, Jen. You don't have to look, if you don't want to, you know? We could just leave."

Reciprocating the stare, Jen pulled her hand back and hugged him. Whispering into his ear, she said, "I know, Jack. I know. Thanks for being here with me. I just really need to know what he was keeping in here."

Relinquishing the hug, she continued, "I *have* to look. You know that. It'll haunt me forever if I don't. It could be nothing at all, or it could be something very important. Important to *him*. And if it *was* important to him, no doubt it'll be important to *me*."

Jack nodded.

"I get it. Of course, I get it. But... I can open it if you'd rather?"

"Thanks, but no. I have to do this."

She inserted the key. She hesitated. Her hand trembled.

"You, okay?" said Jack.

She took a deep breath, exhaled slowly, and turned the key. It turned effortlessly.

The box was released.

She pulled it from the column, set it down on the floor and opened the steel lid.

"What the..."

Inside were two items: a black gym bag and a sealed envelope which sat upon it.

The envelope had three handwritten letters scrawled across it:

'Jen'.

Looking over Jen's shoulder, Jack was shaken. His mouth, all of a sudden dry, frozen in an involuntary 'O' shape. Jen looked up at him with a mirrored expression.

Trembling, she grabbed the envelope and peeled it open.

Inside was a letter.

Her hands trembled as she read:

Jen,

If you're reading this, then something has happened to me. I'm so, so sorry to have left you and I can't imagine what you're going through.
I've got myself in some trouble. Lots of trouble. You may even know what I'm talking about, but whether you do or not, just know that I never meant to hurt anyone and I wouldn't have done this if I wasn't in the most desperate of states.

Not only had I put my own life in danger, but I'd also put yours in danger and that is something that I would do anything to undo

and cannot forgive myself for.
I'd backed myself into a corner and I was given a lifeline to get out of that corner.
I took it, but only because I had no other choice.

I'm so sorry.

The contents of this box I stowed away for you, in the event that anything happened to me.
The money that I received for completing this despicable deed allowed me to free myself from the grips of the people that were after me and there remains around half a million pounds, which I've stashed here for you.

Please take the money and may it enrich your life.
I pray you are well. I miss you. I love you, sis. Xxx

May God forgive me.
Your brother,
Nathan.

Author's Note

If you've made it this far, I want to say a massive thank you—for sticking with my story to the bitter, twisted end. And not just that, but for also taking a moment to read this—my chance to speak directly to you, the reader.

She's Not The Only One is my first real labour of love, my true foray into the world of creative writing. Blood, sweat, tears, solitude, illness, recovery—the usual clichés—all played a part in bringing Jack's world to life.

But beyond that, this book represents a risk. The leap from the familiar routine of the 9-to-5 into the unknown, chasing something I truly believed in.

It all started during the pandemic. The passion erupted, and this story *had* to be told. It consumed my days and nights, growing stronger with each passing moment, until finally, the first draft was complete.

I believe in the words on these pages—not as a factual account, of course, but as proof of what's possible when you pour your heart into something and push past the doubt that tries to hold you back. They say everyone has a book in them, and I believe that's true. All it takes is a spark of imagination and relentless pursuit.

Hence the dedication at the start of this book: **For those who dare to dream.**

AUTHOR'S NOTE

I truly hope you enjoyed this journey, and I'd love to hear from you. My metaphorical door is always open, so if you'd like to reach out and share your thoughts, feel free to email me at: **RADpublishing.author@gmail.com**

On to the next...

Also by Rob Delplanque

If you enjoyed 'She's Not The Only One' I'd love it if you took a look at my novella - Echoes Of Reality:

Echoes Of Reality

ALSO BY ROB DELPLANQUE

Acknowledgments

There are so many people to thank for helping make this book a reality that I couldn't possibly do them all justice in just one page—so I'll keep it brief.

To my endlessly patient wife—my muse—who tolerates my rambling soliloquies about my characters, their motivations, idiosyncrasies and story arcs. She's my first reader, my toughest critic, and the one who keeps my head above water.

To Debbie & Greg, for allowing me to stay at their beautiful home in France, giving me the space and solitude I needed to focus—before illness temporarily stopped me in my tracks. That trip was a turning point, and I'll always be grateful for it.

To my early beta readers—your invaluable feedback helped shape this book into what it is today. You know who you are.

To the many baristas who fuelled me with caffeine and genuine curiosity about my work, keeping me sharp and motivated.

And finally, to you—the reader. I hope this story gave you some satisfying escapism, and perhaps even lingers in your mind long after you turned the last page.

Made in the USA
Middletown, DE
19 April 2025